CHRISTINA
THE
ASTONISHING

CHRISTINA
THE
ASTONISHING

MARIANNE LEONE

A NOVEL

AKASHIC BOOKS

BROOKLYN, NEW YORK
Publishing books since 1997

Published by Akashic Books
©2025 Marianne Leone

Hardcover ISBN: 978-1-63614-261-6
Paperback ISBN: 978-1-63614-273-9
Library of Congress Control Number: 2025933494

EU Authorized Representative details:
Easy Access System Europe
Mustamäe tee 50, 10621 Tallinn, Estonia
gpsr.request@easproject.com

Akashic Books
Brooklyn, New York
Instagram, X, Facebook: AkashicBooks
info@akashicbooks.com
www.akashicbooks.com

*For Ginny, Patsy, Mary Jane, and all the other
parochial school parolees from this particular era*

THE SHAPE OF THINGS TO COME

The harlequin-patterned tiles in the Precious Blood convent are always immaculate. Christina Falcone's outsized fear makes the long hallway seem to stretch on forever and tilt upward crazily, like a scene from *Alice in Wonderland*. The high-ceilinged music room has a grand piano and a bench where the nun sits holding a ruler. Christina splays her five-year-old baby starfish fingers as far apart as she can to play the scales, but they always fumble and the nun is always there with the ruler. At home Christina blinks her eyes rapidly and clears her throat over and over. She never tells her parents about the ruler, but one day an upright piano is delivered to their basement den and a nightclub performer is hired. The nun with the ruler stays in her lair, banished forever. Christina becomes a tiny torch singer and performs at recitals, redeemed. "*Man of my heart, I love you so,*" she croons to a packed house of bemused parents, her enlarged tonsils adding a sultry vocal tone that calls to mind a pack-a-day habit of unfiltered, manly-named cigarettes.

PART 1

SIN EATER

R ita holds the round loaf of bread dangerously close to her chest and saws away, wielding the long knife like a suicidal violinist. The hard crust crackles. Christina, her little brother, Vinny, and her grandfather sit around the red enamel-topped kitchen table eating dinner. Christina's mother and her father, Joe, will eat later, at a more civilized time in the dining room, with a white tablecloth and the wine Joe makes every year from Montepulciano grapes and stores in round oak casks in the cellar cantina. Rita places the bread on the table. President Kennedy is on the radio saying something important about underground testing in his queer accent that everyone says is a Boston accent, but which sounds the way no one speaks in Christina's city seven miles outside of Boston. Rita turns the dial abruptly to a station playing the kind of music she likes, fruity pop songs sung by almost-crying men. Christina's nun teachers would gasp at the disrespect. They practically genuflect every time they speak the name of the first Catholic president. The music isn't helping to drown out the enthusiastic chewing and gulping going on around her. Christina tries to lose herself in her comic book but now her grandfather's slurping is getting on her nerves. She reads the same panel three times and looks up. Vinny, directly opposite, chews with his mouth open, smiling at her to better reveal the mess within. Christina pushes away her pasta fagioli.

"I can't eat! I'm gonna throw up!"

She glares at Vinny, who is now guzzling his drink and making a little humming sound of delight. He smiles again, orangeade glistening on his chin.

"You're a pig!"

Rita points the knife at her. "I got a knife in my 'an'." Her voice is low and dangerous.

Christina's grandfather, his mouth also full, rumbles out his all-purpose mollifier, the only phrase he knows in English: "Eh, s'all right. S'all right."

"Miss Prim," her mother mutters. Rita's truthful assessment of her finicky nature always enrages Christina. Her mother is anything but prim. She wears snug black Capri pants and flirty little blouses. Her pillowy lips are always enhanced with Revlon's Fire and Ice, even around the house.

Christina grabs her comic book and flees. She hates Friday nights. Meatless Friday nights mean pasta fagioli, the mushy beans, the red iridescent soup that surrounds the slimy little elbow macaroni and increases the slurp factor at the table to intolerable levels. Her mother's shriek follows Christina up the stairs.

"You gonna ge' sick!"

Christina slams the door to her room. "I HAVE HOMEWORK!" she yells through the closed door.

"I'm takin' you to the doctor!" Rita's ultimate threat seeps faintly through the door.

"You stupid plebeian," Christina mutters under her breath. Plebeians are commoners, Sister said. Patricians are aristocrats. Christina is an aristocrat, trapped in a family of plebeians who make pigpen sounds at dinner.

Christina lies on her frilly bed, the pink nylon coverlet itching her back. The coverlet catches her curls in its staticky grip. She flings the creepily grasping bedspread on the floor and rolls over onto her stomach. She gazes at the picture of Christ above her bed. He looks about the same age as Christina in the picture, nine, maybe a little younger, with dreamy brown eyes and blond curly hair. He seems a little sad and afraid, His girlish lips pressed together, as if to hold back tears. His eyes follow you, asking shyly for love. The background of the painting is a somber brown except for the thin line of light surrounding His angelic head. It looks like Jesus is wearing a cowboy hat with a glowing brim. In fact, until just last year Christina believed the picture was of a random kid in a cowboy hat that her mother had picked out because Christina had a crush on Dick West, the all-American boy cowboy on TV. It was her chunky friend Rose who had set her straight one day when they were playing house and Christina announced that the cowboy above her bed was going to be her husband. Rose stared at her.

"You can't be married to *Jesus*. Unless you're gonna be a nun. Are you gonna be a nun?"

Rose was so dense.

"That's not Jesus. That's a kid in a cowboy hat. That's my husband and he's a cowboy, stupid."

"It's Jesus," Rose repeated.

"Shut up and go home."

Rose was on the brink of hysteria. Her eyes brimmed with tears. Her voice quavered. "It is too Jesus. Nonna Rose has that picture in her bedroom and she tol' me it was Him!"

A visit to Rose's house had finally convinced Christina. There it was, the same picture in Nonna Rose's room. Nonna Rose blessed herself in front of the blond child, murmuring in Italian. Christina doubted she was praying to Dick West, all-American boy.

Christina stares at ex-cowboy Jesus above her bed. Did her blond preteen boyfriend have any idea He would end up splayed on a cross with spikes through His hands and feet and not just one thorn, but a whole mocking crown of them digging into His scalp?

Of course He did. He was God, so He already knew everything.

The nuns say they should strive to become saints. What does that mean?

Christina is afraid of hell. She is equally afraid of eternity. She fears burning in hell in a place where there is no time. Her mother doesn't believe in hell. Neither does her father. They are foolish to tempt the powers of a God who sees everything and has the power to condemn you to hell for all eternity. Her parents won't listen to the nuns' stories of hell. They laugh at her when she tells them about the tortures that await them. Her mother even commits blasphemy by saying that the nuns are full of shit, that they should see what it's like to fry in a field with the sun beating down on you, trying to grow vegetables from rocks and soil that is *secco,* dust, and then giving most of what you have grown to the *padrone* as payment for working on his land. That is hell, according to her mother. Christina is a voice crying in the wilderness, like St. John the Baptist. Well, *she* isn't going to hell. She will become a saint and go straight to heaven, sailing right by purgatory, heaven's waiting room, which could go on for hundreds of years.

Christina grabs her flashlight, the one she now keeps under the bed to confront ghosts and read covertly at night. She kneels on the bed, the sheet draped over her head as a makeshift veil. She flicks the flashlight under her chin for a haloed effect. She admires herself in the mirror on her bureau directly opposite her bed. She looks like a regular saint.

Her mother opens the door. Rita, queen of her domain, never knocks.

"Miss Prim, this 'ow you do 'omework? Go downstairs an' eat. I make you somethin'."

On the kitchen table is a BLT, Christina's favorite. With chips, extra love. Rita sits heavily across from her, sighing. Christina grabs a comic book from the stack on top of the radiator. She tries to concentrate on her perfect sandwich, but her mother's black eyes bore through the adventures of Little Lulu. All is obviously not forgiven. Christina closes the comic book and looks up, but she is severely undermatched in eye-to-eye combat with her mother.

"I dunno." It is her mother's "Let us pray," the prelude to a well-worn litany of Christina's many failings. Christina bites into her perfect sandwich. The bacon is crisp, the way she likes it. The tomato is juicy and ripe, one of her grandfather's miracles from the backyard garden. Then she remembers. She drops the sandwich back onto the plate.

"Oh no, it's Friday. I can't eat this and receive on Sunday."

Rita shrugs. "Eat. I take the sin." She smirks. She thinks the Friday no-meat rule is *pazzo,* an insane dictum from men who don't cook. What do they know? Did they have to keep an entire family strong to face the hardships life hurled at them? The priests back home in her Italian village are all well-padded little waddlers, their florid complexions shining with health and liters of *vino.* They eat meat every day, not once a month like Rita's impoverished mother and father, and they take the choicest portions offered by their cringing congregants. *Beh.*

"It doesn't work like that. I have to go to confession."

"Eat. God wants you to eat. It's not a sin. It's a sin to waste food." Irritation propels Rita to jump up and stir Joe's dinner, simmering on the stove. "Eat, 'urry up before you father come 'ome." She looks over her shoulder and sees Christina unmoving, staring at the sandwich. Predictably, she snaps: "JESUS, MARY, AN' JOSEPH!"

A car door slams in the driveway. Joe, diverting for a moment the path of Rita's lava-flow rage, throws open the front door. Vinny hurls his cannonball body at his father's knees. "RICO!" Joe cries joyously, hefting him aloft, grunting with the effort. "Pa," he nods to his father, immovable in his rocker, entranced by what he can't understand a word of on television. The soundtrack tells him when to laugh, and he does, obediently, mindlessly, cackling in his old man way. It drives Christina crazy. Now, in the kitchen, she hopes her father, with his bar owner's ability to break up fights, can end the BLT standoff. Rita continues to yell.

"WHAT? I GOTTA FEED YOU LIKE A BABY NOW?"

Christina's eyes sting at the unfairness of the baby comparison. She isn't a baby! She is nine years old! Joe enters the kitchen and kisses Rita, gingerly. Rita doesn't acknowledge the kiss nor shift her withering stare from Christina.

"She no eat nothin'. I make this special for her, and she no eat!"

"Daddy, it's a sin," she whispers, her chin trembling.

"I tol' her I take the sin!" Rita snaps.

"But Sister said—"

"OhhhOHHHohhh," Rita sings her full-throated aria of scorn. "*Sister say! Sister say!* She too much with the fockin' nuns. She got bad dreams every night. They make her *pazz'*! She cut alla you roses. She put the . . . the . . . thorn in her head so she look like St. Rita! Next time she's gonna nail Vinny to the cross, for Chrissake!"

"*For Chrissake?*" Joe laughs.

Rita doesn't get the joke. She never lets Christina forget her misbegotten effort of a few years back to present a picture of herself to God as St. Rita. On that occasion, Christina had solemnly gone about recreating the holy portrait of St. Rita that hangs in the Falcone hallway. The portrait is in a fancy oval frame, the first thing visitors see upon entering their modest house. St. Rita, her mother's namesake, looks transfixed by tiny Jesus's body attached to the wooden cross she holds in both hands. Healthy-looking pink cherubs carrying spills of roses float above her head, and just below the pudgy angels hovers a crown of thorns about an inch above St. Rita's black veil. The white wimple covering her forehead has as its focal point a thorn that is sticking into the flesh beneath the wimple. St. Rita doesn't appear bothered by the thorn, even though it looks more like a spike; she is too busy venerating the tiny Jesus.

Christina had intended to present a picture to God of herself venerating the cross. Christina plans to become a saint and guarantee her place in heaven. She had hoped that God would fill her with grace, especially if she endured the thorn in her forehead, like St. Rita. She had knelt before her father's rosebushes, partially denuded to provide decoration for the crucifix that she removed from above her parents' bed. Two of Christina's plastic baby dolls, naked, also decorated with cut roses, were smashed sideways into the bushes above her head. Christina herself wore her mother's Niagara Falls scarf in place of a wimple. She had gritted her teeth and stabbed herself in the forehead, but instead of grace all she'd earned was her mother's screeching threats and a small scar between her eyebrows.

But that was two whole years ago. Christina is older now and knows more about what pleases God. Following the rules about meatless Friday is one of the important things God demands. The impossibility of explaining this to her mother leaves Christina on the verge of tears.

"In three years, I'll be confirmed. I'll be a Soldier of Christ! I can't eat this!"

Joe utilizes his superior peacemaking skills. He pretends to have an idea: "Heyyy, dolly, speakin' of soldiers, guess what's on tonight? *Sgt. Bilko*! You wanna watch it with me?"

"Okay," Christina sniffs.

The standoff over, Rita whisks away the plate with the BLT. She reaches into the freezer and places an ice cream sandwich in front of her daughter. "'Ere. Eat. No meat." She smiles at Christina, sits down, and takes a big, devilish bite of the BLT, consigning her soul to hell, or at least purgatory.

Christina unwraps her ice cream sandwich and nibbles it. "I'm gonna be a Soldier of Christ," she mumbles. She feels sorry for her mother. Not for the first time, she pictures Rita burning in hell for all eternity, the tongues of fire licking her sinful black Capri pants. Christina's father winks at her, and she takes a big bite of her ice cream sandwich, cheered by its gluey sweetness, and the thought of her mother in flames.

GOOD WORKS

Cecilia Moriarty stands in front of the classroom shrine to the Blessed Virgin wearing her well-practiced fake-humble smile. She has just donated her candy money for the third week in a row to buy a pagan baby, whom she has named Cecilia. Pictures of African and Asian kids renamed Bridget, Timothy, and Graziella are thumbtacked on poster board behind the statue of the Virgin. Sister Isaac Jogues gushes over Cecilia's sacrifice until her voice becomes a swarm of bees around Christina's head. The nun tells Cecilia to take her seat, her eyes moist with fondness, then turns to the class, all business.

The nun stands in front of the blackboard addressing the fourth-grade class of Precious Blood Elementary School. Her chapped moon face looms over the children, haloed by the starched white wimple. Above her head, like the crest of a warrior standard, is a large black crucifix with a silvered dying Christ bolted to it. The old-fashioned classroom has wainscoted walls that are lined with large windows no one is allowed to so much as glance at, under penalty of expulsion.

"Catechisms away. Hands folded. Miss Moriarty, when does the Church declare you a saint?"

Cecilia stands at once and begins reciting in the rote, singsong voice used by all the students to answer catechism questions: "The term for declaration of sainthood is canonization." She takes a self-congratulatory pause for perfectly articulating the word. "A person is canonized when the Church determines that he or she led a life of heroic virtue and is with God in heaven." Cecilia sits down, smoothing her uniform skirt, blithely unaware that she has the starring role in her classmates' daydreams of her slow demise.

Sister Isaac Jogues beams at her. "Very good, dear." She turns her predatory gaze back to the rest of the class, who squirm as one. Those who have not spent the night before memorizing catechism questions pray silently that the nun's gimlet eye will pass them by. "What must be present in a saint's life that makes him holy enough to be canonized? Mr. Grillo." The nun pounces like a lioness thinning the herd.

Danny Grillo is easy pickings; always in trouble, a chronic underachiever, and a junior wise guy in league with Dennis Dempsey, the Worst Boy in the School. He stands and looks down at his scuffed shoes. "Dunno, S'tah," he says, smiling in a way that he hopes is placating but which in fact makes him look like a smarmy rug dealer.

"Get out," decrees the nun, pitiless as a Mongol overlord.

Exile is the worst fate to befall a Precious Blood

student. A banished kid has nowhere to go. The out-cast wanders the dim halls like a soul between worlds. Eventually a nun walking the hallway beat will dis-cover the deportee, and then the enhanced interro-gation will begin, only to escalate into a good cop/ bad cop scenario when the offender is returned to the classroom. It always ends in tears.

Sister Isaac Jogues, taking no chances, calls on Ce-cilia's male counterpart, Timothy Mosher, who trills out the answer, his high-pitched voice cracked with the glory of pleasing Sister: "The evidence of good works must be present in the life of a saint to be canonized."

By sliding her eyes slightly to the left, Christina can see poor Danny Grillo wandering the hall, his eyes darting left to right, scanning for patrollers, knowing he will be nabbed in a matter of minutes.

"Very good, Timothy. God wants all of us to become saints. And, boys and girls, we will have a chance to perform our own good works after school on Thursday. How many here play a musical instru-ment? Stand, please."

Five kids straggle to their feet.

The nun smiles at Cecilia. "And Cecilia, dear, we all know that God gave you a beautiful singing voice. How many take dance lessons? Stand, please."

Rose D'Angelis stands. She looks quizzically at Christina, who scrunches down in her seat, staring straight ahead.

"Fine. We will assemble in the cafeteria after school on Thursday. Mr. Moriarty will drive us to St. Lucy's Home for the Aged Blind, and we will display our talents for all the poor afflicted who live there."

Rose raises her hand. "'Scuse me, S'tah. Uh, Christina Falcone takes tap with me."

Christina transmits thoughts of mayhem and destruction at Rose, who, instead of being struck dead as intended, smiles sappily at her. She's really happy that she has "reminded" Christina. Why does she have such a stupid best friend?

Sister Isaac Jogues glares. "Stand up, Miss Falcone, and tell us why you're deliberately refusing to perform good works."

Christina stands on shaky legs. "Uh, S'tah, I have to help my mother cook. For, uh, my father's restaurant."

Sister Isaac Jogues stares at Christina for a full thirty seconds. Then she takes out a pen with a flourish, flinging back her wide black sleeves, and begins to write. "Come here. Give this to your mother. She's to sign it and return it to me. There are child-labor laws in this country!" And then, in a lower voice, muttering: "These immigrants—no idea of the way things work in *this* country . . ."

Christina fights the urge to cover her eyes. This is scarier than the scariest parts of *Fiend Without a Face*. She pictures the scene at home: her mother laboriously deciphering the note, giving up and handing it to her father, her father blowing up about lying to the sister, bringing shame to the Falcone family and probably a visit from the cops as well. She stutters a reply: "Uh, S'tah, no, it's okay, uh. I'll do it. I don't have to help." She is talking with her hands. Sister Isaac Jogues hates when kids talk with their hands.

She wills her hands back by her sides. "I mean, I don't have to. I was just being like, uh, St. Therese, you know, practicing humility, and praising God with everyday tasks . . ."

Sister Isaac Jogues continues staring at her. Christina withers.

"Be there on Thursday with your tap shoes or stay after school every afternoon for the rest of the year. And be sure to confess your sin of omission to Monsignor Boyle this Saturday. Be seated."

Christina sits heavily and darts a vengeful look at Rose, who seems clueless. Cecilia, who sits behind Rose, glints a nasty smile her way when the nun turns around, alerted by a knock at the classroom door.

"Gonzo!" The subterranean murmur rumbles through the class. Sister Aloysius Gonzaga, the principal, has been the one to capture the unfortunate Danny Grillo, who shuffles in after her, prepared to meet his doom.

The entire class rises. "GOOD MORNING, SISTER GONZAGA."

Sister Gonzaga is highly distractible, or as the pupils of Precious Blood have deemed, *mental*. She doesn't acknowledge the bellowed greeting of the class, but speaks directly to Sister Isaac Jogues, disbelief beetling her brow. "Sister, I found this young man *standing* in the *hallway*," she says, as if he'd been flapping his wings and flying instead.

On cue, Sister Isaac Jogues picks up the script: "Yes, Sister. I'm sorry to say that Mr. Grillo doesn't belong in this class. He didn't know his catechism today!"

This news brings Gonzo to the brink of tears. Her bulgy blue eyes mist over and she shakes her head, unable to speak. Danny Grillo stands between the nuns, staring at his shoes. The two sisters do their duet about Catholics who don't learn their catechism. They harmonize perfectly on how Catholic boys and girls who can't be Defenders of the One True Faith will be helpless against the godless communists. Sister Isaac Jogues goes solo at that point so she can detail the gruesome tortures that the communists will surely inflict on Defenders of the One True Faith, lingering on the bamboo slivers rammed under fingernails and garden hoses turned on full blast and placed against fragile eardrums. Gonzo sings counterpoint on the happy rewards of floating around in the afterlife once you refuse to renounce your faith and are released from torture into blissful, welcome death. Suddenly, Isaac Jogues seems to remember poor Danny Grillo standing between them and zeroes in on him.

"And *you* can't even take the time to learn one catechism lesson. No, you'd rather renounce your faith and spend eternity with your flesh sizzling in the fires of hell. Give up without a fight. Take the coward's way out." She bends closer to Danny and drops her voice to a whisper that is louder than a shout: "And suffer the remorse. That would be worse than the actual physical agony you would feel every second for eternity. The regret, the anguish you would feel that would burn worse than the flames of hell, the torment of knowing that you could have prevented all of this—by knowing what to say to those godless communists." The nun stands tall again and smiles like she's just remembered where she stashed her winning lottery ticket. "Class, I want you to say a prayer for Mr. Grillo. Maybe it's not too late."

Danny Grillo breaks. He blubbers, a snot bubble ballooning from his left nostril. Christina thinks Dennis Dempsey won't let him hang around with him anymore after this. The good cop/bad cop routine winds up to a big finish and no surprises. Gonzo assures Sister Isaac Jogues that Danny Grillo hadn't meant to disappoint her. Sister Isaac Jogues assures Gonzo that *she* isn't disappointed, God is. Danny continues to sob. Sister Isaac Jogues sends him to his seat. The class stands again.

"GOOD MORNING, SISTER GONZAGA."

Sister Gonzaga takes her dithery leave of the class and Sister Isaac Jogues returns to the subject of good works. Cecilia's hand shoots up and she offers that her mother would make cookies for the poor afflicted at St. Lucy's, as if she needs any more brownie points with Sister Isaac Jogues.

"Isn't that wonderful, class? A mother with four little ones at home still finds time for the afflicted at St. Lucy's. While other, *smaller* families are too busy—making spaghetti, I suppose—to be real members of the Christian community."

The nuns are all, with one French-Canadian exception, Irish-American women, despite the absurdly male names bestowed upon them when taking their final vows. They disapprove of the Italians, whom they consider superstitious, mentally subpar, and members of suspiciously smaller families than the Irish, who pump a steady supply of students into Precious Blood's elementary and high schools. It makes Christina depressed. It's all true. The Falcones are not good members of the Christian community, especially her mother. Her father at least sends a turkey over to the nuns at Thanksgiving. If she asked her mother to make cookies for the afflicted blind, she would at first be incredulous. Then she would ask Christina if she was *pazza*. Next Rita's voice would rise to a shriek as she listed all the things she had to do: make meatballs for her father's bar, take care of Vinny, iron the *brutta* uniform they made her buy for the sister school—she would work herself up until the inevitable cursing of the nuns and Precious Blood Elementary. Christina is sure that Cecilia's mother wears a poofy pink shirtwaist while she bakes cookies. And that she has never told the nuns to go fuck themselves.

But Rita could be unexpectedly kind, and isn't that a Christian virtue? A memory comes unbidden to Christina: Coming home from school and finding a brand-new baby doll wearing a long white christening gown in its own little crib on the dining room table. Her mother is standing over the doll and smiling at Christina. It isn't her birthday. It's just an ordinary Tuesday after school when her mother usually takes her afternoon soap opera break to watch *The Edge of Night*, with its thrilling and ominous intro music.

Sister Isaac Jogues is talking through Christina's racing thoughts. "Now, can anyone tell me why St. Lucy is the patron saint of the blind?"

Christina shoots up her hand, quivering. She stands to answer before the nun calls on her. "Isn't St. Lucy an Italian saint?" Her voice rings shrilly in the silent classroom.

A little taken aback by Christina's intensity, the nun nevertheless explains haughtily that St. Lucy lived in the Roman era. And Romans were not the same as Italians.

"My mother's from near Rome, S'tah." She doesn't know why she says this. It comes out like a challenge, somehow.

"Are you being *bold*, Miss Falcone? I don't tolerate bold girls in my class. Be seated."

Dennis Dempsey pretends to have a coughing fit just at that moment, his favorite trick. The big finish comes at the end, where he manages to make "Fuck you" sound like a sneeze. The class loves it, especially when Sister Isaac Jogues says "God Bless You" to Dennis. Christina looks gratefully at Dennis, who glances away.

Sister Isaac Jogues tells the class the story of St. Lucy, early Roman saint. She was a beautiful young Christian woman whose bridegroom-to-be was Jesus. But her unbelieving parents betrothed her to a pagan who had lustfully admired Lucy's beautiful eyes. When Lucy heard his lewd compliments, she plucked out her own eyes and handed them to her suitor.

The class erupts with horror, or in Timothy Mosher's case, a kind of gleeful high-pitched giggle that is more disturbing to Christina than the eye-plucking story. Dennis Dempsey emits another joyful "Fuck you" sneeze. This time Sister blesses him, but with an edge of suspicion. She stares at the class until they are quiet, so she can deliver the punch line to the St. Lucy story.

"But God miraculously restored St. Lucy's eye-balls so that she could go on to experience a glorious martyrdom. The Romans tried to burn her, but the flames had no effect. Finally, she was stabbed through the throat, but she didn't die until a priest came and gave her Holy Communion. She stood there, rooted to the spot with that sword stuck in her throat, until she could receive the Host. Then, and only then, did she finally die."

A filmy curtain rises on a pair of tap-dancing feet. Tinkly, slightly off-key music vamps along to the fren-zied feet as the curtain lifts to reveal a gauzy dress decorated with sequins and stars. The curtain rises farther to reveal a hand swinging a glittery wand in time to the music. The music reaches a crescendo as the curtain disappears; on center stage stands an eye-less horror wearing a top hat, a sword impaled in its throat. The phantom gurgles, "Wouldn't anybody like to kiss a sweet old-fashioned girl?" The eyeless horror is St. Lucy! She extends her skeletal hand to Christina. Lucy is holding a platter, her eyes rolling around on it like loose marbles.

Christina sits up, gasping for breath. She stares into the dark of her room. Nothing looks familiar. The closet door is open. Was Eyeless Lucy hiding in there? Christina gabbles a prayer, her lips too frozen to pronounce the familiar words: "HailMaryfullof-gracetheLordiswiththee."

A gust of wind scrapes the branches of the apple tree against her bedroom window. Lucy's skeletal hand! It was coming through the window! Christina leaps out of bed and runs to her parents' room across the hall. She lingers at the threshold, watching her parents sleep. Her father snores on the far side of the bed, his back to her. She is torn between the need to wake her mother and the fear of invoking a too-familiar late-night scenario where she is blamed and shamed. Her mother will bolt upright, then curse. Christina has nightmares at least twice weekly, mostly starring the martyred saint of the week or communist torturers with garden implements or the one-way escalator to hell.

Christina hears a noise. Is it the house creaking? Or has St. Lucy followed her? She plucks at her mother's nightgown sleeve, whispering, "Ma. Ma."

Rita bolts up, then focuses on Christina. "Oh no. Not again. Sominabitch. Jesus, Mary, and Joseph, you too big for this." She swings her legs to the floor, her head in her hands. "Nonna was givin' me a number to play in the dream, an' now I forget." Rita is a big believer in dream messages from the departed for the lucky numbers she places every day with Chickie, her bookie. She heads for Christina's room without a word. Christina follows, chastened but relieved.

Five minutes pass that are longer than the fourteen stations of the cross, longer than Lent, longer than the wait for Christmas morning. Rita is already snoring lightly, lying on her back. Christina hooks her leg over Rita's for extra protection. She remains alert, her brown eyes scanning the room. She looks at her mother. Her black hair falls back in crow wings on either side of her head, and the moon shining through the window makes it blue and magical. She has a widow's peak, like the evil queen in *Sleeping Beauty*. If St. Lucy comes back, Rita will kick her ass.

Christina and Rose look like pink satin versions of the roly-poly bugs Christina finds under rocks in her grandfather's tomato garden. They are curled uncomfortably into the wayback of Mr. Moriarty's 1957 Chevy station wagon. Tiny Anna Bonfiglio is crushed in with them, her giant accordian attached to her side like a devouring appendage from *Attack of the Giant Leeches*, a memorable horror movie Christina saw the previous summer at the South Shore Drive-In.

Rose and Christina hold their sparkle-encrusted top hats on their laps and Christina shifts uncomfortably as the tulle underskirt to her tap costume bites her bottom in first one place, then another, like a swarm of angry mosquitoes. Four other kids crowd into the backseat, two unencumbered lucky ducks who play piano and two sad sacks clutching flutophones. Cecilia, radiating self-satisfaction from every pore, is up front in the catbird seat, between her dad and Sister Isaac Jogues. Christina can't stop staring at the back of the square-shaped black veil in the front seat, so out of place in the real world of station wagons.

Added to the surreal sight of the incongruous Sister Isaac Jogues is the growing apprehension she feels when she pictures tap-dancing for blind people. She hopes their hearing is acute and that they appreciate syncopation. She and Rose are going to perform a routine to "Be My Little Baby Bumble Bee," sung by Doris Day. Christina clutches the record album and prays there will be a phonograph in the performance hall. She doesn't have high hopes that she and Rose will actually be in sync. They will sound more like an impersonation of popcorn. They will be a huge flop. She starts to feel warm, then dizzy. The tulle under-skirt bites savagely at her rear end. The suffering is a part of doing good works. Sister says to offer it up for the souls in purgatory when you fall in the schoolyard or get German measles. The souls in purgatory are freed by your suffering, like the vampires made stronger by drinking blood in *Horror of Dracula*.

They pull up to St. Lucy's Home for the Aged Blind, a grim-looking redbrick building incongruously squatting on lush, flowering grounds. Sister Eudes, who answers the door, is an old pal of Sister Isaac Jogues's from her novitiate days, and the first jolly nun Christina has ever met. Maybe the ones at Precious Blood just hate kids and everywhere else they are kind and sensitive, like Ingrid Bergman in *The Bells of St. Mary's*. The nuns screen that film every year at Christmas for the students at Precious Blood, an advertisement for a parish that exists nowhere in the actual world.

Sister Eudes ushers them all into the performance room, eager to get rid of the students so she can revisit the good old days with Isaac Jogues, fond memories of kneeling on sand when they were nuns in training. Sister Isaac Jogues tells them all to wait there until she summons them and bustles off with Eudes. Christina can hear them tittering in the next room, a cozy library lined with Catholic books that none of the inmates of St. Lucy's can read, and a pristine fireplace that has never held a fire.

The performance room has about thirty folding chairs set up and a grand piano on the improvised stage, which is really just a space cleared of furniture in front of the piano.

"Sister Eudes. Sister *Huge* is more like it," Cecilia says, irritated at being left with the common herd. But suddenly, she cheers up. "Hey, Christina, look at the floor. What a lovely carpet! Wall to wall, too! Oh, but—they won't be able to hear you, will they?"

There isn't a patch of hardwood floor anywhere in the room. Terror propels Christina on stick legs into the next room, where she can hear the nuns cackling together. Eudes and Isaac Jogues form a black impenetrable arch, their heads tilted toward one another.

"You kissed the floor for penance so many times I lost count!"

"'Scuse me, S'tah," Christina whispers. She doesn't exist. The nuns swoon in the rosy dance down memory lane.

"'SCUSE ME, S'TAH."

Sister Isaac Jogues comes out of her trance. Sister Eudes drops her jolly persona and glares at Christina.

"What *is* it, Miss Falcone? Go over and tell the others we're about to begin."

"It's the rug. We can't tap-dance on a carpet. They won't even hear it!" The words come out in a breathless rush, making Christina dizzy again when she thinks of the silent tap dance she and Rose are about to perform.

But Sister Isaac Jogues is already walking away. "Offer it up for the souls in purgatory," she orders.

The nun sweeps into the performance room, clapping her hands, corralling the do-gooders of Precious Blood Elementary School. Christina lags behind, arriving just in time to see Rose, who suffers famously from stage fright, throwing up on the carpet. Cecilia is at her side, sympathetic as a viper poised to strike.

"Looks like you get to do a solo."

Thirty minutes later, the recital is in full swing. The elderly blind residents have already suffered through an excruciating flutophone duet, and back-to-back piano performances of the ever-popular "Für Elise." Next, Anna Bonfiglio wrestles with her accordion, pumping out "Lady of Spain," until the accordion eventually overpowers her into a throwdown; she is pinned to the floor by the tearful finale. Cecilia, clearly the headliner, belts out "You'll Never Walk Alone," which, Christina thinks, could be very true of her audience. Sister Isaac Jogues claps vigorously at the end, rousing the elderlies from their flutophone-accordion-piano torpor. They join the nun, applauding as loudly as their parchmenty old hands will allow. One elderly firecracker gives an earsplitting whistle through his dentures. Cecilia milks the crowd, pealing "Oh, you're won-

derful!" and "God loves you," like a Lilliputian Judy
Garland before a sold-out audience at Carnegie Hall.
Sister Isaac Jogues beckons to Christina, and she is
suddenly reminded of the skeletal branch of the apple
tree scraping her window. She hands Isaac Jogues the
Doris Day record and prepares to meet her doom.

But once Christina hears the opening bars of "Be
My Little Baby Bumble Bee," Doris's syrupy voice
mesmerizes her. She loses herself in the routine, counting out the steps, managing the tricky flap-ball-change
part without a skip, and only occasionally filtering
the smothered giggles of the other kids through her
dreamlike moves. She misses the comforting clacking
sound of her taps, which in Miss Haggerty's dance
class often rebelled by straying off the beat. The elderly blind sit crumpled and unmoving, though one
vigorous old man hums along with determination,
harmonizing with the "*buzz around, buzz around*"
part of the song, getting in on the act. Christina is
comforted by the humming. The old man is like the
Good Samaritan, lifting her cross. She will go up to
him when she gets through this ordeal. She will even
kiss him, she thinks, as she goes into her big finish,
tapping backward and into a crouch, then spring-
ing up with a final flourish, arms akimbo, pooching
her lips into a big, smacking kiss. Sister Isaac Jogues
tsks reflexively at that whiff of sex. The old people
are tired; they want their afternoon cookies and tea.
They applaud listlessly, except for the hummer, who is
thrilled and says so to the world at large.

"That little girl sounds just like Doris Day!"

* * *

The instructions are to circulate among the old people, pass the cookies, and make polite conversation. Then they'd be done with their good works and could go home. Rose knows how to act around old people; she lives with two grandmothers, another reason she is overly familiar with cookies. Nonna Rose competes with Nonn'Antonia to be Rose's favorite. Christina's grandmothers are both dead and buried in the Old Country. She is jealous of Rose sometimes, when she sees how Rose gets to have her special favorite foods whenever she wants, and how the nonnas could overrule Rosa's mother. Christina usually has to eat what's on the menu at home and she hates almost everything but macaroni and meatballs. But sometimes it's like Rose has not one but three mothers, the way they all yell at her to wear her snow pants or always want to brush her hair or hover around feeling her forehead in case she's getting a fever, or how they do the anti-*malocchio* ritual on her because they're sure someone has given her the evil eye at school. If Christina had three Ritas she would definitely run away and find the *Father Knows Best* family with the reassuring all-American last name Anderson and ask if they would take her in.

She tries to make herself inconspicuous, slouching on a chair near the door beside an old lady who sits in her wheelchair apart from the rest and who doesn't seem to want to talk. She is the prettiest old lady in the room. There is something glamorous about her, too, a Glinda the Good Witch look about her, like she's wearing sparkles, when really she is just wearing a plain gray sweater and skirt. But the skirt shows her legs and her legs don't look blue and bumpy like the other old ladies, they look long and pretty, and the sweater clings to a pair of oversized breasts. Her white hair is wispy but stylish, cut into a cap that frames her face. And she has red lipstick on her wide mouth. She has her eyes closed now and looks asleep. Sister Isaac Jogues and Cecilia weave their way over to them, and the old lady's eyes fly open like a china doll someone jarred on a shelf. They are deep green, mermaid green. Sister Isaac Jogues's voice booms, as if the old lady is deaf, too.

"HELLO, DEAR. I THOUGHT YOU MIGHT LIKE TO MEET THE LITTLE GIRL WHO MOVED US ALL SO DEEPLY WITH HER MARVELOUS VOICE."

There is no response from the old lady. She stares straight ahead. A string of saliva dribbles scarily from the side of her mouth.

"WELL, GOD BLESS YOU, DEAR. I'LL RE-MEMBER YOU IN MY PRAYERS."

"I WILL, TOO," Cecilia pipes up, and the two of them beat a hasty retreat.

They are barely out of sight before Christina hears the old lady, her voice surprisingly raspy: "Stick it up your ass, ya little twit."

Christina gasps.

The old lady inclines her head. "So which one were you? The flutophone? Give it up, kid. Ya got no future in show business."

Christina just sits there, frozen in place.

"Not the one with the accordion?" She begins to sing.

Christina looks around for rescue. The old lady is crazy. Just her luck to get the crazy one.

"*Lady of Spain, I adore you. Pull down your pants, I'll explore you.*"

The old lady stops singing. She smiles with the corner of her mouth pulled down, as if she and Christina are in on a private joke. Christina feels equal parts joy and terror bubble up in her. She might be *good* crazy, like a character in a *Bugs Bunny* cartoon. Christina is on the edge of her seat and for once forgets about the stiff underskirt biting her behind. The old lady shifts in her wheelchair, suddenly irritable.

"Well, which one? Hurry up, I might croak any minute."

Christina clears her throat, after her first attempt to speak fails. "The last one," she gasps.

"The Doris Day record? What the hell was that supposed to be?"

"A tap dance. But the floor was carpeted, so I—"

"So you bombed." The old lady whoops with laughter. Now she's laughing at *her*. She's just like all grown-ups, after all.

"I was performing good works," Christina replies with all the dignity she can muster.

"You really wanna perform a good work?" The old lady looks directly at her as if she can see her. "Push me outta here, *tout suite*."

* * *

The old lady's room is at the end of a confusing maze of corridors, but she guides Christina left and right, never getting lost once. Christina keeps glancing over her shoulder, expecting a peremptory voice to ask her what she thinks she's doing. She goes over excuses in her mind. The old lady felt sick and wanted to go back to her room. She wanted to lie down and Christina was helping her. She was here to perform good works and couldn't refuse a charitable request, under pain of possible mortal sin.

"This one."

Christina wheels her into a bare, ugly room with walls painted a queasy green, a chipped iron bedstead, and beige linoleum floors. Above the bed is a picture of the Sacred Heart of Jesus. Jesus, looking sultry, points to His exposed red heart, encircled by thorns, the X marking the spot at the end of the treasure map for martyrs. The old lady rests her hand on the wall near her chair, a look of pleasure on her face.

"Pretty, huh?"

Christina doesn't know what to say. "You mean the picture of Jesus?"

"I mean the décor. I redecorate every week. This week's a jungle theme. Tiger-skin walls. Feel 'em. Go ahead. And big flowering plants and vines. Maybe a half-naked man will swing in on one of 'em and take me outta here." The old lady emits a sexy Tarzan yell.

Christina begins edging toward the door. "Um, I better go."

"Stick around. What's your name, kid?"

"Christina Falcone."

The old lady extends her hand as if she's an adult and Christina has a fluttery thrill. "Mellifluous name. That means *sweet-sounding*. My 'Christian' name is Mary Frances Fogarty. Sounds like a fart. But you can call me Babe. That was my stage name at the Old Howard. Babe N'arms. Get it?"

Christina gets only that she is in a room with a strange and wonderful creature from another world. "You were onstage?" She doesn't think she said it out loud. She isn't sure she is still in the room. She feels detached like she's dreaming or levitating. Christina peers down at her feet. Her tap shoes are there, touching the floor. She taps one shoe for the reassuring clicking sound of reality.

"An exotic dancer, kid. The best in the business. Okay. Now, here's what I wantcha to do." Babe goes on to rasp out rapid-fire directions. "In the closet, top shelf. There's a tin box shoved way in back. Bring it down."

Christina hates following directions from adults. She usually gets flustered, and almost always gets it wrong. She is still pondering what it meant to be an "exotic" dancer. What does that mean? She has a feeling it doesn't mean following a tap routine to "Be My Little Baby Bumble Bee."

"Didja get it?" Babe says impatiently.

Christina drags the one chair in the room over to the closet and scrabbles around the top shelf, moving aside scrapbooks and hatboxes, momentarily distracted by a pink feather boa. Finally, she finds the tin box.

"There's a pack of Luckys inside and some matches. Light me one. And one for yourself," Babe instructs.

Matches! The holy grail of the future child martyr. Christina has filched a few matchbooks in her time and narrowly avoided setting the basement on fire on one notable occasion during a reenactment of St. Joan burning at the stake. Rita has banned matches since the basement event, and Christina only gets near fire when her mother is feeling generous and lets her light one of her votive candles in front of St. Pantaleon, the patron saint of lotteries who sits in a place of honor on Rita's bureau.

Christina opens the box and lights the match with a flourish, but getting the cigarette to work is a problem. Babe looks right at her again, as if her sight has been miraculously restored, and tells Christina to stick the cigarette in her mouth, draw in, and light the match. Christina follows orders and stifles the overwhelming urge to cough when the searing smoke reaches her nose. She gives Babe her cigarette and lights her own, affecting an insouciance she doesn't remotely feel. Immediately, a rush of dizziness almost pitches her headfirst onto the beige linoleum floor. She feels as if birds should be twittering over her head, like they do in cartoons when people are knocked out. She drags herself over to Babe's bed and collapses.

"Get the pisspot under the bed. For butts." Babe snorts. "Get it? For butts." She leans back in her chair and blows a perfect smoke ring, utterly content. Christina watches her in a luxurious haze now that the dizziness has passed. This is better than the drive-in. This is really happening. To her.

Christina crawls under the bed. She places the bedpan reverently in Babe's lap. She wants to stay forever and watch the old lady blow smoke rings.

"You better take off, kid. That nun'll be looking for you."

"She's not. She's probably still with the twit." Christina shivers, thrilled at her own boldness. *Twit.* She could hardly wait to use the word on Vinny. She settles herself on the bed, leaning against the wall, her head tipped back like Babe's. The ash on her cigarette telescopes, then tips onto the bed. Christina rubs it into the faded pink chenille bedspread, her eyes on Babe in case God decides to restore her sight that minute.

"Usually, I only get to do this when Clemmie's on nights," Babe growls. "She's the only one around here with any Christian charity." She inclines her head toward Christina. "You too, toots. You're a regular saint."

Mr. Moriarty's station wagon rings with the glad voices of kids basking in the glow of good deeds over and done until next year. All except Rose, who sits forlornly, knees drawn up to her chin, thinking of her aborted performance and the cookies forsworn in favor of flat ginger ale, all she had been allowed by the unrelenting nuns.

Christina is plotting a bike route, memorizing the number of big streets to cross if she ever wants to see

Babe again. The fact that visiting the woman would also be in the category of a "good work" is like scamming God, or at least her nun teachers. Babe is definitely an occasion of sin.

Christina can't wait to see her again.

PART 2

PART 2

STIGMATA

A month before she is to become a Soldier of Christ in the year of Our Lord 1964, Christina's main concern is not her knowledge of Christian doctrine; it is her legs. Specifically: would she be confirmed in front of the entire Precious Blood congregation with the dread "mohair leg" visible to all, or would her mother Rita finally allow her to shave her legs so that she could wear nylons and not be an object of scorn, like Grace Benari, whose arms and legs are so furry the boys follow her home from school grunting and yipping like howler monkeys, calling her Hairy Benary.

Sister Odilia, her tottery eighth-grade teacher, warns the class daily of the awesome responsibility of being called upon by the Cardinal of Boston to answer specific questions relating to the Catholic faith. On the solemn day of their confirmation, the girls will wear special white billowy robes and cover their heads with red beanies. The boys wear red robes, as if they belong to the bird kingdom and are entitled to flashier plumage. They have been rehearsing every week, single file up to the communion rail and then kneeling, cued by the nun's clicker. On the actual day, the cardinal, wearing his satin-embossed fish hat and ceremonial cassock, will go to each of them and anoint their foreheads with holy oil. He will slap each kid's face lightly, murmuring, "Soldier of Christ," which means that the Holy Ghost will then come to them "in a special way," according to the Baltimore Catechism they have memorized slavishly. They will from that day forward profess their faith as strong and perfect Christians and Soldiers of Christ. The "light blow," according to Christina's catechism, means that she should now be ready to die for her faith.

Christina will die if she doesn't shave her legs. She will die if she doesn't grow breasts. She will die if she advances to ninth grade with Rose still her only friend. She will die if she remains invisible to boys in high school.

Today Christina is once again posted on lookout because Sister Odilia has wandered out of the classroom abruptly and with no explanation. She does this at least three times a day, unnerving the class. All the shortest kids sit in the first few rows, and Christina hasn't grown an inch since sixth grade, to her sorrow. Her desk is nearest the door right beside another unfortunate eighth-grade miniature, Steven Costello. She hovers by the door, scanning the hallway and the entrance to the cloakroom while behind her the class sails paper airplane notes to each other and the rolling murmur of their voices crests like an excited audience before a public execution. Margaret Mary Feeney fled the classroom fifteen minutes ago after urgently waving her hand and telling Sister Odilia in a frenzied screech that she had to see the school nurse now, immediately, this minute. Then, without even waiting for permission, she ran out the door in a funny, duck-like way. Sister Odilia had looked confused for a moment, her pebbly blue eyes distracted. She droned on for another ten minutes about the confirmation ceremony, clearing her throat a few times, edging closer and closer to her desk. Then she opened her desk drawer and slipped something into the voluminous pocket of her habit. Finally, she, too, opened the door and walked out.

Patsy Gilli, eighth-grade heartthrob, fires a note to her best friend, Mary Agnes Griffin. Dennis Dempsey intercepts the note and reads it to the class, standing and declaiming like an old-style hammy actor, "Margaret Mary got a visit from her friend and had to go down to Nurse Bug Eyes." He looks at Patsy and wiggles his eyebrows, speaking in his normal bad-boy voice: "For what? Dracula tea bags?"

Patsy and Mary Agnes shriek, horrified and thrilled. Patsy knows just how to toss her boyish cap of dark-blond hair so that it flutters around her face like petals. Her lips, shiny with colorless, nun-deceiving gloss, gleam over perfect teeth. Patsy has three big brothers and boys don't mystify her at all. They relax around her, even when she teases them. Christina studies her, trying to decipher Patsy's alluring ways, but like her Latin homework, they remain lost in translation. Mary Agnes, Patsy's best friend, has perky freckles and lush curly red hair, and Patsy's boy-drawing luster spills over to her, pulling almost as many boys into her orbit.

Patsy holds out her hand to Dennis, a queen demanding tribute. "Gimme that, ya big jerk."

Dennis drops his eyes and hands her the note, yanking it away from her a few times, smirking.

Mary Agnes looks at Christina, who is watching the little scene, enthralled. "Aren't you supposed to be the lookout?"

"Yeah, go see what she's doing," commands Patsy.

"What if she sees me?"

"Get going," Patsy says.

Christina tiptoes to the other end of the cloakroom and carefully cranes her head around the door. She peers inside and thankfully sees that Odilia's back is to her at the far end of the room. The sister stands in the dusty cloakroom wedged on either side by lightweight spring coats. She removes a bottle of cough syrup with codeine from her pocket and tries to pour out another spoonful after spilling an entire precious dose on what looks like Cecilia's tightly woven navy-blue blazer. She gives up on the spoon and swigs the medicine straight from the bottle, then bends down to massage her knees which look like they pain her.

Christina can hear the buzz of hormonal voices rising from the classroom. Odilia lifts her head in a listening position. She caps her cough syrup and looks up. She becomes transfixed by the dust motes dancing in the cloakroom's stale air. She turns, widening her heavy eyelids, an effort that appears to take all her remaining willpower. Christina pulls back cautiously but Odilia is staring up at the dust motes as if they are a message from God she is bound to decipher. The cough syrup finally works its magic, banishing the knee demons. Odilia stands taller, renewed. She staggers forward with determination, an avenger bent on taming the pagan hordes next door. She looks purposeful, as if she will drain the dangerous miasma of sex rising from Christina's classmates like mist from a swamp. As she nears Christina, her left shoulder raking the coats on the girl's side, the coats drop obediently to the floor behind her like penitential dominoes.

Christina slides around the corner and signals the class, wildly waving her arms. "Odilia!"

The class returns to their seats. The nun enters, ignoring them. She reaches down and stealthily returns the cough syrup to her desk drawer. She sits, facing them. The students rise as one, as they have been taught to do since kindergarten, whenever an adult enters or leaves a classroom.

"GOOD MORNING, SISTER ODILIA."

Sister Odilia stares at the class. She clears her throat a few more times, then opens the drawer of her desk and gazes with longing at the cough syrup lying there. She takes a deep breath and closes the drawer. "Today we are discussing stigmata. What is stigmata? Hands, please."

Christina knows everything there is to know about stigmata from her one-track reading of saint biographies. She has since moved on to Gothic horror and science fiction, but still remembers the long list of saints who bled from their hands and feet and sides in imitation of Christ's wounds. Some, like Catherine of Siena, prayed to make their stigmata invisible so they could feel Christ's pain while practicing humility. Christina thinks of them as the show-off saints, gilding God's lily. If she had bleeding palms and feet, she would go on *Community Auditions*, the local televised talent show broadcast every Sunday, and win first prize. She would wear her confirmation robe and let the sleeves fall back in a dramatic flourish as the audience gasped. She waves frantically at Sister Odilia, the *Community Auditions* theme song playing in her head in a continual loop as she mutters, "S'tah, S'tah."

Sister Odilia scans the class, finally settling on Christina with a sigh. "All right. Miss Falcone."

Christina stands, letting her imaginary robe fall back, the words tumbling out: "It's when real blood gushes outta your hands and feet and side and even your forehead sometimes just like Jesus on the cross, and just by thinking about it you can make it spout like a geyser, and—"

"That's enough, Miss Falcone," Sister Odilia interrupts, distaste pulling her features into a rictus of disapproval. "We are discussing a gift from God, not a vampire movie."

Christina sits, shame rising like a red tide. The class giggles. The theme song continues playing in her head, mocking her now.

Star of the day, who will it be?
Your vote will hold the key.
It's up to you, tell us who . . . will be star of
the day!

Sister Odilia moves on to her mainstay, Cecilia. "Miss Moriarty, what is the definition in your catechism?"

"The stigmata are wounds in the hands, feet, side, and forehead like the wounds of Jesus. They are gifts from God to heroic souls allowed to join in the physical suffering of Our Lord." Cecilia sits, after an imperceptible nod in Christina's direction, the kind of blank look children give to unfunny, creepy clowns at a birthday party.

Sister Odilia stands unsteadily and writes *stigmata* on the blackboard in big, loopy letters and begins numbering the effects. Margaret Mary's pale freckled face appears outside the classroom door. The class murmurs her name just low enough to be off Odilia's radar, excited at the small ripple of drama in the middle of a boring day. Christina grabs her moment of redemption while Odilia's back is turned; she jumps up, points at Margaret Mary, and hisses, "Stigmata!" The class roars. Margaret Mary stands outside the door, rooted to the spot.

Sister Odilia turns from the blackboard, outraged. "STOP THAT! DO YOU THINK THE WOUNDS OF CHRIST ARE SOMETHING TO LAUGH ABOUT? YOU DARE TO MOCK THE AGONIES OF PADRE PIO AND ST. FRANCIS OF ASSISI?" She bursts into tears. "GET OUT! ALL OF YOU!"

The class stands, unsure of where to go. They stare at her like a bobble-headed herd of devil-eyed goats. Suddenly exhausted, Sister Odilia opens her desk drawer and looks down. The cough syrup bottle beckons, winking at her like an old friend. She moves with purpose, sweeping the bottle back into her pocket, her eyes never leaving the class.

"Never mind. I'm leaving. You don't deserve my teaching and you don't deserve to be confirmed by the cardinal in June. And you don't deserve to take part in the May procession."

Cecilia gasps. "Oh no, Sister, *I* didn't laugh!"

Sister Odilia lurches through the door, nearly knocking over Margaret Mary on her way out. The stunned class remains silent. Then, some smothered giggles.

Patsy dares to speak first: "She's *mental.*"

"Off the deep end," Mary Agnes, her loyal ally, agrees.

The rest of the class snickers. Cecilia, though, is weeping inconsolably. She had been a lock to crown the Blessed Virgin during the May procession, as she has done every year since fourth grade.

As the giggles mount, Cecilia wails, "It's not funny! We'll be the only eighth-grade class who didn't get to crown the Blessed Virgin. It'll be a disgrace!"

Patsy tells her to shut up, and Danny Grillo pretends to crown Cecilia by whacking her over the head with his math book, which only makes Cecilia cry harder. Now Timothy Mosher pipes up, his soprano voice as yet untouched by male hormones, rising even higher in the grip of his panic. He is headed for the seminary next year when he turns fourteen, his one-way ticket to celibacy having been punched since kindergarten, when the only game he ever wanted to play was priest and he insisted on baptizing everyone with sand during recess. The nuns thought it was darling.

"What about confirmation? We have to be confirmed! They won't take me at the seminary if I'm not confirmed."

Dennis sneers at him. "My heart pumps piss for you, asshole."

The mood in the room turns ugly as the hysteria spreads. Danny Grillo bemoans the loss of at least fifty bucks in cash prizes from relatives if the confirmation is off and Rose speaks with sad resignation of the surf and turf she had planned to order at Anthony's Pier 4. Cecilia continues to cry. Kids wonder aloud if Monsignor Boyle will make an appearance.

Finally, Mary Agnes Griffin turns to Christina and passes sentence with the steely conviction of a cardinal at the Inquisition: "This is all your fault."

Christina, jolted out of an elaborate fantasy based on last Sunday's afternoon movie at the Paramount, manages an aggrieved "It is *not*!"

Forty-eight pairs of accusing eyes fix on Christina, delighted to have someone to blame. Her mind races, flipping through the many plotlines that clutter her brain, looking for redemption.

"I got an idea, you guys."

Christina's offer to save the class is met with groans, snickers, and Patsy's flat-voiced threat: "You better have a plan. You got us into this." She rams a piece of gum in her mouth, and pops a huge bubble, without taking her eyes off Christina.

Ignoring the roller-coaster dip in her confidence, Christina blurts out the plan, hastily drawn from a movie she's seen a dozen times during her saint-obsession phase. "We're gonna do *Song of Bernadette*." She turns to Cecilia. "You're Bernadette. Even though Jennifer Jones had dark hair."

Without stopping for breath, she speaks over the jeers. The class will be on their knees in the corner of the room, praying to the "apparition" of the Blessed Virgin. Cecilia, the obvious choice, will be the one answering the Blessed Virgin, who will demand to be crowned and that the class should be confirmed next month. The plan is foolproof because in the movie adults can't see the apparition, only children, the pure of heart.

Patsy rolls her eyes, snapping her gum. "Are you for real?"

"Off the wall," Mary Agnes chimes in.

The rest of the class sits there, speechless. It takes only a minute for the fear to ramp up again. Rose, sounding hysterical, pictures Odilia returning with the monsignor huffing behind her, furious at missing his lunch. "Then we'll all get killed!"

"Christina's as nuts as Odorous," Mary Agnes says.

Dennis Dempsey steps forward. "That's why it might work."

With the imprimatur of the Worst Boy in School, Christina sees her opening. She leads Cecilia to the spot where she wants her to kneel and points out where she is supposed to see the apparition.

Cecilia balks. "What if I get in trouble?"

"You'll brown-nose your way out of it like you always do," Patsy fires back.

Christina reminds Cecilia that the *News Tribune* features an angelic picture of her every year placing the wreath of flowers on the statue's head. Cecilia falls to her knees like she's been shot.

Christina looks her over, frowning. There's something missing, the ineffable final touch that will convince Odilia that she's in the holy presence of Our Lady. "Got your rosary beads on you, Cecilia?"

Dennis drawls, "Does the pope shit in the woods?"

Confident now, Christina describes the rest of the scenario in detail. She has the backing of the Worst Boy in School.

Sister Odilia hears the chanting before she opens the door. Something is wrong: the students aren't in their seats. She fumbles at the glass doorknob, turning it the wrong way. When the door finally opens, she lurches into the room, off-balance. The entire class is kneeling behind Cecilia, reciting the rosary and staring up at an empty space on the wall in the corner of the classroom. She walks toward the cluster of kids, but is suddenly walking on water like Our Lord, the floorboards turning into waves beneath her feet.

Cecilia is speaking to the air about eight feet above her head. Odilia wades through the kids until she is standing beside the girl.

"White carnations and red roses. And you want *me* to crown you." Cecilia, breaking character, can't resist a sidelong peek at the nun beside her. Odilia stares at the designated place high up on the wall, like everyone else. Christina, on Cecilia's other side, pinches her hard. Cecilia squeaks. "Okay, anything else?" Her face reassumes its radiant expression. "Sister Odilia's class must be confirmed as soldiers in My Son's church. Okay, got it."

Odilia starts to sway on her feet. "Wha . . . what is going on here?" she croaks.

The class begins singing, their voices joyous and, for once, in perfect pitch: "*Oh Mary, we crown thee with blossoms today / Queen of the angels, Queen of the May.*"

Odilia sinks to her knees. Now comes Christina's cue. She tugs at Odilia's sleeve, barely able to contain herself. The plan is working!

"The Blessed Virgin is speaking to Cecilia. Can you see her?"

Odilia looks up. "Oh my God! Oh my God!" Is that a sparkling light in the corner of her eye? Yes, it is! A light! But wait—was it only a reflection from the window? Odilia leans back on her wobbly knees to find the light, but that makes her dizzy. She drops her head forward. The waves rise higher and the sun-lit wooden floor comes up to meet her. Then, as if abruptly switching religions, she salaams forward, her forehead clunking the floor.

There is a collective gasp from the class. No one moves toward the heap of nun on the ground.

Finally, Danny Grillo dares to speak: "Holy shit!"

Christina has only one thrumming thought: *I have killed a nun.*

Like an echo outside her head, Cecilia begins to wail: "She's dead!"

Suddenly Odilia lets out a loud snort. The class jumps back as if she has just burst into flames. Odilia, sound asleep, settles herself more comfortably, her wimple askew, face mashed sideways into the floor, legs straight out behind her. She resumes snoring.

After the flooding relief of Sister Odilia's resurrection, spiky new thoughts of being led away in handcuffs root Christina to the floor. The rest of the class stand like prisoners at a roll call, as if confirming Christina's jailhouse future.

Mary Agnes recovers first. Nuns hold no particular mystery for her. She has seen a nun eat. Not one of the other kids at Precious Blood has ever actually seen a nun put food in her mouth, then chew and swallow it. They have seen nuns receive communion and swallow the Body of Christ, of course, but that doesn't count. The mysteries of nuns are many, and to see one of them asleep on the floor in front of them, like a run-over crow on a highway, renders the entire class mute. Except for Mary Agnes, elevated to insider status by having a nun aunt, one who comes to family funerals and celebrations and sits down at the table and eats food like a normal person. She gives Christina a little shove.

"Go get Gonzo."

"Me?" Christina responds. Her mind pinwheels with excuses spun by sheer terror.

The loud pop of a giant pink bubble breaks the tense standoff. Patsy's face emerges from the deflating pink goo and she niftily tucks the gum back into her wide mouth with an expert tongue. "Nah," she says to Mary Agnes. "You go. You got the nun aunt an' all." She turns to the rest of the class. "And all of yis better keep yuh mouths shut. Or we're all screwed."

The class nods as one, rapt, as if they are receiving messages from the Mother of God.

All the way home Rose blubbers about the bunny-fur jacket. No one could understand how, in the course of that strange nun-knockout afternoon, Rose's jacket had been found on the hall floor near the cloakroom with black scuff marks and missing a pom-pom. Rose talks on and on about the nonnas, how upset they will be, how they'll start chanting the anti-*malocchio* to ward off whatever enemy has destroyed the jacket, how her mother will be so mad she'll probably slap her. Christina thinks of suggesting a visit to her father's bar, with its trove of lollipops for bored kids, just to shut her up, but she is too depressed to face him, and afraid she might blurt out what's on her mind: that he will soon find out he is the father of a girl destined for reform school, a *disgraziata*, a daughter who has disgraced the Falcone name. The class had been spared the sight of Sister Odilia being hauled up onto her feet and lugged back to the convent. Sister Gonzaga had hustled them over to the church to recite a

rosary for Sister Odilia's recovery, led by Father Mc-
Mullin, the junior parish priest, an imposingly bluff,
red-cheeked young prelate who only seems engaged
when contact sports are happening somewhere. After the endless repetition of Hail Marys and Glory
Be's, the shell-shocked class had dispersed and began
trudging home, making a wide circle around Christina
and Rose, her loyal, oblivious sidekick.

The minute Christina opens the front door, she
gets into a fight with her mother. She has barely slung
off her heavy book bag before Rita informs her that
she'd better get ready for an early dinner (the zombie return of the hated, slurp-inducing Friday-night
staple, pasta fagioli). Rita stands before the hall mirror in her white nylon slip, her housecoat open, applying makeup. Joe is taking her to Blinstrub's, an
old-person nightclub her mother thinks is the height
of glamour, to hear dipshitty Lawrence Welk music
in the company of the same people they eat polenta
with around picnic tables at the Sons of Italy outings,
Lena and Rocco and Anna and Dibby, all of whom
think yelling is friendly banter. Christina has seen
the formal pictures at a table taken by a wandering
Blinstrub's photographer, the women in low-cut satin
dresses, the men in suits, waving cigars around like
big shots. Her mother is so ignorant. Has she learned
nothing from all those years of watching *The Edge of
Night*? No one on *The Edge of Night* tells dirty jokes
in another language or laughs like a screaming sea
bird. Glamour. Christina snorts, unwittingly mimick-
ing her mother's favorite expression of contempt.

Her mother notices the borderline disrespect, and parries with a low blow, meant to enrage: "Nonno gonna watch you an' Vinny."

Christina's voice rises, even as she is at the same time infuriated with herself for her own predictable reaction. She screams over the banister, halfway up the stairs to her room, "I'm thirteen! No one needs to watch me!"

Now her mother snorts, having scored a defensive cut—not the coup de grâce, but a worthy effort. Rita returns to applying her trademark Revlon Fire and Ice bloodred lipstick, blotting her full lips onto a tissue, then letting the tube fall onto the hall table, a perfect kiss-off for her snotty daughter.

Christina sulks on the nubbly sofa, refusing to say goodbye when her mother and father take their leave, her mother dressed in a slinky number that shows plenty of in-Christina's-face cleavage. She ignores both Nonno and Vinny all night, waiting impatiently for them to go to bed so she can watch her favorite show, *The Twilight Zone*, in peace. Nonno and Vinny chortle throughout *The Flintstones*, but start to fade sometime after the snappy opening song of *77 Sunset Strip*. Nonno loves Edd "Kookie" Byrnes almost as much as Christina does, which kind of takes the luster off. Still, she is drawn to Kookie's smart-aleckiness, which reminds her somehow of Dennis Dempsey. At last, her grandfather rises creakily from his rocker, his old farmer knees snapping like kindling, and says his nightly benediction: "Eh. I go to bed." Christina nudges Vinny ungently with her stockinged foot where he lies dozing in a crumpled heap on the other end of the sofa, and he stumbles up the stairs sleepwalking behind Nonno. She is about to remind him to pee so he won't wet the bed, but then thinks better of it, exacting her own petty revenge against Rita, who will be yanking urine-soaked sheets off his bed tomorrow morning, muttering curses to herself in Abruzzese dialect.

Now she sits riveted as Rod Serling introduces that night's episode, "Nightmare as a Child," starring a Cecilia-like little girl named Markie. Markie is really the grown-up main lady, a pretty dark-haired teacher's actual self as a child. The pretty teacher has buried her childhood memory of seeing her mother killed and now the killer has returned to see if she remembers him. Markie is there to warn her to face her fear and recall what really happened so she can escape the killer. Christina wonders if fear could actually cause you to recreate your younger self, a three-dimensional replica that can go around interacting with other people. She pictures waking up next to a living copy of her nine-year-old self in the morning, the one who wanted to be God's best friend, a saint. A hot bolt of fear passes through her body. She doesn't want to see that Christina. Now she's afraid to go to bed. Great. She will have to stay up until her parents get home.

Her parents open the door around midnight in a burst of meaningful giggles and sexy murmurs cut short when Rita notes with disapproval that Christina is still up. Christina flees to her room, away from any disturbing hint of parental congress. She jumps into bed and squeezes her eyes shut, willing instant sleep, to no avail. If she stays awake, she might hear something that will make her head explode. But nine-year-old Christina is waiting to materialize if she sleeps. She keeps dropping off, then bolting awake and checking the bed, feeling around in the dark for her child-interloper self. Asking her mother to sleep with her is out of the question. She thinks of climbing into Vinny's little bed in his cowboy-themed room, but by now his sheets will be sodden with urine. She resigns herself to lying awake and tries not to picture Monday morning and the announcement at school that the police have come to take her away.

On Monday morning, Christina drags her feet all the way up Derby Street as if she's already on a chain gang. She can't hear a word Rose is saying, not with the clanking of leg irons in her head. They cross the big street before the long one that ends at school, Christina barely making it to the other side before the light turns red again. Mary Agnes and Patsy appear on the corner, preceded by a shocking blast of celestial strings as "Will You Love Me Tomorrow" blares forth like a royal fanfare from Patsy's turquoise transistor radio.

"Falcone," Patsy calls.

Christina doesn't hear her over Shirley Owens's big bad-girl voice singing, *"So tell me now, and I won't ask again / Will you still love me tomorrow?"* Patsy and Mary Agnes have always ignored Christina and Rose as lesser beings unworthy of notice even though their paths cross on the way to Precious Blood every day.

"FALCONE, YOU FISH, I'M CALLIN' YOU!"

Christina halts, eyeing her father's bar a few feet away with trepidation.

Patsy runs up to Christina and blurts, "Guess what happened to Odilia?"

Before Christina or Rose can reply, Mary Agnes, who has been taking drags off, then cupping a cigarette, drawls like a television bad guy: "St. Dymphna's. The loony bin for nuns."

Patsy shoots an aggrieved look at Mary Agnes. "*I* was gonna tell her that. Anyway, she's gone for good, and we're getting Sister Bernie!"

Mary Agnes has gotten the scoop over the weekend from her nun-aunt connection. Christina tries to digest this news through Rose's screams of delight. Everyone knows Sister Bernadette, a new nun who is a substitute teacher on days when the regulars have a doctor's appointment or some other mysterious reason for not being in class. Sister Bernadette is young, pretty, and soft-spoken, a nun from central casting, and the single days when she is the surprise teacher have been little snippets of grace for the beleaguered Precious Blood inmates. But this welcome turn of events hasn't registered with Christina yet; she is bathed immediately in sweet relief. She will not go to jail! Her family will not be disgraced! And maybe, just maybe . . . the whole class will no longer hate her. She feels the urge to scream with joy, to dance a jittery tarantella of utter release.

Rose throws her arms around Christina. "You're not in trouble! An' we're getting Sister Bernie!"

Mary Agnes peers at Rose, squinting as she takes a surreptitious drag of her cigarette. In a voice of doom, she reminds Rose that they would only have Sister Bernie for about two months, until the end of eighth grade. "And next year is Thecla Marie," she says. Sister Thecla Marie is legendary in the annals of horror stories told and retold by PB students. The older kids call her "Captain Queeg" after the obsessive-compulsive commander in *The Caine Mutiny*, because of the quirky-even-for-a-nun rules she enforces around posture, answering questions in class, and arranging desks. Her face is eerily tiny and dominated by a pair of oversized front teeth with a huge gap between them; she looks like a demented beaver that chews human flesh instead of wood.

"She broke a kid's arm, y'know," says Patsy.

All four girls scream and clutch each other, jumping up and down in an ecstasy of adolescent terror.

"We're goin' to Mr. Pup's after school. Wanna come?" Patsy says. Mr. Pup's is a hole in the wall that serves Cokes out of dusty bottles and stale candy at a peeling plastic counter. The omniscient nuns, who appear to have extrasensory perception, have forbidden the Precious Blood students from hanging around at Mr. Pup's. How do they know it's a place where ninth-graders flirt with each other on a clumsy adolescent learning curve, where senior boys make leering comments about the girls under their breaths? Nuns never leave the convent except to go to the dentist or the doctor in safe pairs, so how do they know about Mr. Pup's? Christina fears their alien-intelligence capabilities.

"Sister Odilia says that Mr. Pup's is an occasion of sin," Rose ventures, timidly.

"Who gives a shit. She's officially nuts," says Patsy. Rose giggles.

The girls fall into step and walk four abreast like a squadron that means business. Christina feels their collective power—they are the four Musketeers! The Marcels are singing "Blue Moon" on Patsy's radio. Christina's happiness surges and she steers the conversation back to the exciting Sister Thecla Marie problem.

"Y'know what? I think Thecla Marie's not even a nun. I think maybe she's a morlock like in *The Time Machine* and we'll all turn into the Eloi, and we'll all become blond *stoonad* zombies, an'—"

"Two things, Falcone," Patsy interrupts, her face stern as a nun's. "If you wanna hang around with us, stop sayin' weird things and"—here she looks Christina up and down—"start shavin' your legs."

BRIDE OF CHRIST

The eighth-grade class blesses the hour, prompted by the bell. They put down their pens at once and cross themselves, raising their eyes to the crucifix above the blackboard, flanked on one side by Pope John XXIII and the other by John Fitzgerald Kennedy. The class sings, *In the name of the Father, and the Son, and the Holy Ghost. Amen.* Sister Bernadette smiles at them. The class smiles back, captivated. Sister Bernadette is a nun so far from the usual coven of harridans teaching at Precious Blood Junior High, it's as if Tinkerbell or the tooth fairy has donned a habit and decided to grace them all.

Sister Bernadette holds up a picture of a body reclining in an enclosed glass coffin, like Snow White. She explains to the class that the body is St. Catherine Labouré, a French nun who had received a message from the Blessed Virgin to tell people to wear a medal she described to the saint, the miraculous medal that many of the class have received at their First Holy Communion. Sister Bernadette goes on to explain that St. Catherine Labouré died in 1876. Fifty-seven years later, the Church exhumed her body and it was found to be incorrupt: there were no signs of decay and her limbs were still supple. St. Catherine Labouré isn't the only incorruptible saint, their teacher says. At one time, the Church used incorruptibility as a requirement for sainthood. The Little Flower, St. Thérèse of Lisieux, was incorrupt, as was the nun's namesake, Bernadette of Lourdes, and many, many others. Sister Bernadette bestows another gleaming smile on the class.

Christina has heard very little about the incorruptibles. Normally she would've been all over this deliciously grisly subject, but so entranced is she by the way Sister Bernadette's delicately feathered black eyebrows lift above her indigo eyes when she smiles, Christina can think of nothing else but the nun's radiant beauty. She pictures Sister Bernadette's matching coal-black hair, shiny and straight, underneath her wimple. It is probably short, like Audrey Hepburn's in *The Nun's Story*, and wispily fine, not coarse and horsey, like her mother's. She wishes Sister Bernie were her big sister. She looks like an adorable elf. She is an elf of God, Christina decides.

"This, class, is a miracle. Can anyone give me another example of a miracle?"

Christina's hand shoots up before she thinks through her answer. She has to get on Sister Bernie's radar.

"Yes, Christina?"

Christina stands to answer, averting her eyes. She can't speak and look at Sister Bernie at the same time. She swoons to think that Sister Bernie uses first names for students without the formal, condescending "Miss" in front of their last names like the other nuns. She realizes the moment she stands that what she has to say is ridiculous and might actually provoke the class to uncontrollable mocking laughter, but she plunges ahead anyway, speaking all in one breath, as quietly as if she is confessing to murder.

"Once when I was at Norumbega Park I spent all my money on rides and then I couldn't get home because I didn't have money for the bus and then I found a quarter right under the witch at the haunted house like it was a sign from God and I could take the bus home and it was a miracle because I needed to get home." She clears her throat. "On the bus which cost a quarter," she adds. She sits down and stares at her scuffed wooden desktop. She ventures a peek at Sister Bernie, who is still smiling, except now her smile looks fake, like the smile on a department store dummy. Christina looks around at the class gingerly. She sees Patsy rolling her eyes at Mary Agnes and shaking her head.

Sister Bernadette nods. "Er, well, God works in our lives in many ways. I'll tell you a story from my own life."

The class stirs with interest. Nuns never tell you anything about their personal lives.

"When I wasn't much older than you, I prayed very hard to hear God's special voice telling me I had a vocation. You should do the same, boys and girls."

The girls in the class shift in their seats, disap-

pointed. This is no juicy insight into Sister Bernadette's pre-convent life. Instead, it's the same tired
pitch to sign up.

Noting the audience drifting away, Sister Bernadette picks up the pace: "And . . . at that very second,
Elvis came on the radio singing 'I Want You, I Need
You, I Love You.'" The nun stares at the class expec-
tantly. "Do you see? It wasn't Elvis speaking to me.
It was really Jesus's voice telling me He wanted me,
loved me, *needed* me as His divine spouse!"

It is possible to get radio messages from God,
Christina thinks, with a kind of wonder she hasn't felt
since the Christmas mornings of long ago. Elvis could
change into God, like bread and wine could change
into the body and blood of Christ. It is thrilling. There
are messages that are trying to come through to Christina, maybe. She just has to pay more attention to the
pink plastic radio in her room. She has probably been
tuning in to the wrong station, and God is having a
hard time coming through Arnie "Woo-Woo" Ginsburg on WMEX. As if from a distance Christina hears
Mary Agnes asking Sister Bernadette if she had boyfriends when she was a teenager, and her friend Rose's
excited high-pitched giggle.

Sister Bernadette explains that she had lots of
dates when she was in high school, but that she wanted
something more.

Patsy raises her hand and stands. "But . . . didn't
you have fun, S'tah?"

"Oh, yes, dear, I had fun, but the dates didn't make
me happy. What made me truly happy was to give

myself entirely to God and experience the fullness of His love away from worldly distractions. Because, boys and girls, today we are discussing miracles. And God's love is a miracle! Love is a miracle!"

The boys begin chasing the girls before they even get out of the schoolyard, trying to hit them with their green book bags. The girls shriek with delight and simulated fear, coming close then zigzagging away, all except for nuns-in-training Cecilia and Margaret Mary who walk away, their squared shoulders signaling disapproval. The boys ignore them; they have no love for Cecilia and her wannabe-saint sidekick.

Dennis Dempsey catches up with Christina and scores a direct hit on her shoulder. She turns, squealing, and lifts her bag, but before she can land a return shoulder slam, he reaches in and gives her nose a Three Stooges–style tweak. They stand, panting, facing each other in a limitless time zone of adolescent possibility. Giddy anticipation pushes Christina's lips into an almost-kissable pout. She wants to burst out laughing. A boy wants her! The worst boy in school wants her! Dennis's blue eyes are intent on her face. Christina marvels at the adorable cinnamon freckles scattered over his tiny, up-tilted nose. She loves his nose; she wants it for herself. If she had Dennis's nose she would be cute, perky, American, like Tuesday Weld, the blond beauty on *Dobie Gillis*. Dennis lifts his hand and, in a reverse salute, places it on Christina's forehead, above her eyes. He looks at her. Christina thinks he will tell her then. He will say, *I want you, I need you, I love you*. This is the moment.

"Your eyes are brown. That means you're full of shit up to here," he says.

She turns and runs, the rush of disappointment pumping her legs higher and higher, until she catches up with Patsy and Mary Agnes and Rose.

Christina slumps on her bed after dinner, the scenes from that afternoon running through her mind in a headachy loop. She had gone to Mr. Pup's with Patsy and Mary Agnes and Rose and watched from a corner as the senior boys eyed Patsy and Mary Agnes, ignoring Rose and Christina. One of the seniors, a squat boy with a brush cut and bad skin, even bought Patsy a Coke. She ignored him with enviable restraint. How did Patsy always know how to act with boys? The brush-cut boy was now dazed with love for her. Danny Grillo came in with Dennis. Christina turned away from Rose, her lifeline, and faced the wall, pretending to stare at a dusty, out-of-date calendar. Danny struck up an awkward conversation with Rose, asking to copy her math homework. Christina smirked at the wall, hearing that one: Rose got sixties in math. Mary Agnes gave them the invisible signal to leave, and Christina and Rose got up, like drones following the queen. Christina had to squeeze by Dennis, who acted like she was a person with a contagious disease, not even looking at her, his body leaning farther away than was necessary as she edged by him, eyes to the ground like a penitent.

Through her closed bedroom door, Christina can

hear her mother's teasing faraway voice responding to something her father said. Christina will never get married. She will never talk to a boy in a special voice. She hates boys, which is good, because they hate her back. She thinks of Sister Bernadette and Audrey Hepburn in their little cells, away from the world. She wants to be shut away from the world and not have to talk to anyone.

Christina leaps up and turns on her pink plastic radio. If Sister Bernie can get a message from Jesus over the airwaves, maybe she can, too.

> *Adventure Car Hop is the place to go*
> *For food that's always right*
> *Adventure food is always just so*
> *You'll relish every bite!*

The jingle goes on for another two verses, then Arnie "Woo-Woo" Ginsburg comes on urging kids to order the "Ginsburger" that is served on a record you get to keep. And if you say "Woo woo" to the car-hop, you get another Ginsburger for free. Christina is disgusted. She turns off the radio in the middle of an avalanche of cowbells and Klaxon horns. Obviously, she is just a joke to Jesus. She will show Him she is serious. Suddenly determined, she runs downstairs.

"Daddy, I'm gonna be a nun," she blurts.

Her father is distracted, his eyes on the television news. "Huh?" he says.

"I'm gonna be a nun. Like Audrey Hepburn in *The Nun's Story*."

Joe smiles at her. "Over my dead body. I wanna walk you down the aisle someday."

Her little brother looks up from his coloring book. "You're ugly enough to be a nun," he says.

Christina makes her witch face at Vinny, the one that always makes him go limp with fear. She walks slowly toward him, adding an eerie laugh. Vinny tries not to cower, but the scary voice gets to him and he begins to whimper.

"Eh, s'all right, s'all right," says her grandfather, employing one of the few English phrases he knows, his skinny body lost in the depths of his chair.

Joe loses his patience. "I'm tryin' to watch this! RITA!" he calls.

Rita rushes in from the kitchen in time to hear Christina and Vinny stake out their positions.

"He called me ugly!"

"She tried to scare me, Mummy!"

Joe looks up at Rita. "Now your daughter wants to be a nun," he says.

Rita looks at Christina and smirks. "*You* gonna keep your mouth shut?" She mock-blesses herself in Italian, then says to Joe: "She wants to wash the priest's *mutande* for free for the rest of her life!" Rita and Joe both have a good laugh at the idea of Christina washing the priest's underpants.

Christina storms up the stairs to her room, yelling over the railing to her stupid, insensitive family: "You'll all have to visit me behind bars when I join the Carmelites!"

"YOU BETTER SHUT UP OR YOU WILL BE

BEHIND BARS! IN THE NUTHOUSE!" Rita shoots back.

Christina slams the door to her room and flings herself back onto her bed, her mother's shrill "Sominabitch! No slamma the door!" muted and distant, like a bad memory. She lies back on her pillow, picturing herself in a flattering white habit, her features transformed into Audrey Hepburn's, nose slimmed and tilted, her now flawless complexion enhanced by the white wimple and flowing veil. Her family would come to visit and she would receive them, seated behind the grille. They would be nervous and insecure at her calm, saintly bearing. Her mother would beg her to pray for them, and ask her for a winning lottery number. Christina would agree to pray for Rita but would warn her mother that her Bridegroom, Jesus, is unhappy with Rita, that she never goes to church and says too many swears. Rita would fall to her knees, weeping, asking for forgiveness. Then Dennis would come in. He would be struck dumb by her radiant beauty, enhanced by the habit. He would be unable to look at her. He would also beg her forgiveness for his rude behavior. He would tell her that every time he looks into her brown eyes, he can hardly keep from fainting, he is so overcome with love for her, that his love for Christina is making him mad with desire, that she has to be his girlfriend, that he will buy her a Ginsburger and a charm bracelet and a friendship ring to wear around her neck. Christina would be demure, murmuring that her Husband didn't want Dennis to speak to her like that. Then the voice of

God would boom down at Dennis and her heavenly Husband would tell him to GO TO HELL, that he is cursed and can only be redeemed by doing penance for the sin of insulting Christina, the Bride of Christ.

The phone rings in the hall. Christina races to get it before her mother picks up. It's Patsy. "Dennis Dempsey likes you," she says.

BABE

Christina takes a quick drag of Babe's cigarette before passing it to her. By now she is able to light up like a pro, without coughing. They are sitting companionably side by side, Christina on a stone bench, Babe in her wheelchair, sheltered by a giant rhododendron in the scraggly back garden of St. Lucy's Home for the Aged Blind. Babe sits with her face upturned to the sun. Christina stares at the tiny wrinkles lining her closed eyes. Babe's skin looks translucent, like her mother's prized miniature milk-glass animal collection.

"So where'dja tell your mother you were?"

"Confession. But this time I really shoulda gone. I got in trouble at school."

Babe's doll eyes fly open at that. Then she cackles with delight, hissing out a stream of thin blue smoke.

Christina has been visiting Babe for four years now, ever since her fourth-grade class had been dragooned into performing at St. Lucy's. Christina doesn't like to think about her disastrous tap-dancing performance, but she has been richly compensated by her friendship with Babe. Babe is still the most glamorous old lady Christina has met, and Christina never tires of Babe's trove of stories that don't seem to run out, each one more fantastical than the next.

Before Christina had met Babe, she was used to tiny little nonnas dressed in black, their white hair skinned back into buns, their outsize voices gruff and gravelly, urging her to eat, eat, eat. Babe is long and lean, with a feathery gamine cap of silvery hair and eyes as green as the land of her Irish ancestors.

"Do tell," Babe says. She takes a long drag of her cigarette and double-dragon exhales, smoke flowing upward to her nose and back again to her lipsticked mouth, a move that never fails to impress Christina.

"It was bad. Everyone knows I started it and I'm afraid someone's gonna tell. And then I'll get killed. And maybe expelled. And everyone's mad at me at school." Christina feels the relief of saying it out loud. She has never felt this lightening of spirit after actually going to confession, when she recites the same unvarying list of venial sins: talking back to her mother, sneakily assaulting her brother, being mean to Rose, her best friend since babyhood. Always omitting, of course, the strange, exciting, and wrong, so wrong impure acts of touching herself every night when she is lying in bed after first running her hands over her breasts to check for any growth and suffering the daily crushing disappointment when the status quo remains unchanged: flat, flat, flat as a board. But you can't go to jail for touching yourself, Christina is pretty sure of that, although what do "sodomy laws" mean? She heard that on the news or somewhere. She thinks sodomy is just about some woman being punished by turning into a pillar of salt for being too curious and looking at what she shouldn't. The murky sixth commandment is in there somehow, though. That salt woman was probably staring at someone's privates, like when Vinny was a baby and Christina peeked at his nether parts when her mother bathed him in the sink.

"Well? You gonna just leave me hangin'?"

Christina hastily abandons the disturbing brain-picture of Vinny's snaillike penis. "All we were doing was turning cartwheels during recess. Some drippy girls were talking about sodality and I started a cheer for the Blessed Mother to make fun of them. Then I turned a cartwheel, then Patsy did, then all my other friends did, too. Then when we came in from lunch, Sister sent the boys to study hall, and then the priest came in, too."

"Geez, they called in the Gestapo," Babe says, mock-impressed.

"Father McMullin asked us if we could imagine the Blessed Mother turning cartwheels."

That gets a loud snicker from Babe.

"I still don't get what the big deal was all about," Christina says.

"Were the boys watchin' ya?" Babe asks.

Christina, suddenly uncomfortable, shrugs. Then she remembers Babe can't see her shoulders, so she mumbles something noncommittal. She doesn't like where the conversation is going.

"It was about sex, kiddo," Babe declares.

Christina is sorry she told Babe about the cartwheel episode. She wants to drop it, this sex talk. She assumes a frosty teachery tone. "I don't think so, Babe. The priest said it was because Our Lady wouldn't ever turn cartwheels." She leaves out the part about the priest telling them to confess their sins of impurity.

Babe is unmoved. "Trust me, kid, it was about sex."

"I don't think so. I gotta go now. My mother's probably worried about where I am."

Babe can be mean sometimes, making fun of Christina in a way that Christina can't exactly pinpoint, but she knows Babe is laughing at her all the same. Still, Babe is experienced. Christina's mother has only had one boyfriend: her father. Babe has had too many to even remember. They are reading Colette now during Christina's visits. Babe told Christina how to get a book past the hawk-eye librarian if she decided it was "too old" for her and refused to check it out. "Just stick it in your schoolbag—they'll never miss it. I bet no one's checked it out in years," Babe said.

Christina is afraid to steal a book. There is no absolution for stealing until you make restitution. That is easily solved in the case of a library book, but what if the theft bans her forever from the library? It isn't worth the risk. Instead, she brought Colette up to the desk, and the librarian had just stamped it and handed it back to her. Possibly, she thought *Gigi* was about an innocent young girl, not a courtesan in training. Christina is learning about courtesans. When she looked up what it meant, the first definition was "prostitute."

She understands from the book that if you are pretty enough, some man will pay your rent and take you out to dinner and give you jewels and furs. But you have to be nice to the man all the time. Christina doesn't think she could do this. Neither does she think she's pretty enough. Sex is involved but Colette isn't too specific about how and in what way. This is frustrating to Christina, but she doesn't want to ask Babe in case Babe laughs at her. Yet that is the least of her worries now. Christina needs Babe's worldly assurances.

"What if I get kicked out of school and arrested for . . . for impurity? Probably it'll be Cecilia who squeals that it was me. An' then I'll be kicked out of school and arrested," she finishes glumly.

The more she says it out loud, the less likely it is to happen, she hopes, in accordance with the magical "Step on a crack, break your mother's back" rule. She waits for Babe's reaction. There is none. She just sits there with her eyes closed. At least her enviable chest, wasted on an old lady, is moving up and down. Her cigarette falls from her hand. Is she asleep? Is she . . . in a coma? Has Christina's story put Babe in a coma? Is this God's punishment for lies and sins of impurity? Fear shoots up her arms, and she shakes Babe like a jerky, uncoordinated puppet.

"Babe!" she barks.

"Jesus Christ on a cracker, whadja do that for?!" Babe's voice is mild, though she's scowling.

"I thought you fell asleep."

"Just takin' a breather during intermission."

Christina breathes deeply and asks again: "So, do you think Cecilia will squeal that I started it, the cart-wheels, and I'll be kicked out of school for . . . for impurity? And maybe arrested?" She garbles the words in a rush and awaits Babe's verdict.

Babe holds the pack of cigarettes out to Christina, who lights another one and hands it to her. "You got a get-outta-jail-free card, kid. Stop worryin'."

"But what if—"

Babe cuts her off and floors her with her next remark: "I was in jail once, y'know. It's not that bad. Better than this place."

Christina's mouth hangs ajar. "What? You were arrested?"

Babe hisses out a stream of smoke along with a dry chuckle. "The bluenoses at the Watch and Ward complained about our 'sinuousity.' After they got a real good look, of course. Ann Corio bailed us all out. She was Italian, like you. Her old ma useta say, 'Long as they look-a, but no touch.'"

Christina is confused. Who were the bluenoses and how could they throw dancers in jail? "So they put you in jail just for dancing?"

Babe sighs. "Speakin' of jail, you better wheel me back in. And stop worryin', kid. You're already in jail in case you didn't know, and in a few years you'll be paroled into the big wide world and you can tell them all to piss off."

A WOMAN OF POISE,
MYSTERY, AND ALLURE

On the first weekday morning of summer vacation, Christina meets Patsy at the entrance to Nonantum Park. They make final checks on their outfits. Both are wearing white shorts and a pink ruffled sleeveless top. Neither Patsy nor Christina is disturbed by their unplanned twin outfits. Instead, they are comforted by the sameness, as if they are still wearing their Precious Blood school uniforms, members of a powerful club. Together they survey the tree-less expanse of the park cordoned off by a chain-link fence ripped in several places and offering an easy escape for cherry-bombers during police raids. There is a prison yard–like square of cracked cement with two basketball hoops missing nets on either end, and a small concrete building where the little kids can make pot holders and key chains when the recreation director bothers to show up. Feral-looking children swarm over the four available swings, jostling and elbowing for turns. Most of the older kids are sprawled in the stingy shade offered by a few skinny maples at the far end of the park. That's the sweet spot, the destination that will provide an infinity loop of possibilities for fun.

Patsy pulls out her lipstick and slathers on some Frosted Bubblegum Pink without even looking in a mirror. Christina watches her with admiration. It's a skill she hasn't acquired yet but one she hopes to perfect this summer. That very morning, Christina had luxuriated in bed, going over her plan to reinvent herself as a person of poise, mystery, and allure in time for freshman year next September. She is gaining confidence on the allure front, since Dennis Dempsey's off-and-on interest seems promising, but poise and mystery will take all summer to attain. There are plenty of hints for becoming poised in her June copy of *Teen* magazine, and she has decided to add mystery to the mix. Becoming a woman of mystery will be the most difficult because she is by nature a blurter, always volunteering too much information and saying the wrong thing at the wrong time.

Just before the noon deadline for meeting Patsy, Christina's fresh mouth has almost curtailed the visit to the park. Her mother lists all the things Christina has to do before she can go to the library (her alibi for the park): clean her room, dust the parlor, dry-mop the hall. Christina informs Rita in her haughtiest movie-queen voice that maybe slavery is still legal in Italy, but in *this* country, Lincoln freed the slaves a hundred years ago. The convenient arrival of her aunt Connie has averted full-scale war. Connie, heavily pregnant, huffs in carrying her snotty toddler, Dommie Boy. Rita hisses, "Take 'im!" jerking her chin. But Christina, skeeving his leaky nose and grubby little paws, pretends not to hear. Rita bites her hand, glaring, and then scoops up the baby, nuzzling the rolls of his moist-looking neck.

Connie collapses into a kitchen chair. "Don't have kids, honey," she says to Christina, smiling to show she's kidding. Christina looks at her and sees a pretty face, now almost unrecognizable, puffy and blotchy with heat. Her eyes travel down to her aunt's looming belly, taut and distended, her swollen ankles. Christina feels equal parts irritation and pity. In this way she is the same as her mother and father, who often sigh and cluck over Connie and Big Dommie's ongoing dramas.

Big Dommie works for Christina's father at the bar and she hears occasional muffled rantings from Joe behind the bedroom door about what a *mammaluc'* Big Dommie is, how he blows his pay on bookies, how he gives away drinks at the bar, how his poor sister has ruined her life. Connie and Big Dommie are fallen idols. Once, they were Cinderella and her prince and together threw a radiant light that drew Christina like a magic spell. Christina, dressed in her own pink princess gown and matching bonnet, had scattered rose petals down the nave of Precious Blood Church as a three-year-old flower girl at their fairy-tale wedding. Christina's father hated the wedding. Connie had been eighteen at the time, sixteen years younger than Joe. Joe didn't like Big Dommie, a callow, swaggering, handsome boy exactly the same age as Connie. Christina loved Big Dommie, who took her with them for rides in his souped-up car and for ice cream at Howard Johnson's. At six, she wanted them to adopt her so she could bask forever in their reflected glory. Now she feels like someone who has narrowly escaped from a house made of candy hiding the evil hungry witch inside.

"I won't," Christina says.

Connie, already distracted, unpacking the log of provolone she brought for Rita, looks at Christina. "What?"

"I won't. Have kids," Christina replies as if her hand is on a Bible and she's taking a solemn vow.

Connie laughs, and Christina sees her opening. She races out the door, leaving Rita and Connie to their clucking housewifely concerns. Christina runs all the way up Derby Street toward the promise of romance until she is gasping like a woman in the throes of passion, or at least the ones she has read about over and over in everything from the sublime *Wuthering Heights* to the trashy *True Story* magazines she gets from Connie. Christina isn't reading romance for its literary value, though; she wants instruction in the ways of men.

Patsy smacks her lips, finished with the lipstick, and squints across the park. She needs glasses but refuses to wear them. "ANGIE!" She begins waving frantically at the group under the trees.

Christina sees orange-peroxided hair in the distance, glinting in the sun like the helmet of a Norse invader. "Is that Angie Vasolo?" she asks, trying to keep the quaver out of her voice.

"Yuh. She's my third cousin, on my mother's side."

"I thought public school has two more weeks."

"She probably skipped," Patsy answers, a glow of pride for her cousin's daring in her voice.

Angie is sixteen and has been *kept back*. She goes to Wizzie, Wiswall Junior High, where she commands a gang of ninth-grade tough girls, who are to be avoided at all costs in case you look at them funny by mistake and wind up wearing a cast on your arm. Eye contact is the worst. Eye contact results in the dreaded "What are *you* lookin' at, girlie?" challenge that never ends well. Christina had just such an encounter with this same Angie once when she took a detour to avoid an overly frisky police dog on her usual route home. Angie had been making out with Jimmy Halloran in the doorway of the Hibernian Boxing Club and Christina stood on the sidewalk staring, mesmerized by the way Jimmy's hands seemed to be everywhere at once, like some kind of magic trick you'd see on *The Ed Sullivan Show*. Angie, moving with the stealth of a panther, thumped her on the chest and pushed her over. "What are *you* lookin' at, you fuckin' little skank?" Christina sat on the ground catching her breath, too dazed to cry.

Now, remembering that humiliation, Christina digs into her pocketbook and pulls out her oversized sunglasses and puts them on. Maybe Angie won't recognize her.

Patsy looks at the sunglasses with approval. "Where'dja get those?"

"Liggett's. They're just like the ones Jackie Kennedy wears."

Patsy is already heading through the gates of the park.

"Rose isn't here yet," Christina stalls.

"Well, where is she? I'm not waiting for her," Patsy flings over her shoulder at Christina.

"I'll wait for her here," Christina ventures, but at that moment Rose emerges from the recreation building. She is waving two red, white, and green pot holders and calling to them.

"Look what I made!" She runs up to them.

"You were in there makin' pot holders with the little kids?" Patsy says, incredulously. "Put those away, for Chrissake, what's *wrong* with you?"

"What? They're for my nonnas," Rose says, hurt. "They're in the colors of the Italian flag!"

Patsy just shakes her head and keeps walking. Rose and Christina follow. Rose looks crushed.

"They're nice," Christina mumbles. She takes the pot holders and shoves them in her pocketbook. "I'll hold them for you." She pictures the nonnas over the moon at the gift: *You made-a? For me?* The hugs and kisses, the gathering into their old, doughy arms. She can't remember the last time she made her mother happy like that. Everything she does disappoints Rita. It isn't her fault! What is she supposed to do? Stop reading? Become ignorant, like her mother? Put a kerchief on her head and move back to Italy and squash grapes with her feet, like Lucy in that embarrassing *I Love Lucy* episode?

"Hi, Angie," Patsy says. Rose and Christina hang back.

Angie looks them up and down. "Lemme try those on," she says to Christina, offhand, cobra-still.

Christina hands the glasses over. Angie shows no recognition of Christina; she is as meaningless as a fly Angie once batted away. Angie puts the glasses on and turns to Frankie, the leader of the pack, playing cards a little distance away. Christina notices that Dennis Dempsey and Danny Grillo are among the boys flipping cards in some incomprehensible game.

"Whaddaya think? Frankie!" Angie calls in her foghorn voice.

Frankie looks up, annoyed. "You look like a bug."

"Kiss my ass, Frankie." Angie takes off the glasses and holds them out for Christina, turning her back on Frankie.

Dennis catches Christina's eye and jerks his chin at her in recognition. Her heart flutters in return, and she blushes as if he has offered her a sonnet. Dennis goes back immediately to the game, crowing in triumph as he lays down a winning card.

The afternoon wears on. The boys move from cards to knife throwing. Patsy brings out her transistor radio and Angie shows them some dances she knows: the Stroll, the Mashed Potato, the Monkey, and the Twist. Patsy seems to learn the steps at once and so does Rose. An idiot could do the Twist. It is the stupidest dance Christina has ever seen, bar none.

She pretends to turn her ankle after the first dance and sits down on the grass, covertly watching Dennis. Angie never looks at Frankie, not once, but she seems to be dancing only for him, writhing, shaking her shoulders, and lifting her chin, her mouth open, inviting. The boys, including Frankie, are absorbed in their game, yipping and shouting insults at each other. Then on some secret signal Christina can't decipher, Frankie stands up and Angie stops dancing in the middle of a song. They walk off together without a backward glance, taking some of the glow of the summer afternoon with them.

There is some more dancing after Angie leaves, but without the danger and excitement of her presence, the girls eventually sink to the ground and the day begins to dwindle into boredom. The metallic tinkle of the ice cream truck galvanizes everyone into action. The little kids run over first, then Patsy, Rose, and Christina, and finally the rest of the boys. Christina finds herself beside Dennis in a cluster of kids.

"You goin' to the Paramount on Sunday?" Dennis asks Christina. "They're showin' *The Terror*."

Danny sticks his head between them, his face contorted into a monster's mask. "BWAHAHAHAHA!" he howls.

Rose pokes him shyly and tells him to stop, he's scaring her, which propels Danny into a full-blown Boris Karloff impersonation. Rose keeps begging him to stop, although it is clear to anyone watching that this exchange is the highlight of her day. Encouraged, Danny moves on to Bela Lugosi and tries to bite

Rose's neck. Her bleats of delight are breaking the sound barrier.

Christina, digging in her purse to avoid looking at Dennis, tells him she'll probably go to the Paramount. Inside she feels the spreading warmth of rising joy. He's asking her for a date! Isn't he?

"Got an extra quarter I can borrow off you?" Dennis asks.

Christina hands it over, feeling that the moment is somehow tarnished. As far as she can tell, no romantic hero ever said, *Got an extra quarter I can borrow off you?* Dennis mumbles that he's caddying tomorrow and will pay her back. She gives him the quarter, covering it in her hand like it's a secret message. He doesn't say thank you and turns immediately to the ice cream truck, scanning the menu.

Christina can't stand the crush of kids another minute. She mumbles, "I gotta go," and squirms out of line. Rose calls after her, but Christina pretends not to hear and keeps walking. She hopes her sudden departure will mark her as a woman of mystery and make Dennis wonder about her. She turns the corner and sneaks a look back at him. He is already halfway through his Rocket Pop, his lips rimmed blue; there is no resemblance whatsoever to Heathcliff. With his prominent ears wiggling as he sucks his pop, he is a dead ringer instead for Alfred E. Neuman.

"I am possessed of the dead," says sultry Sandra Knight as the Baroness Ilsa in Boris Karloff's creepy old castle shrouded in mists that might or might not be evil spirits. *The Terror* turns out to be more boring than terrifying, and most of the audience at the Paramount Sunday matinee, all kids, are throwing popcorn at each other instead of watching the movie, and keeping the ushers busy shushing them. Christina, however, is enthralled. She shivers as she imagines herself possessed of the dead—or, as the nun-drilled grammarian part of herself corrects, possessed *by* the dead.

Christina sits with Rose, Patsy, and Mary Agnes, who are more interested in the boys, including Dennis, sitting directly behind them. Danny Grillo has already been sanctioned by the usher-guards for unrelenting fart noises. The ushers, gangly older teens, are more officious than prison guards and overzealous in their mission to keep order during showtime even when a grade-Z movie is playing. Just as Jack Nicholson, the dashing Napoleonic soldier, draws the undead Baroness Ilsa into his arms, Dennis snakes his hand around Christina's neck, causing her to shriek and bolt from her seat.

An usher runs down the aisle and passes his sentence: "Okay, you. You're outta here."

"Me?" Christina squeaks.

Dennis jumps up. "Leave her alone, asshole! It was my fault!"

The usher sweeps his merciless stare over to Dennis. "You, too. Outta here."

Rose issues a protest, faint enough to escape the bulldog radar of the usher, but strong enough to demonstrate friend loyalty. Patsy and Mary Agnes are too busy lobbing popcorn back at the boys behind them to notice Christina's expulsion. Christina glares at Dennis and follows the usher up the aisle, her eyes on the dusty flowered carpet. Dennis straggles behind her. A hail of Jujubes pelts them, like rice at a wedding.

They reach the lobby. "Want some Junior Mints?" Dennis asks, as if sensing her black mood.

"No," replies Christina. She is still furious at missing the romantic/scary part of the movie, although *Leave her alone* reverberates in her brain, a thrilling echo of courtliness, if you leave off the *asshole* part. She considers the Junior Mints. He does still owe her for the Rocket Pop. She looks through the smeared lobby doors at the still-bright afternoon and walks out. Dennis follows, as she wills him to, silently. She feels powerful, defended, the royal recipient of candy tributes.

Her new shoes are killing her, but that is just a minor irritation, the price of walking with Dennis, who after a while begins walking beside her, not behind her. The foot pain is worth it; the white patent-leather shoes perfectly match her new red and blue polka-dotted sundress. They are headed up the wide boulevard toward the park, an unspoken pact. Again, without words, they both turn into a Brigham's along the way; Dennis buys Christina a double-scoop black raspberry cone, and a double-scoop chocolate chip for himself. As they reach the side streets, black-clad nonnas fan themselves on porches, nodding sleepily after their midday dinners. Christina begins walking a little faster, distancing herself from Dennis; some of these old sentinels know her mother, though their hooded hawk eyes show no recognition. Christina is sure her presence is noted, and with an Irish boy beside her, *disgraziata*. None of it—the expulsion from the movie, the pinching shoes, the nonnas' unvoiced disapproval—can dim her swelling excitement: she is on a date with destiny.

The park looks transformed, its shabby edges softened by a low-rolling fog. They have it all to themselves, a miracle befitting this magical day.

"Let's take off our shoes and run through the grass," Christina says.

Dennis looks dubious. "There's dog shit."

Christina takes off her shoes, ignoring Dennis. Her feet have become identical pain pockets and she almost moans aloud at the sweet relief of wiggling her toes in the cool grass.

"You're just chicken!" Christina throws out the challenge as she begins to run, her shoes dangling awkwardly from one hand, the other clutching the ice cream cone. The inevitable happens a few minutes later: the ground comes up to meet her with astonishing speed as she stumbles and falls. When she scrambles to her feet after a dazed few seconds, her left breast-bud is smeared with black raspberry ice cream and her new sundress has grass stains on the skirt. Her shoes are somewhere in the grass, flung aside.

Dennis is laughing so hard he's doubled over, gasping for breath. "Too funny!"

Christina freezes her features into a Baroness Ilsa

mask and comes toward Dennis, zombielike. "I am possessed of the dead." She makes her voice flat and otherworldly, like Sandra Knight's in the movie. She keeps advancing toward Dennis, who keeps laughing. "I am possessed of the dead," she repeats. Dennis continues to laugh, but now it sounds a little forced. "I am possessed—"

Dennis stops laughing. His face now registers alarm. Christina bursts out laughing. Really, he's as easy to scare stiff as Vinny.

"I got you! I got you!" she screams. "You were SCARED! YOU—"

Dennis grabs her and kisses her, hitting the side of her mouth and stepping on her martyred toes in the process. Christina tries belatedly to turn her involuntary cry of pain into something resembling passion, as befits her first ever non-family kiss. She breaks away and looks around for her shoes. And suddenly she just wants to be alone in her room, contemplating what just happened. As if to underscore her thoughts, there is a low rumble of thunder in the distance.

"I gotta go," she mumbles.

Dennis hands Christina her shoes. The tips of his fingers graze the tiny bump that is her left breast. "You got—" indicating the ice cream stain.

Christina freezes. Both avoid looking at each other. "I gotta go home," she says again. They head their awkward, separate ways.

All the way home, Christina's heart thumps along with her loosened shoes in a clacking, shivery metronome of joy and terror. She relives the kiss, recreating the scenario, and now it is perfect: Dennis hadn't missed her mouth, hadn't stepped on her toes; instead the kiss was a mutual pledge of undying love and had taken place in a shimmery garden free of dog shit.

In the morning, Rita the slave driver volunteers Christina to babysit for Dommie Boy, while she and Connie go shopping. Christina stands in the hall, her arms folded across her chest. She will keep Dommie Boy from electrical outlets and falling on cement, she informs her mother, but she draws the line at actually touching him.

Rita feigns shock. "What kinda mother you gonna be someday? Huh? You no touch? Hah! When you were a baby I chew the food and put inna you mouth!"

Christina squeezes her eyes shut to blot out the disgusting image, puts her hands over her ears, and screams. Rita smiles. She enjoys Christina's tantrums, as predictable as the laugh track on the Lucy show, as dramatic as the firecrackers they set off when the Sons of Italy parade the Madonna del Carmine bedecked with dollar bills down Adams Street.

Connie appears at the door, shepherding Dommie Boy, who races inside, more blur than boy. She looks at Rita, puzzled, when she sees Christina standing with her hands over her ears.

Rita shrugs and says, "Eh," her all-purpose comment, this time signifying, *See what it's like to have a girl?*

Connie kisses Dommie Boy, panting with the exertion of bending down, uncomfortable at the idea of Christina babysitting, but even more desperate for a few precious minutes in the company of an adult. "You be good," she says to the toddler. "We'll be right back," she reassures Christina, who isn't reassured.

"We bring you cannoli," her mother adds.

They leave in a hurry, before Dommie Boy, whose face is already darkening, throws his own tantrum.

"I'm NEVER having children," Christina yells after them. "I HATE cannolis!"

Her outburst has stopped Dommie Boy in his tracks. He looks up at her with wonder, as if she is some mythic goddess of rage. Christina peers at Dommie Boy and sighs. She takes his sticky little hand, leads him over to the couch, and turns on the television.

"Wanna watch cartoons?"

Her goddess moment is over. The cartoon-watching lasts five minutes, if that. Dommie Boy squirms away from the sofa and Christina turns off the television. She turns on the radio. Skeeter Davis comes on, singing "End of the World." Christina serenades Dommie Boy, who pays no attention at all when she sings, *"Don't they know it's the end of the world 'cause you don't love me anymore."* Christina sings it to the end, anyway, liking the sound of her own voice, though Dommie Boy starts babbling nonsense when she does the speaking part.

After an hour of steering Dommie Boy away from potentially lethal dangers like the sculpted-glass candy bowl on the coffee table and the stairs to the cellar,

Christina hears Rose calling her at the screen door. Christina yells for her to come in. She has finally distracted Dommie Boy by letting him bang on Rita's already battered pots and pans. He sits on the kitchen floor adding more dents to the colander with a wooden spoon, hammering away like a miniature tinsmith.

"Where were you yesterday?" Rose asks. "Angie and Frankie had a big fight after the movie. It was horrible! You missed it!" She notices Dommie Boy on the floor and melts, predictably. "Awwww," she says. "C'mere." She scoops him into her arms and kisses him.

Christina shivers reflexively. Rose can't wait to get married and be a mother and become an indentured servant. Rose is insane.

"I have big news," Christina says. "But I can't tell you now." She gestures toward Dommie Boy. "But it's big. My whole life has changed."

"TELL ME," Rose yells, almost dropping Dommie Boy.

"I can't. Not right now," Christina says.

Rose sniffs and hands Dommie Boy to her. "I think he did something."

Christina receives the toddler as if she's dismantling a bomb. She sits him on the floor, telling him to bang the pots.

Rose keeps looking at the door; she seems anxious to go. "Well, if you're not comin' . . ." She edges toward the door.

"I'll tell you later. I'm not kidding. It's big. My life is forever changed."

Rose looks at Christina, her brows beetled. "This something you wanna read me again from *Withering Heights*?"

"No, no, this is a real thing that happened to me. So real."

Rose moves closer to the door, saying that she doesn't want to miss when Frankie and Angie first see each other after the big fight. The screen door slams. The kitchen rings with the clanging of the colander. Christina stares at Dommie Boy, absorbed in destroying the pots and pans. A viscous teardrop of drool sways to the rhythm of the brain-numbing beat.

The morning drags on. Christina eats a peanut butter and jelly sandwich and gives one to Dommie Boy. He finds a way to pound the sandwich along with the pots and pans and little blobs of sandwich paste are scattered over the kitchen like buckshot. Christina finally hears the familiar nervous clatter marking the return of her mother and Connie. She bets they feel guilty for saddling her with Dommie Boy, who now smells worse than pecorino romano. But her mother isn't at all concerned about wrecking Christina's morning. She drops her bags on the counter and yells at her daughter for not changing Dommie Boy.

"I gave him a sandwich!" Christina screams in self-defense. They have even forgotten to bring her cannolis. She hates her mother, the slave-driver witch who only loves her porky brother Vinny.

Christina stomps upstairs to her room for a final check on her outfit (the same sundress from yesterday,

Day of the Kiss, now miraculously spotless thanks to Rita) and hair (a perky ponytail that doesn't make her look like Sandra Dee, as she had hoped). She dabs some Evening in Paris behind her ears. Her toilette complete, she races back down the stairs and out the door to meet again her Fair Love, the private name she has given to Dennis. The name is never to be spoken aloud even under threat of torture. Maybe if they get married someday she will say it to his face. When she gets married, it will be different from when Rose gets married. Rose has planned everything already, down to the color of the bridesmaid dresses and the wedding favors (candy-coated almonds wrapped up in pink mesh like her bridesmaids' dresses). When Christina marries her Fair Love, they will elope to a place where they can gallop together over the moors. Christina's steed will be black. Her hair will turn black to match her stallion and it will stream out behind her in the wind as she rides.

She arrives at the park too late to see the reunion between Frankie and Angie. Rose meets her at the gate and tells her they made up the night before so there wasn't really a reunion. They just walked in with their arms around each other. The big news is that Angie has three hickeys. Christina doesn't care about the lovebirds, and she doesn't know what a hickey is. She is craning her neck to see if Dennis is there, in the usual cluster of boys. He isn't. Rose and Christina walk over to the spot where Patsy and Angie are huddled, discussing something so serious they have to whisper even though the boys are way over by the fence playing cards and aren't even looking at them.

"C'mere, c'mere, c'mere," Patsy hisses, beckoning them over. "Angie's gonna tell you somethin'!"

Angie is lounging on the grass looking sleek and satisfied. There are two greenish-purple bruises on her neck. Rose sits at her feet in a listening posture like the RCA dog in the advertisements. Christina drops beside her, careful of her sundress.

Angie sits up and takes a long look at both of them. She shakes her head. "Nah. Yis are too young," she says.

Rose protests that she's only a month younger than Patsy. She points to Christina. "She's the youngest. She's a whole year younger than the rest of us."

Christina stares at Rose with disgust. Is there no end to her betrayals?

Rose feels the stare. She looks guilty, at least. "Well, you're still only thirteen," she says.

Angie overcomes her scruples after a second or two and tells them the big news: she and Frankie have gone all the way. Christina and Rose know right away that this means Angie and Frankie have *had sex*. Angie smiles down at their shocked faces from her new lofty place as a woman, a grown-up, a person who has had intercourse with a man.

Rose speaks first: "Is . . . is that why you have *those*," she whispers, pointing to Angie's neck.

Christina hopes not. She's never seen bruises on her mother's neck, and she knows for a fact that she and her father have sex, even though she doesn't like to think about it. Still, there is no denying the barnyard noises that sometimes come from behind her parents' closed bedroom door on nights when Christina is up late reading. Is this neck-sucking some new vampire component? Maybe only teenagers get bruises. Maybe Angie is possessed of the dead. All her nerve endings light up at once and Christina suddenly has to stand up, then sit down again. She feels like slapping her own face to calm herself down.

Angie laughs. "I can't even show you where the other one is," she says.

"It's on her ass!" Patsy whisper-shrieks.

Rose and Christina inhale sharply, their eyes huge. Christina feels queasy, and the world tilts off its axis a little. "But," she blurts, "weren't you embarrassed to take your clothes off in front of him?"

Angie looks at Christina with something like pity. "We were so hot we couldn't wait," she responds, like she's ordering fries to go.

"Hot?" Christina says.

Angie's lip curls.

"Oooh, *hot!* I get it. I didn't hear you," Christina says before Angie can rank her out for being stupid.

Angie just looks at her like she is Dommie Boy, an annoying toddler not worth answering.

Patsy dares to ask what they are all thinking: "What if you get pregnant?"

Angie shrugs, then tells them she's okay with that, it would get her out of the friggin' house and out of school for good. Christina thinks about telling Angie how boring it is to chase a toddler around all day, more boring than school, but she notices that Dennis has arrived and is playing the knife game with the other boys. She gets up while Patsy, Rose, and Angie are discussing their dream weddings and walks over to where the boys are playing. She smooths out her sundress. She hopes Dennis will see it and remember yesterday, the Day of the Kiss.

They are sitting in a circle throwing a knife into the dirt. They look like cavemen or dangerous young primates. Christina thinks they'd probably like it if she told them they look like apes, instead of being insulted. A few of them would even jump up and start beating their chests and butting heads. As she draws closer, she knows they notice her, but they pretend she isn't standing there. She hears mumbling and fragments of words, dirty-sounding words like "finger fuck" and "tits." Then, "What tits?" and an idiot falsetto laugh.

She pretends not to hear and says, "Hi, Dennis."

Some of the guys mimic her, calling out a high-pitched, girly "*Hi, Dennis.*"

She wishes she had never come over here. What is wrong with her? Why didn't she know she shouldn't have come over here, so close to the boys-only circle? Only Angie can walk right up to the boys and not be mocked. Dennis ignores her and concentrates on his turn at throwing the knife. He misses and swears under his breath.

"Whoa. Don't get all excited 'cause your girl-friend's here," Frankie says.

"She's not my girlfriend," Dennis mutters, not looking at Christina.

There is nothing left to do but turn around, like someone possessed of the dead, as she stumbles toward the giggling future brides a million miles away across the park.

TWIRLY SHIRLEY

Sister Eudes greets Christina with her usual measure of equal parts suspicion and distaste. Christina always feels an amorphous guilt in return, along with a burning resentment that she isn't being recognized for her selfless good works in visiting Babe. It is a corporal work of mercy to visit the sick. She isn't sure if bringing Babe cigarettes and racy books should actually count as "visiting the sick," but Babe is very happy when Christina brings her smokes. Babe will be thrilled with the meatball sandwich and ginger ale she's bringing, courtesy of her father, who feels sorry for the old lady. Babe complains all the time about the swill they serve at St. Lucy's.

Sister Eudes doesn't move from her gatekeeper post. *My shorts are disrespectful*, Christina thinks, suddenly alarmed. She looks down. The meatball sandwiches have leaked through the paper bag, leaving an oval grease stain in the center of her T-shirt, like a shame medallion. Sister Eudes is staring at the grease stain. Christina's toes curl inside her sneakers. Greasy guinea.

The nun looks at the paper bag Christina carries with distaste. "Miss Fogarty is on a bland diet. I hope there's no greasy food with garlic in that bag."

"Uh, yes. I mean, no. This is my lunch," Christina stammers.

Sister Eudes sniffs and directs her to the bench Christina and Babe sit on in good weather, pointing her finger toward the garden area like the specter of death, although Eudes's pudgy finger is more like an Italian sausage than the Grim Reaper's bony digits.

"She has another visitor," Eudes says, as she waddles away, shaking her head.

Christina hurries down the path to the cluster of trees, her curiosity aroused She's never met any of Babe's family or friends. She is always vague about her family. Her parents are dead, of course, but Christina doesn't know if she has any brothers or sisters. Babe loves to regale Christina with her tales of men and being on the road and traveling all over America and Europe, and being arrested, but she acts as if Christina has suddenly turned back into a pesky fourth-grader when she asks personal questions. The conversation ends abruptly and Christina feels like a babbling child whose intrusion is only tolerated instead of a grown-up equal, trading wonderful stories at some fancy soiree.

Christina rounds a corner and sees Babe in her wheelchair beside a woman with crayon-red hair in an elaborate updo. She looks around Babe's age. She is shaking all over, helpless with laughter, Babe joining her, cawing her raucous cry. Her friend is crammed into a shiny green dress, her breasts bobbing above her low neckline like cling peaches in a Jell-O dessert. The woman looks just as delicious somehow. Rita would think she looks like a *putana*, Christina realizes.

"She couldn't take her eyes off them!" the friend gasps, snorting, as the laughter dies down.

"If you had your tassels on ya, you could've done your showstopper and sent her to her final reward," Babe cracks.

"Open up the pearly gates, Sister!" her friend cries, cupping her melon breasts and jiggling some more.

Christina stares.

The friend finally notices her. "Hiya, kid. What's your tale, nightingale?"

"I brought meatball sandwiches. And ginger ale." Christina holds out the bag.

"Shirley, this is Christina Falcone. She wants to be a saint," Babe says.

"No I don't!" Christina is peeved. "I really don't," she says again to Shirley. She begins clearing her throat over and over, a nervous tic that makes Rita threaten homicide. *Che tu possun' uccidere!* she always yells when Christina starts her nervous habit. *I'm gonna kill you,* she always adds, in case Christina missed her drift.

"I'm kidding. Christina's a good kid. She's my smuggler," Babe says. "Keeps me in smokes and news bulletins from the world of junior high—"

"I don't want to be a saint anymore because I have a boyfriend now," Christina cuts in.

"You have a boyfriend!" Shirley exclaims, like she's announcing the winner of the Irish Sweepstakes.

"This the kid who burned down the confessionals?" Babe asks.

"Oooh, a bad boy!" cries Shirley. "Momma likeee," she says, wriggling in her seat.

"It's all fun and games until someone gets hurt," Babe sings.

Babe and Shirley elbow each other and burst out laughing, two old girls from the schoolyard of hard knocks.

"'Member that guy who passed himself off as a count or a duke or some bullshit royalty?" Shirley says.

"You were gonna marry him and be a countess," Babe rasps.

"Yeah, Countess Twirly Shirley! Kiss my ass, peasants!"

This pronouncement sends them into more gales of laughter.

They are impenetrable, bound by years and years of good times. Watching them makes Christina lonely for Rose. Despite being her oldest friend, Rose sometimes now seems like a giggling stranger, someone possessed not by spirits of the dead but by the need to be liked by everyone and anyone. Rose will have a real boyfriend, not the fantasy one Christina has. It will probably be Danny Grillo, wiseass sidekick to Dennis Dempsey, Christina's not-real boyfriend.

Twirly Shirley notices Christina staring at her. "Well? Tell me about the boy. Is he cute? Is this boyfriend of yours a good kisser? That's important, ya know."

Christina feels trapped in a truth beam, like she's in a *Twilight Zone* episode and Shirley is zapping her with alien powers compelling her to reveal all. She shakes her head. "No. We kissed once but he missed my mouth and stepped on my foot and it really hurt. Then the next day, he dumped me and said I wasn't his girlfriend."

This unvarnished version of the kiss tragedy is the first time Christina has admitted the truth to herself. Now that she has said it out loud, some of the misery that has settled over her like an evil miasma begins to dissipate. She hopes Babe and Shirley won't laugh at her. She will die if they laugh. But Shirley surprises her by delivering a throaty version of "The Man that Got Away." Babe applauds vigorously and they both laugh, which leads Shirley into an upbeat encore. "*Knockers up . . .*" she croaks, to Babe's delight.

Christina begins looking around nervously for the reappearance of Sister Eudes, puffed up with outrage, like a maddened toad. But Shirley completes the entire song and at the end gets off some high kicks while she twirls her giant breasts in a jaw-dropping climax.

"Well, didja at least coax a smile outta the kid?" Babe asks.

"I dunno. She looks more shell-shocked."

Christina comes out of her stupor and applauds. "That was really good," she says, insincerely.

"Come by my newspaper stand in Brighton Center. I'll slip ya some magazines and smokes and you can bring 'em to Babe here."

Babe says she's tired and Shirley has to get back to her newsstand. They say their goodbyes and Christina begins to push Babe's wheelchair back to her squalid little room.

Babe tells Christina she has changed the décor in her room again and asks her how she likes the new color on the walls, but today Christina isn't in the mood for tests. The liberation she felt at admitting the truth about the kiss fiasco has been fleeting. Now she's just depressed. Again. She guesses blue, listlessly, for the wall color.

"Blue? Blue would make me look dead!" Babe says. "They're pink. Abalone pink, inside-of-a-peach pink, palazzo-on-the–Grand Canal pink! Save your pennies, kid, and make sure you see Venice before you die. At Carnevale."

Christina doesn't answer. Babe is content to be quiet, drifting along the serpentine green canals of adventures long past. After a few minutes she rouses herself and does that uncanny stare at Christina, as if she can see her clearly instead of a blurry kid-blob with brown tangled hair and a smear of too-big-for-her-face features.

"What's up with you, kid? You're turning mopey again. If you keep going like this, you're gonna be the biggest party pooper on the planet by the time you're twenty-one. Then you'll be a mean old lady pissed off everyone else is having the fun you missed out on. You'll be just like one of them, the nuns you're always bitching about."

"I'll never be like them," Christina replies, out-raged. She isn't mopey. Her mother calls her *mezzo mort'*, half dead. More and more Babe seems like a clone of her mother, but in a better mood and without the indecipherable accent. They just don't know her. She is like Catherine's ghost on the moors, roaming around and no one can see or hear her. She tells Babe she's leaving Precious Blood next year for sure.

Babe snorts. "I'll believe that when I see it. And I can't see anything. You've been sayin' that you're leav-ing for two years. What's stoppin' you? Your mother calls them the 'fockin'-a nuns' and you got your daddy wrapped around your little finger, it sounds like."

Christina opens her mouth and closes it. She had been about to tell Babe that she was afraid, that the public high school was too big, that she wouldn't know anyone besides tough girl Angie Vasolo, who would probably pretend not to know her or might beat her up, if Angie is even still in school next year and isn't pregnant or a dropout. Even if her friends don't like Joan Baez or folk music or poetry, they're still her friends and sit with her at lunch and walk with her to and from school. She pictures herself alone in an enormous overly bright public school cafeteria, eating by herself, the food sticking in her throat, picked on by tough girls who knock her stack of books off the table, then laugh at her, snapping their gum as they saunter away. And the kids like her, the ones who read poetry and play guitar and listen to folk music and wear black armbands for the civil rights workers who got killed down south? They'd probably think she's mopey and want nothing to do with her.

"Let's break out those sandwiches," Babe says. "I'm hungry."

"I'm gonna," Christina says, her voice trailing off uncertainly. "Next year, I'm going to public school."

MARTYRDOM

Christina plunges her hands into the murky water. The squid bodies mass around each other like alien extras in a science-fiction movie awaiting instructions from their director. She holds her breath and pulls off the first tentacled head. She shudders. The tentacles are a vivid purple and match the speckles on the opaque white bodies of the slimy creatures. The squid's guts are yellow and held together in a membrane, like mustard in a see-through packet. Christina has volunteered to stand at the sink and separate squid heads from their bodies. She is sick of herself, sick of brooding in her room, sick of not answering the phone when Rose or Patsy call, even sick of listening to Joan Baez sing "Silver Dagger" over and over until her mother screams that she has a splitting headache, what's wrong with her, Christina is *pazza*, she is taking her to the doctor, Jesus, Mary, and Joseph, and on and on, her high notes outdoing Joan's. Christina hums to herself at the sink, the words to "Plaisir d'amour" in her head punctuating the squoosh and rhythm of the squid decapitations.

Joy of love is but a moment long
Pain of love endures the whole night long

Christina is hands-deep in squid guts as an offering to whatever gods or saints or guardian angels
prevented her mother from breaking in on Christina's
shameful lapse into babyhood last night. She winc-
es when she even thinks of it now: she had actually
barricaded her door after supper, dug deep into her
closet, retrieved her Ginny dolls and played with
them. Though she hadn't actually played with them,
not really. She felt sorry for them, tucked away in the
closet. She wasn't playing with dolls. She is way too
old for that. Freed from the recesses of the closet,
the dolls came to life. Nurse Ginny took Valentine
Ginny's pulse and diagnosed her as sick with love.
Bride Ginny was hanging around like a ghoul waiting for Valentine Ginny to die and asking the other
Ginnys if they liked her dress. Cowgirl Ginny called
her a fucking show-off and a snot. Cowgirl Ginny
began stomping Bride Ginny, calling her a dipshit for
wanting to marry some neighborhood *divya* and start
having one kid after another and being so stupid, so
incredibly stupid and ignorant. Christina realized
suddenly that her voice was getting loud. She felt like
she was coming out of a trance. She flung the dolls
one by one back into her closet, then buried them
under some old pillows. She could just picture Rita
if she could see her now. She would stand with her
arms folded, shaking her head. *Oh, Madonn', now*

she's goin' backward. What are you, fifteen? (Rita often pretends Christina is older when she yells at her.) *Playin' with dolls? I dunno whatsa matter with you. When I was you age . . .*

But today Rita seems thrilled with signs of life from her long-dormant daughter. Christina has moped around the house for the entire summer, except for the family vacation in Green Harbor. She made everyone miserable there, not even going to the beach with Rose and Patsy, whose parents rented cottages nearby. Instead, she remained in her hot, stuffy room reading stacks of books and listening to the same dreary music she plays at home. Christina's discovery of folk music is another station of the cross for Rita, who likes rock and roll and has a secret crush on Elvis. Now all that comes from Christina's room is the same high keening voice singing songs of death. And Christina never leaves her room, except to go to the library. She refused to go to the christening of Aunt Connie's baby girl even when Joe yelled so loud the neighbors heard. Now it is the Friday before the first day of school, and Rita is ironing Christina's uniform.

"Good, good, *mamarella,* you doin' a good job."

Rita leaves her ironing and stands beside Christina at the sink. She puts her arms around her. Christina squirms away, but Rita keeps talking, determinedly, cheerfully. Rita has performed the anti-*malocchio* in secret on her daughter's behalf. Christina overheard her mother telling Connie that she thought someone had put the *malocchio* on her daughter. Christina once spied her late at night, after the whole house was quiet and she thought everyone was asleep, pouring the water and the oil and the salt into a bowl and murmuring the ancient chant in dialect, moving her left hand in a circle over the bowl. Then she plunged her fingers into the oil and broke it up into a million tiny eyes, proving that her daughter had been cursed. Christina, who had snuck downstairs to read and not be discovered by the light under her bedroom door, stared at her mother's crone-like bent back over the bowl of oil and water. She wanted to laugh but was also unnerved by the sight of her mother invoking a spell.

But the spell hasn't lifted the evil eye. Christina is still miserable. Now in the kitchen, her mother's fakely cheery voice is irritating.

"We gonna have a big birthday party for you an' we have alla you friends—"

"I want to go to Club 47 in Harvard Square and hear Joan Baez for my birthday," Christina interrupts her.

"Oo? Oo's that?"

"Joan Baez, the folk singer."

"That *mezzo mort'* sounds half-dead alla time?"

"To you. Because you're ignorant."

"Don' let you father hear you talk to me like that. He's gonna give you an election when he gets home."

Christina smiles, a demon grin that never reaches her eyes. Rita inadvertently puts her hand over her thrumming heart.

"An *election?*" Christina places the last of the decapitated squid bodies into a colander by the side of the sink. "I think President Johnson has a couple more years in office," she says, wiping her hands on a dishrag.

Rita goes back to her basket of clothes, banging the iron harder than is necessary on Christina's *brutta* uniform. She slams the iron down on the uniform as if she's branding it.

"Anything else you want me to do?" Christina says, making it sound somehow like a challenge.

Rita lifts up her iron and stares at her cursed daughter. "No. Go read you books, you so smart. You so smart, you *stupid*!"

Christina leaves, fighting back tears. Her mother's words sting, even though *she*'s the stupid one, not even knowing the difference between *election* and *lecture*. Rita goes back to her ironing, allowing her tears to spill only when she hears Christina's heavy footsteps on the stairs.

The phone rings, and Christina hears her mother answer it. She pauses on the stairs, eavesdropping. She hears her mother sniffling and murmuring to someone.

"I dunno, Rosa. Whatsamatter with her? She make me cry . . ."

Rita is talking about her to Rose! Now her mother's taking over her own friends! Christina runs upstairs and picks up the extension.

"Hello, Rose," she says, her voice flat. "Hang up, Mumma." Her mother slams down the phone.

"School starts Monday," Rose says.

"No shit, Sherlock."

"Well," Rose says, in a breathless rush of words, "Patsy and Mary Agnes and I are all goin' to Grover Cronin's tomorrow and we're all getting madras blazers and saddle shoes for the first day! We decided we're gonna be *colleege*! Wanna come?"

"I dunno," Christina replies. She is thinking of her new book from the library, *Jane Eyre*. She is working her way through the Brontës and is now on Charlotte. Maybe Jane Eyre was like her, stuck in a strange place with unenlightened former friends who are now strangers, people who actually gave a shit about being *colleege*, whatever that is.

"Well, if you don't come, you're gonna be the only one in our crowd who isn't *colleege*. Everyone else will be rats."

"What's *colleeege*?"

"I dunno. Patsy says it's not dressing rat, no teased hair an' stuff. She read about it in *Seventeen*. Oh, an' we're all gonna iron our hair on Sunday so it'll be flat for the first day. You comin' or what? Ten o'clock at the bus stop."

Christina sighs. "Yeah, okay." Maybe she can find a black turtleneck like Joan Baez wears. And blue jeans. She doesn't even own blue jeans. She doesn't want to be *colleege*. She wants someone to listen to Joan singing "Silver Dagger" with her and mourn the tragedy of the girl in the song sleeping alone for the rest of her life. She has to get out of Precious Blood and go to the public high school. The public high school is huge and must have people who listen to Joan Baez and read the Brontës and the poetry of Sylvia Plath. But she's afraid to go to such a big school. She is a coward. She will wear the madras blazer on the first day and walk into Precious Blood High School in a protected *colleege* phalanx of friends who aren't really her friends. She hates herself.

"Wanna walk up the park with me?" Rose is saying.

"Nah. I'm helpin' my mother with the squid."

"That's a first."

"I know. I decided to be good."

They both snicker, a brief return to their old closeness. Christina hangs up the phone and dives onto her bed. The park. The place where Dennis Dempsey, the Worst Boy in School and the love of her life, dumped her the day after he bought her an ice cream cone at Brigham's and then clumsily kissed her. She will never go to that park again. Never. She opens *Jane Eyre* and reads the first words: *There was no possibility of taking a walk that day* . . .

No shit, Charlotte.

PART 3

YOU AND ME COULD REALLY EXIST

It is Saturday and Christina will be free to ride the trolley to Harvard Square after a perfunctory performance of her Saturday-morning chores. These include spraying Pledge and running a cloth over the furniture in all the bedrooms upstairs and passing a dust mop under the beds in the most desultory and marginal way possible. Vinny's bedroom floor produces the most debris in the form of loose army men and forgotten candy wrappers, the flimsy solace of sleepless nights spent worrying about wetting the bed. Nonno's bedroom faces the street. It is monastic and spare, and as neat as if no one lives there. However, the neatness is deceptive, because Nonno has the demented nightly habit of peeing out his window onto the porch roof instead of walking the four feet down the hall into the bathroom. Her mother, self-appointed and sleep-deprived house warden, only allows herself to close her own eyes when her family is all rhythmically breathing and flying safely through the clouds of dreamland. She heard Nonno cranking his window open one night and caught him in the act.

Rita has been on dawn patrol ever since, but nothing will deter Nonno from making his nightly deposit on the roof, not even the subzero temperatures of winter that should give him pause. With the stealth of a sniper, he times his attacks on the roof for when Rita herself is in the bathroom. Rita threatens daily to kill both herself and Nonno over his disgusting habit. Joe stays out of the Great Urine War, but Christina has heard him laughing about it with Vinny. She wonders if Nonno pictures himself at the door of his mountain farmhouse looking at the same comforting moon he used to see in Italy as he lets loose a hypnotic stream of urine, the disappointing sameness of the houses on Derby Street fading into a dreamscape of hard-won rows of wavy garlic stalks and glimmering tomatoes made luminous by moonlight. Still, her mother is right: it *is* disgusting and is more proof that her family carries a dangerous insanity gene. It couldn't be interesting literary insanity like Allen Ginsberg or Sylvia Plath had, Christina thinks resentfully as she thrusts the dust mop under Nonno's bed; no, her family has inbred peasant bathroom behaviors, and expresses themselves not on paper with uplifting verse, but in wavering streams of pee, like out-of-control zoo monkeys.

Christina's first pilgrimage to Harvard Square was two years ago on a mission to find Club 47 and see where Joan Baez played. It was a disappointing, dirty-looking place in a dark alley. The club looked closed and was. Well, what did she think? That she would just saunter down the cracked cement stairs and breeze in and order a drink and Joan would sing "Silver Dagger" just for her? She was fourteen; they wouldn't even let her in without her parents, probably. Harvard and Radcliffe students passed by laughing, confident, members of a secret club, speaking a coded language that Christina was surprised to hear was English. She passed a kiosk with newspapers and magazines from all over the world. The subway rumbled below her, the line into Boston. Christina has never taken the subway. Her trips into Boston, whether to see the Ice Capades or to go shopping with her dad in the North End were always chauffeured by her father in his black and white Chevy station wagon.

Christina passed a grimy window and stacks of barely visible books inside. She backtracked and pushed open the door, and a bell tinkled, but the old man behind the counter never looked up from the tome he was reading. Untidy bulges of books were stacked everywhere, some in leaning towers that looked dangerous. Christina pictured herself buried under a random explosion of books set off by an unwitting customer. Rita would wail at first, then sit at Christina's wake nodding, lips set. Death by bookslide, the culmination of what Rita had always predicted: books would make her daughter blind, make her crazy, make her a spinster, take away her future children.

A silky blonde was flipping through a photography book, checking out pictures of lushly round half-dressed women from another time wearing black satin lingerie. Christina slid her eyes over to the pictures while pretending to study the faded cover of a dull-looking volume of history. Abruptly, the blonde tossed the photography book onto a teetering heap and walked away. Christina stemmed the imminent landslide and picked it up. *Brassaï: Photographs of the Paris Demimonde* was the title. Christina resolved to look up *demimonde* in her French dictionary when she got home. *Half world* is what it meant, but it couldn't mean that. She glanced around the store, trying to appear like she belonged there, leafing through black-and-white pictures of lesbians and prostitutes in Paris in the 1930s. No one was paying any attention to her, least of all the old man wearing Coke-bottle glasses behind the counter. He hadn't lifted his head from *Tropic of Cancer*. The Brassaï book was the most expensive book she'd ever seen: it went for twenty-five dollars. Christina studied it, lingering on a photograph of a woman smoking and tossing back her hair and an attentive man staring at her like he wanted to devour her for dessert, the charged atmosphere enhanced by their mirrored reflections repeating into infinity. Christina wished she could close her eyes and wake up as the woman in the photograph. She looked at the old-fashioned black clock on the yellowed wall of the bookstore and saw that it was time to go if she wanted to avoid questions from Rita. She closed the book and knew she would be back the next Saturday, and the next one after that.

Since Christina's first foray into the demimonde of

Harvard Square two years earlier, she has become bolder, even sitting in a coffeehouse and drinking espresso (it is horrible and tastes like dirt; she likes almond croissants a lot better). She brings home thin little City Lights paperbacks, the poems of Allen Ginsberg and Denise Levertov, just the right size to smuggle between the pages of a textbook and read during class. She has not yet talked to a stranger in Cambridge. Even the bookstore owner only exchanges nods with her upon her weekly visits.

Christina doesn't like the Harvard Coop, but she feels funny asking for a book with a lot of sex in it from the bifocaled old man who runs her favorite no-name bookstore, the one she haunts every Saturday. This book she wants has tons of sex in it. The outraged article in the *Pilot* goes on and on about the disgraceful book by an Irish Catholic woman, Mary McCarthy, called *The Group*. Christina checks the *Pilot* every week to see what films and books are condemned by the Church, so she can look for them on her weekly sojourns to Harvard Square. According to the article about this McCarthy novel, it will provide a much-needed instruction manual about the mysteries of birth control and passion and, as a bonus, reveal the secret lives of the upper classes.

The Coop is too well lit and has an atmosphere of commerce and tidiness that offends Christina. Two perky-looking Radcliffe girls heading for the textbooks shoulder past her with an air of propriety. What would it be like to go to Radcliffe, Christina wonders, to sit, no, to *sprawl*, in a classroom like you owned the place and maybe you did own a little piece of it because you were a legacy and your mother went there, too, and to smoke cigarettes while an adult asked for your opinion on literature as if you had your own opinion and it was worth hearing by a professor? She doesn't know how to have an opinion. She only knows how to memorize something and parrot it back. That is how she got a one hundred on the English test for *Julius Caesar*, by memorizing passages from the play and reciting them back to Sister Coronada, ten points for each speech. She wasn't asked and she didn't have an opinion on *Julius Caesar*. She is not college material. Unless some professor wants to hear her drone by rote, *Wherefore rejoice? What conquest brings he home? / What tributaries follow him to Rome, / To grace in captive bonds his chariot-wheels?*

She prowls the shelves and finds the fiction section, bleakness settling over her like a caul. She pushes away the clear image of her future self in a gray cubicle taking dictation from a pompous little prick not much older than she. Some insufferable toady like Timothy Mosher who is a reject, not even seminary material, but is still at Precious Blood sucking up to the priests after failing to get into St. John's. She is not college material. She is a future coffee-getter and dictation-taker. Christina looks back at the Radcliffe girls. She wishes she had the reflexive and fearless class hatred of Angie Vasolo. If she had Angie's swagger, she could casually hip-check the snotty coeds so that their textbooks fly out of their Pendleton-sweatered arms, scattering to the floor. As they scramble to pick them up, she would tower over the girls, sneering, *What are you looking at, girlie?* The pair would slink away, afraid to meet her eyes. Angie Vasolo would make them fear her.

Christina finds *The Group* and can't resist opening it right there, in front of the bookshelf, hoping to glean a juicy bit about loose college girls even though she tells herself she is just making sure she gets the title right. She glances around to see if there is anyone nearby who can see what she is reading (and thus know she's looking for racy paragraphs). There is no one except a guy a few feet away from her, chortling to himself over a book he holds open in his hands. Christina notes that it is J.P. Donleavy's *The Ginger Man,* a book she hasn't read. She wonders if this boy is doing the same thing, getting a cheap thrill from random sexy bits on the printed page. He is cute, and looks young, around her age. He is *very* cute, she decides, staring openly now. He looks just like John Lennon, her favorite Beatle. (Christina has no patience with her shallow Paul-loving friends; John Lennon is an *author.*) Christina bought a copy of *In His Own Write* the day it came out. But this guy has red hair. Not the Howdy Doody orange hair despised by her aunt Connie, who warns Christina away from Irish boys who carry like a genetic disease the possibility of ginger-haired future babies. This boy has hair the deep red color of autumn leaves. And no freckles. She wishes he would look up so she can see what color his eyes are.

And then, as if her thoughts are commands beamed

directly into the redhead's brain, he looks up and meets her eyes. His eyes are brown, a foxy yellow-brown. He looks at the book she holds in her hands and gives her a wicked smile, revealing perfect white teeth. He saunters over.

"Are you one of those suppressed psychos who gets a hard-on over stale bird shit?" he says, still smiling at her.

"Uh, I find it impossible to get a hard-on over anything."

His smile grows even wider. He puts out his hand. "John Patrick O'Rourke. Somerville." He pronounces *Somerville* as *Summahville*.

Christina shakes his hand solemnly, though inside she is bursting with glee. "Christina Falcone. Similar working-class slum."

John Patrick cocks his head, considering her. "That's a shock. I thought you were one of those Jules Feiffer–cartoon college girls."

Christina doesn't know who Jules Feiffer is, but she wants desperately to continue this exciting exchange. "Oh, really? And was the mention of hard-ons supposed to excite me in a D. H. Lawrence kind of way?"

He peers at her with pure anticipatory delight, like she's a delicious dessert someone has plunked down in front of him. "You and me could really exist," he says.

He turns around abruptly and begins searching the poetry shelves. Christina watches him pull a slender volume off a shelf and stick it inside his dungaree jacket. He whirls around, smiles at her, and walks nimbly out of the store. Christina feels like she has just taken part in some kind of impromptu performance of a play where she somehow knows all the lines and has played the starring role without a misstep. And now, just like that, the magic interlude is over and the stage is dark and she is alone. But he had said *You and me could really exist* like it's something he really means. So what just happened? He stole a book! Is she supposed to steal one, too? Follow him? All of a sudden, she is irritated at John Patrick O'Rourke. Well, she isn't going to exist with some Somerville guy in a life of crime. His wicked smile flashed at her, taunting. She turns and looks for the cash register. He thought she was a college girl. *You and me could really exist*. She wants more of John Patrick O'Rourke, petty thief.

He is lounging against a wall right outside the Coop when she comes out the door. She expected him to be there. Nothing could go wrong on this day when her thoughts and desires are materializing like wishes in a fairy tale.

"Did ya get your stale bird-shit book?" he asks.

"Yeah, and I paid for it because I'm not a criminal," she replies, a lift in her voice to show she's teasing. "Anyway, it's not for me, it's for a friend."

"This is for you." He hands her the stolen book. It is Lawrence Ferlinghetti's book of poetry *A Coney Island of the Mind*. She can't think of a smart-ass remark. She sticks the book into her bag and looks away. They fall into step beside each other, walking toward Brattle Street. He is tall, Christina notes with pleasure. But not too tall.

"You ever go there?" he asks, indicating the theater. The marquee reads: *Repulsion*.

"Mmmmh," she says, rendered mute by the book of poems crowding her brain. Stolen. Purloined. For her.

John Patrick grabs her hand and runs with her to the back of the alley alongside the theater. She feels like she is flying. She feels like she is in a Beatles movie. She is someone else, a girl in a movie. A foreign movie. He presses her against the wall and kisses her. She kisses him back, loving the feel of him, of all of him against the length of her whole body, giddy, unsurprised by her own passion even though she has never felt it before. They kiss for what feels like a long time; in fact she is getting tired of her lips pressing against his and the slight impediment to her breathing, but she wants the part where he is grinding against her with his hands on her ass to go on and on, wants it more than the kissing, she realizes. And then suddenly, dream over, she is aware of the rough brick scraping her back where her turtleneck and jacket have rucked up and she wants it all to stop, and John Patrick, who by now she's convinced is a mind reader, pulls away. They are both breathing heavily and regarding each other with delight, like Olympic teammates who have just won a relay race.

The trolley back to Watertown Square is a descent into hell. It's packed, and a big man sits down heavily next to her, spreading his knees like he owns the place, and the massive package between his beefy legs demands both his space and hers. Christina squeezes up against the window and tries to squelch her irritation. He has on a blue shirt with the name *Bud* embroidered on his left pocket. Christina stares down at his thighs straining against his khaki work pants. She takes out *A Coney Island of the Mind*, willing herself back into the time and space of an hour before. But she feels such a miasma of seeping belligerence from Bud that it makes her look up. He is staring at the words on the page of her little book, his thick lips moving soundlessly. She shoots up and baby-steps in front of Bud's inflated knees, melding herself into the hard plastic back of the seat in front so as not to make physical contact with him. Finally, she lurches free into the crowded trolley aisle, but not before Bud cops a plausibly deniable feel of her thigh. She looks back at him, angry at herself for what she knows is the look on her stupid, shocked face. He is staring straight ahead, mouth moving again like a herd animal chewing on its own regurgitated lunch. Men are disgusting, Christina thinks.

A vivid memory now surfaces, courtesy of the bovine Bud. Christina, Patsy, Mary Agnes, and Rose, three years ago, arms linked, singing a joyful, off-key version of some Top 40 song she can't remember now, on their way home from Brigham's on an early spring evening, their song turning abruptly to shrieks when a creepy old man standing under a streetlamp exposed himself to them, jiggling his pale-white goods and laughing at their sudden high-pitched yips. When she got home and told her parents, Christina's father became an avenging Old Testament God and wanted to jump in his station wagon to apprehend the pervert who defiled his little girl, while Rita screamed, "*Sozz'!! Disgrazia!*" and other denunciations that sounded enhanced and juicier somehow in her peasant dialect. But then, Rita couldn't help herself—she giggled, shocking Christina, who had been basking in her father's glorious, towering outrage on her behalf. Her noble father thought Christina was precious and worthy of protection and Rita thought some pervert showing her his thing was *funny*? In the end, her father didn't go—"You gotta get up *early*, for Chrissake," Rita said, and suddenly it was all Christina's fault for not getting home before dark. Rita looked at Christina and shrugged. "What can you expect? Men are pigs!"

Her mother and Connie and even the nuns agree about the low nature of men. The nuns make it clear through multilayered code words the girls somehow understand: boys can't control their baser instincts and it is up to girls to protect the priceless glory of their virginity. Aunt Connie is always saying over coffee that men are assholes and Rita mutters, "*Bestia*," in flawless harmony to Connie's theme song. After she and Joe saw *Two Women* in the North End, an Italian movie in which Sophia Loren and her adolescent daughter are gang-raped during wartime, Rita pronounced all men animals. But she didn't say it like she did when she was with Connie; when she was with Joe, it was a sly invitation for him to open the cage door and unleash the beast and a message that she would welcome cavorting with him out in the wild. Rita is disgusting, Christina thinks.

Alone at last in her room, she fights between the urge to devour *The Group* to see if there is a character in the book who could describe what she felt with John Patrick O'Rourke in that alleyway, and the equally desperate need to find out if he has given her a book of poems because there is one in it that reminds him of her. After all, he had stolen it for her, risking arrest and getting a record and maybe going to reform school and ruining his life. But her father would understand. Her father would like John Patrick and recognize that he had only stolen the book because he had the overwhelming need to give it to Christina. Her father would give him a job in the bar. They would get married and live in her room.

She has to see him again. There must be something in the book, a message from him to her. They hadn't exchanged phone numbers. He didn't ask for hers, so she didn't ask for his. That would've been stupid, like they were in some dippy musical or a Rock Hudson/Doris Day movie. John Patrick would never do something like that. She wouldn't even like him if he did. Unless the book is a message that's telling her to meet him next Saturday at the Coop. That could be it.

Christina finds the poem on page 22. It doesn't have a title, but the line "*You and me could really exist*" jumps out at her. Number 9 isn't a love poem;

it's a story about disappointment. The narrator of the poem meets a girl who tells him, "You and me could really exist," but the next day she turns out to have bad teeth and be a poetry hater. Why does it take him until the next day to find out she has bad teeth? Christina wonders. An image of John Patrick's perfect white teeth superimposes itself over the poem. Christina leaps up and stands in front of her glossy-beige laminate bureau. She stares at herself in the mirror, stretching her lips into a wide, fake grin. She has bad teeth. No, she doesn't. Her incisors are kind of long and vampirey, though. She hates John Patrick O'Rourke. She wonders if he will be at the Coop next Saturday.

QUANDO MAI

Sister Juventinus, the first-grade nun who passed back corrected papers marked with either a star for getting it right, or a baby for getting it wrong, and who never told Christina why making all her twos backward was incorrect, who stamped a chubby, curled-up baby on her paper which made Christina forever after associate babies with shame.

(Pray for us)

Sister Aloysius, the second-grade nun who rationed bathroom breaks so severely that the aisles between the desks ran daily with rivulets of pee that no one acknowledged were there.

(Pray for us)

Sister Frederika, the third-grade nun who was an impish hair puller and ear twister, and whose cheery pointed features had the power to make the muscles in Christina's face jump from a distance, even when Christina was home and supposedly safe.

(Pray for us)

Sister Isaac Jogues, the fourth-grade nun who had a martyr fetish and penchant for hanging signs on kids and parading them through the other classes for humiliation and finger-pointing and derisive laughter that would echo forever down the corridors of their lives.

(Pray for us)

Sister Boniface, the fifth-grade nun who declaimed over and over every day the phrase "Woe betide you" in the thunderous voice of an Old Testament doomsayer, and then delivered the woe with the stoic formal sorrow of a masked executioner.

(Pray for us)

Sister Liberata, the sixth-grade nun who told the boys they were the spawn of the devil and loved the girls, except for the ones with vowels at the end of their names, who were the spawn of Mary Magdalene, junior whooers whose breasts came in too early to be decent (except for Christina, freakish member of her own tribe who didn't even have the whispered promise of tits).

(Pray for us)

Sister Benedict, the seventh-grade nun who had a large hypnotic carbuncle in the center of her forehead like the stump of a unicorn horn that gave her the magical power to see out the back of her head and nab transgressors who dared to chew gum or pass notes in her class.

(Pray for us)

Sister Odilia, the eighth-grade nun who Christina drove into dementia, saving the class from disgrace and securing her place among the cool kids, followed by Sister Bernadette, who got messages from Jesus over the radio, but was otherwise kind.

(Pray for us)

Sister Thecla Marie, the ninth-grade nun who was the Beastmaster, aka Captain Queeg, who made Rose feel fat for life and who made Christina come out of her Catholic trance.

(Pray for us)

Sister Mary Margaret, the tenth-grade nun who possessed the chin-quivering outrage of the true bigot when reminded of the two-thousand-year betrayal of her Lord Jesus by the Jewish people, a travesty that goaded her to fulmination when they read Oliver Twist that year.

(Pray for us)

Sister Coronada, the eleventh-grade nun who is melting down what's left of my brain with this stupid, fourth-grade-level school essay contest when I could be reading Howl by Allen Genius Ginsberg. Write an essay about your patron saint! Moloch! Moloch! Nightmare of Mo—

Patsy jerks the notebook out of Christina's hand and scans the page. They are at the big public library along with Mary Agnes and Rose and most of the student body of Precious Blood High School, doing research on the school-wide essay contest due the next day. Patsy has selected the most strategic table, the one next to the cutest senior boys.

"The fuck are you doing? We're never gonna get to Brigham's at this rate. We're not waiting for you. I found my saint already. And she's pisser! Lookit."

Patsy shoves the book of saints in front of Christina, who bats it away. Undeterred, Patsy reclaims the book and begins reading.

"*St. Patricia was from Naples, and a virgin*"— Patsy looks over at Mary Agnes and smirks—"*and a martyr*. But this is the best part: they have a vial of her blood that liquefies every year on her name day thirteen hundred years after her death! Coronada's gonna love that!"

Mary Agnes looks unconvinced. "Nah. She'll just say, 'Those dumb guineas'll believe anything,'" she drawls.

Patsy laughs and pretends to slam Mary Agnes with the book. "How about leprechauns and banshees? That's not stupid?"

Timothy Mosher, two tables away, shushes them, outraged. All four girls flip him the finger without looking at him.

Christina folds her arms. "This assignment is absurd bullshit. I'm not doing it."

Patsy, eyeing the senior boys at the next table, gets down to the business at hand. "Hurry up and write your thing. We're goin' to Brigham's in five minutes." She smiles over at the senior boys.

Mary Agnes, across the table, stares at Christina, unblinking. She picks up Christina's notebook and reads it. She nods, smiling, as if the paper confirms what she has suspected for a long time. "What is this supposed to be?"

Rose sits beside Mary Agnes, oblivious. She is copying the life story of St. Rose of Lima from a sourcebook with the hypnotic diligence of a fifteenth-century monk illuminating a manuscript.

Christina snatches back her homage to Allen Ginsberg, the twin soul who walks skinless with her through the world, who gives voice to the voiceless pain of the outsider. Genius. He is a genius and Mary Agnes can only sit there chortling and nodding like the world's creepiest jack-in-the-box, like she knows something secret about Christina that gives her some advantage.

Patsy puts the finishing touches on her essay, then sweeps her notebook and pens into her green bag. She stares at Christina, who has opened *Howl* and sits reading, absorbed.

"C'mon, I'm not kidding, we're leaving."

Rose steps up her copying speed, complaining as she writes, "I'm not finished!"

Mary Agnes closes her reference book with a *thunk*, smug and happy about her find. "I'm done. And mine's gonna win. Get this: Agnes was from ancient Rome and she had a pagan boyfriend who wanted to marry her, but she refused so she could be a bride of Christ. So, this pagan, who was the governor's son and a big shot, decreed that she had to be sent to a whorehouse and paraded through the streets naked! But God made her hair grow to her ankles suddenly to cover her up. Then this pagan comes up to her anyway—'with lewd intent,' it says—tryna feel her up, probably, but before he can put his hands on her, God strikes him blind. But Agnes forgives him and his eyesight is restored. She still refuses to marry him, so he tries to burn her, but the flames don't touch her, and she's finally beheaded. All 'cause she wouldn't marry the pagan guy."

"I'd marry the guy," Patsy declares.

Mary Agnes is shocked. "That would be like marrying a Protestant or a Jew! You would marry a Protestant?"

Now it's Christina's turn to smirk. For all her wise-guy affectations and cooler-than-thou demeanor, Mary Agnes is as scared to flaunt the rules as the rest of them.

Rose looks up from her work and chimes in: "No way would I marry a Protestant. Then you couldn't be together for eternity. You'd be in heaven and your husband would burn in hell. Forever."

Rose sounds as drippy as Cecilia, who is always trying to get them to join sodality, which has to be the most boring after-school club in the universe. All they do is say the rosary and pretend to be the Blessed Virgin Mary.

"You don't even know any Protestants! Or Jews!" Christina responds. "And all the most interesting people are Protestants or Jews! Albert Einstein! Allen Ginsberg! Joan Baez! Bob Dylan! Dr. King! Gandhi!"

Her irritation is making her voice strangled and loud, which earns them another, louder "SSSHHH!" from Timothy Mosher. They all flip him the bird again.

"Why don't you transfer to public school if you wanna be with Protestants and Jews like you've been sayin' you were gonna do for the last million years, huh?" Patsy slings her schoolbag over her shoulder. "Let's go," she says to Mary Agnes and Rose. "We'll be at Brigham's," she tells Christina. "If you can stand hangin' around with *Catholics*."

Mary Agnes and Rose follow Patsy to the door, trailed a few minutes later by the senior boys.

Christina looks over at Timothy Mosher and gives him the finger again for good measure, then sighs and opens the reference book on saints.

All she can think about is her own cowardice. Patsy is right. How many years has she been making excuses for her timidity? The plain fact is that she fears leaving a class of eighty kids she has known since kindergarten for a school with a graduating class of eight hundred. She would disappear, she would become lost, she would be a ghost floating through the corridors of that huge and confusing place. No one would see her, no one would hear her. She would have to put on a different uniform, only she would have to guess at the right one. There would be different uniforms for different groups and if she chose the wrong one, she would be banished or worse, invisible.

But there would be teachers instead of nuns. And she could openly read books that are banned at Precious Blood, books like *Catcher in the Rye* and

Franny and Zooey. And there would be drama clubs and plays, instead of the spring chorale everyone is drafted into performing at Precious Blood. Her parents would let her go. Rita would make a big deal of it just for the chance to sing her aria of perpetual worry and bask in her operatic moment. Joe would be happy not to shell out tuition and to hear the end of her complaints. Her whining, if she is honest.

The reference book on saints swims into focus. The first St. Christina she finds is crappy, and she isn't even a full-fledged saint, she is only a "blessed," the last step before canonization. This Blessed Christina is from her mother's region in Italy and was just a boring abbess at a convent, although once a Sacred Host in a golden pyx radiated from her breast. Christina pictures herself blasting the kids at Brigham's with her lit-up breasts and watching Billy Evans, star Precious Blood quarterback, drop his sundae spoon and fall to his knees. In her case, however, there would be illuminated bumps where breasts should be, she thinks. She decides against Blessed Christina. Saying *breast* during her reading of the essay would reduce the students to squirmy whispers and giggles, and distract the nun judges. She needs to find a pisser saint, not one who spent her whole life in a convent.

Christina slogs back to the stacks, surrounded by books she doesn't want to open. She won't get to Brigham's today. She isn't missing anything. She pulls down a book and gets back to work. Another St. Christina, this one from Bolsena, Italy, torn by hooks,

fastened to a rack and cooked above a flame in a furnace, where she remained for five days, unhurt. Then
thrown into a snake pit. After that, her tongue cut
out, and, for the grand finale, pierced by arrows that
did her in and earned her the martyr's crown. What
was it about the arrows that the snakes and furnace
couldn't do? Christina wonders. She takes the book
back to the table and copies down the list of tortures
and the important dates and places. This saint's life
was the like the shower scene in *Psycho*, minus the
Bernard Herrmann score, playing on an endless Catholic loop. Come to think of it, Alfred Hitchcock is
Catholic, although not one of the all-stars the nuns
are always bragging about, like Louis Pasteur and
Knute Rockne and Kennedy. Maybe she'll write her
essay about the St. Christina/Janet Leigh shower
scene and make a comparison between torture and
Catholic values. Right. She'd be kicked out, and is
that such a bad idea? It is September, the first week
of junior year, and already Christina is ticking off the
days, like a lifer in prison.

   Christina soldiers back to the stacks. She yawns
and picks up a dusty-looking reference book, in-
trigued by its title, *Great Eccentrics in History*. She
leafs through the book, stopping at an engraving of
a wild-eyed young woman crouched in a tree. The
woman wears a ragged shift bound with saplings.
Two friars stand at the bottom of the tree. They look
like they are begging her to come down and having
no luck. Christina reads the title and a roar fills her
ears. *St. Christina the Astonishing*.

Christina has to expel the roar or burst. It comes out as a high-pitched yelp, as if she's suddenly standing face-to-face with a wild beast and no zoo enclosure between them. She doesn't notice Dennis Dempsey standing a few feet away ripping a page out of *The Catholic Encyclopedia*. He looks at Christina, whose eyes are closed, clasping the book to her breast like a long-lost friend. He folds the paper torn from the encyclopedia and stuffs it into his pocket, staring at Christina, who is evidently lost in the throes of divine book-lover bliss.

"Dipshit," he mutters.

Christina the Astonishing
by Christina Falcone

Christina the Astonishing was born in Belgium in 1150 AD. She was orphaned at age fifteen and became a shepherdess. She had some sort of fit and everyone thought she was dead. But at her funeral Mass she suddenly flew up out of her coffin like a raven into the rafters of the church. It was supposedly right after the Agnus Dei. The priest saying the Mass was yelling at her to come down but she wouldn't. Everyone else screamed and left the church. When Christina came down she told the priest she had been to heaven and hell and purgatory and that she saw a lot of people there she knew from the town. God told her she could stay in heaven or go back to earth and Christina decided to stay on earth. Christina was being really saintly and came back to help people somehow.

After that her life really became Astonishing. Christina hung out mostly in the tops of trees and only spoke to birds, because she couldn't stand the stink of humans, especially men, who smelled worse than anyone else to her. Sometimes she balanced on weather vanes, or sat in holy water fonts or hid in ovens. Many people thought she was insane because she could handle fire and not get burned, or get flung around by mill wheels and not get hurt. She became a beggar and wore rags bound with saplings (which really looked good on her because of her holiness). The townspeople tried to capture her, but they couldn't. She always escaped as if she were magic or maybe God was protecting her from the townspeople who were really the crazy ones, not Christina the Astonishing. People thought she was a witch, but they also came to her for advice. She was never officially made a saint by the Vatican, but her life is a good one to follow for people who live outside of society. Because outcasts need a patron saint, too. Therefore, Christina the Astonishing is my patron saint.

The End

Sister Coronada tells the class that she is satisfied, for the most part, with the essays they handed in on their patron saints, "even yours, Mr. Dempsey." Dennis smirks like he could care less, but the rebellious tips of his ears turn pink at the unaccustomed praise. Some essays will have to be rewritten, of course. The nun reads off a list of names. The not-good-enough students rise as their names are called and file up to collect the offending papers sitting on a far corner of her enormous oak desk. They are the usual suspects, the perpetual dullards and shirkers. Sister Coronada hands each of them a paper marked with corrections in red. Christina's is the last name called. It is a first for her, to be included in the not-good-enough students. She can see the red slash through her essay from half an aisle away. Sister Coronada has leaned on the diagonal line bisecting her paper so hard that it is torn in places. As Christina reaches for it, the nun's voice stops her.

"Miss Falcone," she says, her voice soft as a whispered prayer. She looks directly at Christina and rips her paper in half, then half again, her meaty red face eerie in its utter blankness.

Christina shivers. She hopes the nun doesn't see.

"This mentally deranged soul you wrote about is not a saint. She has never been canonized or recognized by the Vatican. You will write your essay about the saint for whom you were named at your baptism: St. Christina, martyr of Bolsena, who was delivered by the power of Christ to endure inhuman torments including serpents, the fiery rack, drowning, and having her tongue cut out"—here the nun pauses as if ruminating on how much better it would be for everyone if this could be arranged for her present-day namesake—"before her soul was released to go up the shining path to sainthood. You will have this paper on my desk tomorrow morning. Now throw this in the trash where it belongs and take your seat."

Christina drops the remains of her essay in the wastepaper basket and walks back to her desk, ignoring Patsy's mouthed *What the fuck?* She checks the clock. Twenty minutes until the bell rings. Four days until Saturday, when she can take the trolley to Harvard Square and spend the whole day in her favorite no-name bookstore.

Christina's time with her friends now is mostly spent walking to and from school and sitting with them at lunch. Patsy and Mary Agnes resent her odd ways; sometimes their teasing has an edge. Rose is still her best friend, but she, too, is receding like a faded photograph. Sometimes Rose spends more time talking to Christina's mother than to Christina when she calls the house.

"What did you write that made Coronada go mental like that?" Patsy asks, removing her tie and shedding her navy-blue blazer as she walks. Mary Agnes and Rose also remove their blazers. It is September but it feels like August. Christina's hair, grown long in imitation of Joan's dramatic waist-length glory, crackles around her head like a frizzy cartoon halo. She pushes it away from her face with irritation.

"I'm not named after any saint," she says. "My father wanted to name me after his mother but he couldn't bring himself to do that to me, thank God."

"What was her name?" Patsy demands.

"Oh, it's a good one. You're gonna love this." Christina pauses for effect. "Cesidia." She uses a buffoony Italian accent to draw out the name.

They all hoot with laughter, although Patsy and Rose and Christina herself feel guilty. *Why does that name sound so funny and ugly to us?* Christina thinks. Their parents would be baffled and hurt if they could hear them making fun of the names of their old people, mammas left behind forever with an ocean of tears to separate them.

"I'm gonna start callin' you Cesidia and tell everyone that's your real name," Mary Agnes says, an evil glint in her eye.

"St. Cesidia!" Patsy shouts. They all laugh again, their voices chiming as they sing-taunt the name: "St. Cesidia! St. Cesidia!"

"Yeah, well, I'm not named after any fucking saint who got her tongue ripped out," Christina says, hot anger making her voice tremble.

"Coronada *wishes*!" says Patsy.

"If you don't write that essay and flip Coronada out so she's pissed at all of us, *I'll* rip out your tongue," Mary Agnes says.

"Fuck you," Christina responds mildly, and walks away.

"Fuck YOU," Mary Agnes fires back with sudden vehemence.

An old lady coming out of Larry's Superette turns around and gives them both a disapproving glance. She is dressed in black from head to toe and looks like the witch in *Snow White*. She even has a wart on her nose. Christina turns her face away, though it is too late and the old crone has seen her. And might tell her mother. She begins walking so fast Rose has to break into a trot to keep up. Christina doesn't say another word until she reaches her house. She walks up the stairs to her front door, ignoring Rose's tiny-voiced goodbye.

Christina catches a glimpse of her mother at the kitchen table before fleeing up to her room. She hears the clink of coffee cups and guesses that Aunt Connie is there, interrupting Rita's afternoon soaps, but providing better melodrama than *One Life to Live* as she describes in juicy detail last night's fight with Dommie, the *stupidone*.

"I HAVE A LOTTA HOMEWORK," she yells down the stairs before running up to her room. Her mother's sour "*Quando mai*" floats up the stairs, a caustic after-dinner belch to this dyspeptic, endless day of people yelling at her. Christina has no idea what her mother is actually saying, but the intent is clear: *Yeah, right. Sure, you have homework so you can't set the table. Sure, you need money for more friggin' books you keep buying and bringing into the house, put them in your bedroom, makin' a mess. Sure, you only care about yourself. Sure, sure.* Quando mai.

Christina resists the urge to put on her record player before opening her notebook. Dylan's nasal voice penetrates her mother's brain like a jackhammer, causing her to shriek at the first few bars of "Masters of War" the way St. Christina of Bolsena probably sounded before her tongue was cut out. Her eyes scan the list of her namesake's tortures and miraculous revivals before her final demise by arrows and drowning. Grilled on a rack like a hamburger. Thrown into a pit of serpents. Just exactly how is this story of St. Christina's ordeal supposed to be a role model for her future life? It dawns on her so suddenly she gasps at the connection. This is what the Church is preparing her for: motherhood.

Christina has overheard the gruesome labor and delivery stories her mother and her friends intone like sibyls at every coffee session, always the Sorrowful Mysteries between bites of biscott'. The blood, the pain, the ripping of tender flesh, the story told with reverence, in whispers. Christina is invited to join them; she earned the right to sit at the table when she got her first period a few months ago (three years after her other friends). The birth stories make her nervous and ashamed, like Rita and her friends are inviting her to watch them go to the bathroom. Christina will travel to Paris when she finally gets out of Precious Blood. She will sit in a café like that woman in the Brassaï photograph and smoke cigarettes, her head tossed back, and have a man lean toward her, fascinated by what she has to say.

She keeps thinking of her revelation: the Church is preparing her for motherhood with martyr role models. She is exasperated with herself for not seeing it before. She remembers one of Sister Coronada's favorite sayings to the class dimwits when they finally get the right answer: "Light dawns on Mahblehead." On impulse, she rushes downstairs. Maybe her mother and Connie know about this connection.

"You finish?" her mother asks. She holds Denise, Connie's toddler, on her lap.

Christina eyes the biscott' but is too excited to sit down and eat it. She paces the kitchen.

"Take off you *brutta* uniform before it gets wrinkled," her mother orders.

Connie lights a cigarette and also eyes the biscott', but doesn't take any. She complains often that the size of her ass has doubled with each kid. She's right, Christina thinks. Connie's ass looks like it harbors another, unnamed toddler clinging and squirming under her dress.

"I have to ask you both something. It's for homework," Christina says.

Connie laughs. Her mother pays no attention. Homework isn't her job.

"You're askin' the wrong person, honey. I always copied my girlfriend's," Connie says.

"Do you think the tortures of the saints were role models for motherhood?" Christina asks.

Her mother is distracted, feeding Denise teaspoons of her heavily sugared coffee and laughing at the comical faces the baby makes.

Connie provides the answer: "The saints are just to ask for things because they're in good with God, like if you lose something you ask St. Anthony to find it: *Dear St. Anthony, look around. Something is lost and cannot be found.* Like that." She smiles at Christina. "Why? Did you lose something?" she teases, drawing out "lose" and managing to make it sound dirty.

Her mother picks up the tone: "She better not

lose nothing." She and Connie look at each other and laugh. "She better not disgrace the Falcone name," her mother continues, pushing the joke too far like she always does.

Connie stubs her cigarette and blows out her last puff with gusto, revived by the topic of sex. She takes a long glance at Christina, still smiling. "You got a boyfriend?"

Christina shakes her head. "No," she huffs. "I hate boys. Especially the boys in my school. They're all morons."

"How come you don't have a boyfriend? You're cute," Connie persists.

Rita snorts. "She so cute, she like the Irish boys."

Christina freezes her face into a featureless mask, hoping her mother, who makes her father's poker-playing buddies look like giggling little girls with her extrasensory ability to bluff, is doing so now. How does her mother know about her long-ago crush on Dennis Dempsey? Once again, the nuns have it wrong: It isn't God who is the omniscient presence seeing all and judging His creations. It is Rita, has always been Rita. Forever and ever, world without end. Her mother and creator.

Connie reaches for a biscott'. "Listen to me. Stay away from those Irish jerks. They drink and don't respect you, all grabby hands and dirty mouths. If they don't show respect, they're no good." She looks at Denise wiggling in Rita's arms, at her mass of blue-black curls. "An' they're ugly. You gotta think of the kids you'd have with them. You wanna have a buncha Howdy Doodys with freckles an' orange hair?"

"*Brutte*," Rita agrees.

"You're no help. I should've known." Christina turns to go.

"*Quando mai.*"

St. Christina of Bolsena
by Christina Falcone

St. Christina of Bolsena was born in the middle of Italy and we don't know when. We do know she died around 300 AD as a martyr. She looks pretty young in the pictures, probably no more than fifteen. I would list the tortures she went through before she died, but you could also watch "The Pit and the Pendulum" or "Attack of the Crab Monsters" or "The Premature Burial" and understand the depth of St. Christina's suffering, and I am sure many of my fellow students have seen these films. The people who suffered in these movies are not saints, even though many regular people who are not saints suffer every day, some just with mental pain. Or people in the South who cannot go to school because they are Negroes. These people are not saints either. But they suffer, like St. Christina.

St. Christina is the patron saint of Insanity, Psychiatrists, and Millers. Insanity because she probably went insane when she was thrown into a pit of snakes. Psychiatrists because they probably pray to her to help them understand people who have been driven insane by various things. Millers I don't really understand why unless it's because St. Christina finally died after all those tortures when they threw her into a pond with a millstone around her neck.

St. Christina is my patron saint and I will pray to her nightly not to go insane.

The End

STATE OF GRACE

Since September it has been all leprosy, all the time. Leprosy makes Catholic sense. To Sister Coronada, it is the outward manifestation of sin and the body's innate corruption. What matters to Sister Coronada is the soul. The body is a trap, beguiling its owner into sin and eventual decay. The Precious Blood class reads a book about Father Damien, who glorified his immortal soul by establishing a leper colony on the island of Molokai, and then succumbed to the disease himself. It doesn't matter, though, that his flesh rotted: his soul is immortal and in heaven with God because of his sacrifice and his over-the-top even by God's standard good deeds.

Today will be the presentation of the oral reports on the most recent leprosy book the class has been assigned: *Miracle at Carville*. The book is about a happy young Southern debutante who discovers a red spot on her leg one day, and before you know it, her doctor fiancé dumps her, and she's installed in a leper colony in Louisiana. Christina still can't believe it: banished to a leper colony in the continental

United States, where the girl will live until she dies, her young body ravaged, maybe missing some fingers or a nose. There's the promised miracle and a cure at the climax of the book, but Christina and everyone else who reads the book are all fixated on the random red spot and the girl being shipped to a leper colony from which she can never, ever leave.

Despite her rage at Coronada for giving her yet another thing to worry about in her already anxiety-ridden life, Christina delivers the expected composition: a shameless propaganda piece on faith overcoming all, the real miracle not the medical cure but the young girl offering her suffering to the Lord, blah blah blah. She is certain she can get through the grueling afternoon of forty-six other oral presentations exactly as pandering as hers (though not as intelligently and subversively ironic, she reassures herself). If she feels herself slipping into uncontrollable eye rolls or unrepressed snorts of derision, she has the Book to slip under her report, to be read as surreptitiously as an underground broadsheet during the regime of a brutal fascist dictator, someone not unlike Sister Coronada. The Ferlinghetti is a last resort because it isn't as easy to conceal as the thinner, flatter City Lights poetry books. Still, she wishes she hadn't automatically begun checking her body for red spots every night and morning, and sometimes during lunch. Leprosy is now a part of her daily routine, along with thinking about mortal sin and medieval torture devices.

Only twenty minutes into the hour-plus presentation, Christina realizes she has been overconfident about her stamina for leprosy times forty-six. She finds herself slipping the Book out of her desk and under her *Miracle at Carville* paper with the slow precision of someone dismantling a bomb. Sister Coronada sits at her desk like a Roman emperor hearing petitions from the plebes as, row by row, members of the class straggle up to the front of the room to deliver their reports. Winnie Mahoney is presently spending way too much time on the human love story at Carville, bloviating about Betty, our heroine, finding a husband at the leper colony. Her fatal mistake has been not giving enough ink to the part about the love story with God, always the main character. Sister Coronada is beginning to frown. *Improvise for your life!* Christina silently implores Winnie, to no avail. Winnie's love-besotted fantasy will be cut short any minute now. But Winnie, as if sensing the looming imperial thumbs-down, finishes her reading at warp speed, places the paper on the end of Sister Coronada's desk, and scurries to her seat.

Dennis Dempsey is up next. Christina slides the Book open to Ferlinghetti's poem about Christ climbing down off the cross and running away and finding another womb to be born into and escaping his fate on the cross. That poem always cheers her up, and the escape theme is especially meaningful during the midafternoon *No Exit* part of the school day. Dennis's black shitkicker boots with the Cuban heels clomp past Christina. He makes a point of "bumping" into her desk as he goes by, jarring the Book. She rights it and glares at his retreating back and keeps up the eye-murder throughout his report, a ghoulish and detailed catalog of the effects of leprosy on the human body. Even Sister Coronada is starting to look as green as her soul twin, the Wicked Witch of the West, by the time he deposits his paper on her desk. Christina returns to her poem, so she doesn't see Dennis smiling evilly at her as he passes her desk, and isn't ready when he slams it again, knocking the Book to the floor.

The *thwack* of the Book hitting the floor explodes like a pistol shot in the silent classroom. The sound is out of all proportion, considering the slenderness of the volume and the fact that it's a paperback. Sister Coronada stares at it lying in the aisle. It is most definitely not a copy of *Miracle at Carville*. She draws back her lips and inhales sharply. The pages are emitting a foul odor, the stench of blasphemy. She knows when the devil surfaces. She can smell it from where she sits, the filth.

"Bring that book to me at once, Miss Falcone."

In the slow motion of a nightmare, Christina picks up the Book and walks to Sister Coronada's desk, invisible weights dragging her ankles, almost making her crawl. She hands the Book to the nun and stands beside the desk, her invisible shackles becoming heavier by the second. She waits for sentencing in the new zone of elongated time.

After school, Christina and Sister Coronada walk in silence the short distance to the Gothic redbrick horror that is the Precious Blood rectory. Christina waits outside the monsignor's office while Coronada goes in with the Book. She comes out a few minutes later, ignoring Christina. She hitches her heavy black shawl around her shoulders. "You are an evil girl," she hisses, then sweeps out the door without a backward glance. The monsignor calls Christina into his office, his voice ringing with practiced warmth.

"Take a seat, Christina."

She slumps into the low-seated cane-back chair opposite the monsignor's Captain of Industry–sized desk. The Book is there, resting atop a pile of papers on the near corner. The monsignor smiles at her, leans back in his far more comfortable leather chair, and laces his fingers over his stomach that rises like a planet, orbited by his shiny purple sash. He switches off the smile and his puffy red face no longer looks Santa Claus jovial. Now he looks liverish and concerned, as if he were sitting in a doctor's office and the prognosis is terminal.

"Sister Coronada showed me what you were reading, and I knew then that her fears for your immortal soul were justified. Blasphemous books are mortally dangerous, Christina. They are faith killers." He glances at the Book, its contents polluting his office. "Have you lost your faith?"

Christina looks down. "No," she mumbles.

"These kinds of influences pose a great danger to young women your age. Dangerous music, dangerous films . . . all threatening your faith and your immortal soul. Your judgment isn't formed yet. You need guidance from the good sisters, your teachers, and Our Lady. They'll guide you in how to be strong in the world."

Christina shifts in her chair and coughs. Monsignor Boyle, an old hand at sensing audience unrest, changes tactics: "So . . . you're interested in poetry, is that right?" The smile and the jolly-old-elf color return to the priest's jowly cheeks.

Christina parries, flashing her own fake smile. "Yeah."

The monsignor leans in, still smiling. "I, too, am a poetry lover," he confides. "Does that surprise you?"

"No," she replies. The smile was a mistake. She has encouraged him. Now he's about to recite some long-winded poetry.

"I can suggest some excellent Catholic poets for you to read. Joseph Mary Plunkett, for one. '*I see His blood upon the rose. And in the stars the glory of His eyes,*'" he drones, his own eyes closed. "Or Donne: '*Batter my heart, three person'd God; for, you as yet but knock, breathe, shine, and seek to mend; that I may rise, and stand, o'erthrow me, and bend Your force, to break, blow, burn and make me new.*'" He comes out of his trance and peers at Christina, his watery blue eyes glazing into permafrost. "Are you in a state of grace, Christina?"

Christina hears him from far away. She is thinking about *break, blowe, burn and make me new*. She likes that. Okay, if that's what it takes. She wants to be new. Maybe she'll give Donne a try. Is it masochistic to ask God to beat the shit of you so you can be reborn? She is reading Freud, also a blasphemer, she suspects. She realizes the priest is looking at her and has asked a question.

"What?" she says, dazed.

He repeats, "Are you in a state of grace?"

Christina tries to remember the rules for being in a state of grace. When was her last confession? She can't remember. Can she be in a state of grace without going to confession? For how long? She thinks of all that as *their* rules now, she realizes. "I don't know. I think so," she says.

"You *think* so," the priest counters. "Well, if you have to *think* about it, it sounds like you're in need of spiritual renewal. Am I right?"

She has to pay attention. She gave the wrong answer. She is prolonging the interrogation with her daydreams. "No, I am. I know I'm in a state of grace." She tries to sound confident. And to radiate whatever being in a state of grace means.

Monsignor Boyle begins winding it down. At last. "You know, Christina, Our Blessed Mother helps troubled girls like you. I want you to make a novena to her to help you find peace of mind. Will you do that?"

"Sure. I mean, yes. Yes, Monsignor." She forces herself to make eye contact and sound demure and sincere, even though she is insulted by the *troubled girls like you* crap. She isn't some troubled girl, some pregnant girl in trouble! She was reading a book, for Chrissake!

"And I haven't seen you at the Catholic Youth Organization dances, either, Christina. Boys don't like girls who read and study all the time, you know," he chuckles. He doesn't sound amused at all to Christina. "I want to see you next Friday night having a swinging time at the CYO dance! Okay?" He doesn't wait for her answer. He is sniffing the air like a dog. It's true—there's something sulfurous in the air, a cabbage smell. She hopes he doesn't think it was her doing.

"And no more of this blasphemous poetry, right?"

"Right," Christina replies faintly. She wants the Book back. She wonders if she can ask for it, now that he is done with her. But, no, they will never give it back. It is both within sight and lost to her. *Those bastards*, she thinks. *Thieves*. An image gleams, of Christina the Astonishing, her mad-saint namesake, floating up into the rafters of the church, ignoring the priest's commands to come down.

The monsignor takes a deep, satisfied breath. "Well, my nose tells me Mrs. Murphy's good boiled dinner is just about ready. I'll see you on Saturday for confession." He begins to rise, dismissing her.

The phone rings. The priest sits down again, picks it up, and answers. It's someone important, a big donor probably; Christina can tell by the instant tone of bonhomie in the monsignor's voice. This guy has more vocal impressions than Rich Little, the comedian her father loves on *Ed Sullivan*. The priest half turns, flapping her off with his fingers, like snot. *Ta ta!* Christina takes the half-turn opportunity as a heavenly sign from Christina the Astonishing, her patron saint. She snatches the Book in one deft move and flees. *Ta ta! Go with God, Man of Many Voices!*

On the way home, in an excess of joy, Christina

runs and slides on long patches of ice, the freezing blueness under her feet not unlike the gelid eyes of Monsignor Boyle.

"Honest to God, we thought you got kicked out," Rose tells Christina on their way to school the next morning.

The Book incident has eclipsed all other news events at Precious Blood, even Valentine's Day and its built-in drama: who got a measly card, who got a charm bracelet, who was ignored, and who was heartbroken for life. Patsy and Mary Agnes are dying to hear all about Christina's disgrace. They even meet Christina and Rose halfway up Derby Street, instead of their usual place in front of Al's Lunch.

"UNCLEAN! UNCLEAN! THE LEPER QUEEN APPROACHES," Mary Agnes is shouting from a block away. She pretends to ring a bell. She looks more cheerful than Christina has ever seen her in their entire friendship, positively tickled.

Patsy galumphs up to Christina, avid for news, her breath puffing like a runaway train, fur-trimmed boots plowing up dirty snow in her wake. "I was afraid to call your house last night. Did you get in trouble?" she asks, greedy for the details.

"We thought you got kicked out," Rose repeats. This time her voice has a plaintive tone. *She almost sounds disappointed*, Christina thinks.

"Didja have a nice conversation with the monsignor?" Mary Agnes asks.

"No, because your nun aunt was makin' out with

him. She was letting him feel her up," Christina answers, pushing it.

"You suck. Tell us what he said," Mary Agnes presses, all business.

Christina affects boredom with the whole subject. "We discussed poetry. He has drippy taste. And he wants me to go to CYO dances and have a swinging time. And make a novena to Our Lady, of course. That's it."

"Discussed *poetry*," Patsy squeaks, her husky voice gone falsetto with disbelief.

"You were lucky he didn't kick you out," Rose says.

"Did he rip up your book?" Mary Agnes wants to know.

Christina smiles and takes her time removing the Book from her schoolbag. She displays it with a flourish, waving it in front of them. She gets the expected result: they all gasp as if she is displaying the trophy head of a conquered chieftain.

"Don't tell anyone under penalty of death. I stole it off the monsignor's desk when he wasn't looking." She pauses, watching them. "Well, they were gonna steal it. It's mine." Christina returns the Book to her bag and tosses it in with a casual shrug for her awestruck audience.

Even Mary Agnes is impressed. "Geez, you're a regular reform-school girl," she says. "Maybe you and Dennis will end up at the same jail."

"Fucking Dennis Dempsey. This is all his fault. He's a dangerous psycho."

"What's he got to do with it?" Patsy asks.

"He bumped me! You didn't see? He did it on purpose."

"I thought he was *bumping* Angie Vasolo while her boyfriend was away," Mary Agnes says.

Dennis is having sex with Angie Vasolo? That explains the swagger and the Cuban heels. And, *vomit*, Christina doesn't want to picture it, Dennis's puny body subsumed by Angie's lush one.

"You shouldn't bring that book back to school," Rose says. "What if they find it? You'll definitely get kicked out."

Sister Coronada thinks Christina got off lightly with the monsignor, that is clear. She simmers all day whenever she looks at her and refuses to call on Christina even when hers is the only raised hand in the room besides Cecilia's. By the end of the day Christina is relieved the nun hasn't searched her bag, calling on the police-procedural skills she has mastered so thoroughly in her random cigarette pat-downs, usually involving Dennis Dempsey or Danny Grillo. She resolves to leave the Book at home from now on. Rose is right: if she gets caught with it again, she will get kicked out. And she doesn't want to get kicked out. She decides that she will get through one more year and then she'll go to college and live far away from the suffocating neighborhood where everyone knows she's a Falcone just by the shape of her face. This murky idea is just becoming clear, like the message on a Magic 8 Ball. She still has no idea how she can make it a real plan.

When Christina arrives home, it's clear that Sister Coronada has exacted her revenge. The minute she enters the hallway, she hears Rita from the kitchen, her voice vibrating with outrage: "The nun call the 'ouse!" Her mother's voice shakes, the preliminary tremors to a life-threatening earthquake.

Christina pictures Coronada with a battering ram going right through the oak door and piercing the wrought-iron curlique *F* on the bottom half of the screen door. She notes with relief that Connie is also sitting at the table, although it shows how desperate the situation is when Christina depends on her aunt to be the voice of reason. Denise is crawling on the floor even though she's old enough to walk, and Dommie Boy is chomping on a cookie at the table. They provide good distraction, she thinks feverishly.

"Don't worry, I talked to her," Connie says. She places an oily roasted red pepper on some crusty bread and takes a ladylike bite. She looks Christina up and down. "What're you—readin' dirty books in class? I thought you hated boys." She smiles at Christina, the oil on her lips glistening and somehow lewd.

"Books!" Her mother spits the word out with the disgust she reserves for gristle. "Miss Prim!" she adds. "Ha!"

Christina will not engage. This kind of ignorant squabbling is beneath her. "It was poetry," she says with all the dignity she can muster.

"She told me you saw the monsignor," Connie says, unable to keep a tinge of awe from her voice.

"Yeah, and we talked about poems and he likes

poems, too, just not the poems in the book I was reading. And that was it. So, I won't bring that particular book to school anymore. The monsignor quoted John Donne. So, I'm gonna read him." She decides to hit them with the Donne: "*Batter my heart, three-person'd God . . .*"

Connie and her mother stare.

"They better not come 'ere," Rita says. "This my 'ouse!" Her mother seems to think this is the Inquisition and cowled men in black robes are about to appear at 65 Derby Street and carry her off to some dungeon for questioning.

"This isn't fascist Italy," Christina says. "They can't come to your house. God, you're so—"

"Shut up you readin' bad books! *Che vergogna*! *Disgraziata*! I'm tellin' you father!"

Christina leaves the kitchen. At a safe distance, she yells, "Go ahead! He reads, too! He's not like you, illiterate! And the poet I'm reading is Italian! His name is Ferlinghetti!" She heads up the stairs to her room. She can hear Connie reassuring her mother, the murmured word "teenager" bobbing to the surface.

Rita's one-word curse seeps under the closed door of her room: "BOOKS!"

Christina kicks off her shoes and collapses onto her frilly bed. She rolls down her knee socks and begins hunting for red spots, careful not to miss an inch of flesh.

That Friday night, squeezed beside Rose in the front seat of Danny Grillo's Chevy clunker, Christina sighs, disgusted with her own quivering anxiety, the fear that the monsignor will somehow know if she doesn't follow his order to go to the CYO dance and have a "swinging" time. She doesn't want to go. She wants to stay home and read and listen to music, but the monsignor might find out. She has a sudden mental picture of Monsignor Boyle on the gym floor, twisting the night away, his soutane swishing and revealing his black socks and white legs threaded with lumpy varicose veins. She shudders.

Rose, hyper aware of her position as girlfriend of the driver, reacts with proprietary diligence: "You cold, Christina? Danny, turn up the heat."

"You want the heat turned up?" He leers at Rose. "Later, baby."

Rose squeals and punches his shoulder. "Shut up!" she cries, thrilled, glancing sideways at Christina to see if she's heard.

"Glad All Over" by the Dave Clark Five comes on the radio and Danny blares it, singing along. "I'm gonna call you 'Glad' from now on," he says to Rose, as if they are alone in the car, as if Christina is a nonperson. "*I'm feelin' glad all over,*" he sings, looking at Rose, pounding the steering wheel on the downbeat. The car swerves. Christina stares out the window, trying to disappear herself.

Christina and Rose are in the cloakroom off the vestibule when they hear the ruckus. Danny has gone ahead and is already on the dance floor. Timothy Mosher, who is taking tickets at the door, refuses entrance to Angie Vasolo. She is wearing a pink pullover angora sweater. Pullovers are against the dress code for CYO dances; the only sweaters allowed are cardigans buttoned over blouses. Catholics obsess about sex every minute, Christina thinks. Pullovers outline the shape of breasts too vividly. At school, girls are supposed to wear white socks over nylons, a rule that seems insane until you think about it. Someone has figured out that the nylons would have to be held up by a panty girdle and that would keep loose flesh from bouncing around. It is all about stopping the jiggle, taming the female form. The suspicious nuns even check girls' legs sometimes, running a creepy hand up their calves to make sure they're wearing the regulation nylons under the white socks. *Sexual repression*, that's what Freud would diagnose, all this shrouding of women's bodies.

Anyway, it has the opposite effect: everyone thinks about sex all the time. Even class eunuch Timothy Mosher, who is at this moment inciting a possible riot by barring Angie Vasolo from the dance, is addressing her prominent chest instead of her face, stuttering and reddening as he shakes his head. Angie is looking at Timothy as if she can swallow him whole. Coach Flanagan steps in, carrying a brush-cut whiff of law and order that makes Angie back off physically but not verbally.

"Fuck yis all, then! I didn't wanna come to your chicken-shit dance anyways. None of yis can dance for shit, either. Yer all a buncha faggots! C'mon, Dennis." Angie turns on her heel and wiggles out. Dennis shuffles behind like a trained poodle.

Rose and Christina check out the desultory action on the dance floor. Patsy and Mary Agnes aren't there; spending too much time on the dance floor is depressing for even them. Precious Blood inmates are separated by sex all week long; in the classroom, the lunchroom, and at recess, there is a boys' and a girls' side, the lines as defined and unimaginable to breach as the yellow foul lines on the gym floor. No one trades bons mots when they are suddenly, magically allowed to fraternize Friday nights on the dance floor or on a Coke break in the Pope John XXIII room, someone's Andy Hardy fantasy of teen recreation. On the gym floor, the girls cling together in a gaggle until some brave soul trudges across the wide expanse to claim them, whereupon the couple totter in a small circle like windup toys until the slow song ends.

Christina and Rose check the ladies' room first. That is the epicenter of an agonized conversation about tampons. One girl is talking the other one, a first-timer, through the insertion process. "I'm gonna throw up!" comes the plaintive wail from behind the stall. Christina and Rose make a quick check in the mirror, Rose stopping to apply some frosted-pink lipstick. Christina stares at herself. She looks dour and beetle-browed, like someone taking an algebra exam. She wouldn't talk to herself if she saw that grim girl standing across a dance floor. "Let's go," she says to Rose.

They find Patsy and Mary Agnes at last in the Pope John XXIII room, nursing Cokes and having a fake conversation while eyeing the senior boys playing ping-pong under the beneficent glow of the pontiff himself, gilt-framed above the table, his hand raised as if giving advice on how to execute a killer serve. Not that Billy Evans, quarterback for PB's winning football team, needs papal advice on how to score, along with his squat teammate, Jackie Gallotti. Billy Evans reigns as uncrowned boy king of Precious Blood and has his choice of loyal female subjects. Girls vie in the halls of PB for a nod from his chestnut-curled head; they gaze at his perfect profile and forget the answers to their catechism questions. As if his physical perfection isn't enough to incite Beatles-style riots, Billy has a really cool Volkswagen he named the Pea-Green Bug. Patsy's first order of business is to get a ride home in the PGB, followed by an invitation to the senior prom next spring. Her fake conversation with Mary Agnes is putting her on Billy's radar, but there has been no contact yet. However, she and Mary Agnes so far have the advantage of being the only ones in the room, except for Timothy Mosher, who has been reassigned behind the snack counter. He is straightening napkins into perfect, fussy alignment to atone for his recent intimate encounter with Angie Vasolo's double-D's. Christina lets Rose fill Patsy and Mary Agnes in about Angie's banishment by Coach Flanagan. The initial thrill of the Angie event has already begun to wane for Christina.

Patsy feels keenly the slight to her cousin. "What an ASSHOLE," she yells.

"Hey! No swearing in the Pope John XXIII room," Timothy cries, as scandalized as some old biddy dowager in a Three Stooges routine. Everyone, including the two senior boys, ignores him.

"Your coach was mean to my cousin," Patsy says to Billy, pouting just enough to make her full lips fuller.

"No shit, he's mean. He killed Koreans in the war," Billy responds, tossing his curly, crown-awaiting head.

"And that's so cool, right? That your asshole coach kills people," Christina says, her voice loud and hot. But she gets it wrong again, she realizes right after she says it. She means it, Patsy doesn't.

Patsy looks at her, alarmed. "Didja come in the Bug?" she asks Billy, in a desperate bid to deflect the conversation.

Billy doesn't answer. He glares at Christina as if she has just executed a subpar curtsey.

"I don't know how you fit yourself into that thing," Patsy continues, managing to make "that thing" sound sexual and promising. Billy perks up. He bestows a full-lipped smile on Patsy, who smiles back, a promise of things to come.

The strains of "Everyone's Gone to the Moon" filter into the Pope John XXIII room. Rose screams, "That's our song!" She runs out of the room trailed by Patsy and Mary Agnes. The senior boys follow them.

Christina sits alone at the table littered with Coke bottles.

Timothy Mosher looks up. "You're supposed to bring the empties up to the counter."

"Eat it raw, Timothy," Christina mutters. But she gathers up the empties and brings them to the counter.

"Hey, Timothy," she then says, an idea forming, "does the monsignor ever come to the dances?"

"No, never." He brightens. "But Father McMullin comes a lot! He's a really good dancer," he says, practically swooning.

Christina leaves the Pope John XXIII room and skirts the shuffling couples on the dance floor, aware of people watching her. She thinks of Christina the Astonishing, her patron saint who was able to walk through fire without harm. She tries to motion to Rose that she is leaving but Rose has her head burrowed into Danny's shoulder with her eyes closed. Patsy and Mary Agnes are also in a transport of bliss clinging to their newly acquired seniors. Christina snatches her coat and pushes open the gym door. She steps into the freedom of the quiet night, gulping the icy, burnt-smelling air. She wishes the monsignor could see her now, in a state of grace.

FREUD WAS A NUT

"These are the best years of your life," Aunt Connie tells sixteen-year-old Christina at Easter dinner, the tone in her voice braying a challenge.

"Yeah, I know," Christina replies, a big phony smile on her face. "I'm having a blast." That might have been too much, she thinks, the *blast* part. She always overdoes it. It's a tightrope walk, this challenge she has charged herself with—impersonating Sandra Dee in *Imitation of Life*, a black-and-white movie she never misses when it's on the late show. Sandra has a bubbly effervescence, a cuteness that disarms everyone who comes in contact with her. Christina could wield that like a magic shield if she could ever get it right. Rita is also drawn to *Imitation of Life* but more for the heart-wrenching martyr-mother scenes with the long-suffering maid, Annie, and her ungrateful, passing-for-white daughter, Sarah Jane, than the less interesting story of good-girl Sandra Dee and her actress mother, Lana Turner.

Christina and Rita always sit together when *Imita-*

tion of Life is on the late show in the quiet, night-solemn living room, the only light coming from the television and the phosphorescent Sandra Dee, live mother and daughter not speaking, not even acknowledging each other, their eyes on the film mothers and daughters. Rita blows her nose every so often, pulling a soggy tissue from the pocket of her bathrobe and quietly sobbing. While Rita honks, Christina works on her Sandra Dee impression, copying expressions and repeating phrases under her breath. She ignores the pietà looks her mother throws her way whenever Annie the maid suffers another stab to the heart from bitchy Sarah Jane. Arriving too late at her mother's funeral, the ingrate daughter realizes that she had loved her mother after all. Sarah Jane throws herself onto her mother's coffin, mad with grief and guilt. This is the part of the film where Rita always releases a strangled sigh of afterglow contentment, the distasteful sound causing Christina to get up and leave. The instructive Sandra Dee part of the film is over and done with anyway. Rita and Christina don't say good night to each other, nor do they ever refer to the movie in the light of day. It is their nighttime secret, like a blurry dream you can't remember the next morning.

This afternoon is a good time to try out the Sandra impersonation, during the hours-long Easter feast. In the middle of the table is the nod to American tradition, a pink rubbery ham studded with cloves that everyone ignores. They will make sandwiches of the meat later with sharp provolone and roasted peppers and hard, crusty bread; for now, the ham is starring as a photogenic *Good Housekeeping* Easter centerpiece and nothing else. The ham is accompanied by a romaine lettuce salad, bitter greens, roast potatoes, and the real star of the show, Rita's hand-cut ravioli with meatballs. A carafe of Joe's homemade red wine has pride of place at the head of the table.

"Yeah, you think it's a joke," Connie says bitterly, correctly noting the fakeness of Christina's smile. "But it's the truth. These are the best years of your life."

Christina switches off the smile. Clearly, she has to work on her Sandra Dee. She sighs. Everyone is still eating. It will be an hour at least before dessert, coffee, and the arrival of guests, when she can make the escape to her room.

Big Dommie shakes his head. "You got a lotta growin' up to do," he says, fixing his bloodshot eyes on Christina in a Popeye squint. He takes a huge glug of wine.

"More ravioli, Dom?" Rita thrusts the bowl at him, hoping the pasta will absorb the wine.

Big Dommie ignores her. "Sit up straight," he orders his miniature replica, Dommie Boy, squirming in his seat beside Christina.

"You go to that wake the other night?" Connie asks.

The wake of Anna Bevilacqua has received more news coverage during dinner than this year's Red Sox prospects, the recent horrible weather, or the upcoming trial of Albert DeSalvo, the Boston Strangler who is shamefully Italian American. The drama at Carmello's Funeral Home involves Anna's estranged sister, Philomena, making her appearance after forty years of not speaking to her sibling. Neither sister was able to remember the origin of the feud while Anna was alive—in fact, it is questionable if they'd even remembered they were related, since they were both in their nineties—but the scene at Carmello's front parlor rivaled the last act of *Madame Butterfly* for those lucky enough to catch the performance. The wake is sure to be rehashed in its entirety when the neighbors arrive.

"The old lady looked good," Joe grunts.

"I want Ray to do me when I go," Connie agrees. "Anna looked beautiful."

"But you see Philomen'? Madon'—she look like *she* should be in the coffin," Rita says, spooning more ravioli onto Vinny's plate. Rita has yet to take her seat, even though the rest of them are halfway through dinner.

"She had a stupid look on her face," Connie explains to Big Dommie, who was working the night shift and missed the excitement.

"And then, oh my God, it was terrible when they went to close the coffin. LOOK OUT, DOMMIE BOY!" Connie interrupts herself, reaching over to steady her son's tottering glass of soda.

"Philomen' went crazy screaming. She try to pull the sister outta the coffin," Rita reports, on her way back to the kitchen for more ravioli.

"She took it bad," Joe says, shaking his head.

The old-lady drama is taking up the entire meal. Christina's head is pounding. She thinks of the witty repartee in the Oscar Wilde play she's reading. In painful contrast, this is like trying to have dinner conversation with feral beasts of the wild. "She was *ninety*!" Christina blurts.

Rita springs from the kitchen as if shot from a giant rubber band. She tops her daughter's puny outrage without breaking a sweat. She is on familiar ground, like a coloratura soprano delivering the aria that has made her world-famous. "So what! It was her sister! Her *blood*! You tell me now if you brother Vinny die you no gonna pull him outta the coffin?"

Christina looks at her mother. She wishes she could write to Freud and ask him how to analyze Rita. He didn't leave any clues in the books she's read so far. What if she could just write that one sentence and ask him what he thought? That her mother is actually judging how much Christina loves her brother on the basis of whether Christina would someday pull him out of his theoretical coffin.

"Eh, s'all right," Nonno rasps. "S'all right."

Connie picks up the flying saucer–sized loaf of crusty bread and stands to slice off a piece. Dommie Boy's leg jitters again, shaking his glass. Connie points the knife at him, shrieking: "IF YOU SHAKE THAT GLASS ONE MORE TIME, I'LL KILL YOU! YOU SEE THIS KNIFE IN MY HAND? DON'T TEMPT ME!"

Dommie Boy stops banging his leg.

"S'all right," says Nonno, his faraway voice like the faded chorus to an old-timey song. "S'all right."

Connie, satisfied that Dommie Boy is frozen into

submission, stops pointing the knife. Christina thinks again about the hotbed of neurosis that exists around her family table. Freud would be in heaven observing this bunch.

"You're gonna give him a castration complex, Aunt Connie," Christina ventures.

"Huh?" Connie looks at her, still pissy about Christina's failed Sandra Dee.

"I don't want that kind of talk at the table," Joe says to his daughter. "Pass the *insalat'*."

"What? Psychology? Freud?"

"Freud was a *nut*," Connie says.

Rita appears behind Christina like a ghost. "Always talk crazy. BOOKS! Readin' dirty books!" Still harping on that one time the nun caught her reading the Book in class. Rita is still outraged. "The nun call the 'OUSE," she said for days afterward, as if the entire convent had arrived as a militia.

Christina will not engage, she tells herself. But immediately, she fires back: "I told you, that was poetry. Those mental midgets only want us to read about leprosy and the lives of the saints."

Joe looks up from his ravioli. "You're getting the best education you can get around here."

"They all say the sister schools are the best," Big Dommie chimes in.

Oh, that's rich coming from Mr. Fifties Pompadour, who never reads anything but the sports page in the *Boston Herald*.

"Who's *they*? Moe, Larry, and Curly?" Christina sneers.

Joe points his fork at Christina. "Watch your mouth," he says, his tone dangerous.

Christina feels the beginning of tears pricking the back of her eyes. She blinks and clears her throat, the old grade school tic resurfacing.

"Drink your tonic, honey," Connie tells her toddler. Denise wraps both pudgy hands around her orangeade and slurps, like a good girl. Christina is not a good girl.

"You're graduatin' next year," Joe continues. "Then you can go to work until you get married, and I can walk you down the aisle."

"Great. School prison to work prison," Christina mutters.

"Wait'll you get married. *That's* prison," Big Dommie says.

Joe chortles.

Rita gives her endorsement: "Ha!"

Connie plays along, pointing the knife at Dommie. "I'll give you prison, you bastard. First, I'll make you a capon."

Dommie laughs. "Oooh, Connie, you're givin' me a castration complex!"

"You people—" Christina is sputtering when Dommie Boy's jiggling leg finally overturns his glass of orangeade onto her lap. She leaps up. Her new jeans are soaked. "YOU LITTLE BASTARD" she yells. She lurches back from the table, almost overturning her chair, and runs upstairs, her mother yelling behind her, "GOOD! NOW I CAN FINALLY WASH THEM!" echoed by Connie's favorite refrain: "Hey! He has a mothuh and a fathuh!"

And then, very faintly, her grandfather, sounding the last, reedy note to the family sonata: "Eh, s'all right."

Rose raps on Christina's bedroom door and lets herself in. She has arrived with her parents for the dessert-and-coffee portion of the Easter feast. Christina slides her notebook under the bedspread. She is working on a play that combines the hopelessness of *No Exit* with the elegant satire of Oscar Wilde.

Rose is all dressed up, wearing nylons and a filmy Easter dress that swishes when she moves. She stares at Christina's crotch, which is still damp. She laughs. "What'd you do, wet your pants?"

"That little bastard Dommie Boy." Their eyes meet.

"*Hey! He has a mothuh and a fathuh,*" they say together, then giggle. It feels good to laugh, like the old days when they were easy together.

"Where's Danny?" Christina asks. Danny and Rose are inseparable these days, and if Danny can pass his finals he'll soon be her high school–graduate husband.

"He had to go to Easter dinner at the rich aunt's. The one who lives in Weston. Patsy went to the movies with Billy. Mary Agnes has to spend all day at the convent visiting the nun aunt and going to a special Mass. Can you picture that?"

"No wonder she's forever in a shitty mood."

"*You're* the one always in a shitty mood," Rose blurts. They glare at each other, the closeness of a minute ago gone. An uncomfortable silence develops.

Rose wants them to go downstairs and get some dessert. Christina imagines how they would look standing side by side in the dining room, Rose the first-generation dream daughter and Christina the *disgraziata* in her crotch-soaked blue jeans. Rose's parents would direct looks of pity at Rita, and Rita would meet those glances like the Madonna Addolarata exposing her sword-pierced heart; her father would swallow his anger, then order Christina upstairs to change, the whole scene escalating into World War III. She persuades Rose instead to bring a plate of goodies back to her room. Rose agrees and is gone for a long time. Christina can hear loud talk and the high-pitched laughter of the women from downstairs.

Finally, Rose returns. She's carrying a plate of angeloni cookies, two forks, and a slice of ricotta pie. "Your father wants to know when I'm getting married," she says.

Christina shakes her head, disgusted. She grabs an angeloni cookie, her favorite, and licks the icing. Rose smiles demurely in the mirror, rehearsing for the future.

Christina changes the subject before the inevitable monologue on the wedding-to-be: "What movie did Patsy go to?" She wants to see the movie version of *The Group*. She wonders if the instructive sex scenes in the book will be portrayed in CinemaScope. Probably not. The movie is yet to be banned by the Legion of Decency, the Catholic organization that rates films.

"She went to *The Sound of Music*. She couldn't

wait, she said, even though we're all goin' next month."
The nuns are taking the entire school to see the
award-winning movie that portrays nuns as sweet and
chirpy. The girls have all learned the entire score for
chorus.

"She wants to see it twice? Is she a complete
masochist?"

"You hate everything," Rose says. The uncomfortable silence returns. Christina gets up and turns
on her record player. "*Hello darkness, my old friend*,"
sing Simon and Garfunkel, their girlish harmonies re-
storing an artificial peace. Christina sits cross-legged
on her bed. Rose drops down beside her, the plate of
sweets between them. She picks at an angeloni cookie
before popping it in her mouth. She slips her little
kitten heels off and rubs her feet, which look red and
swollen.

"I'm wearing flats for my wedding, I don't care,"
Rose declares.

"Yeah, well, I'm getting my own apartment and
I'm gonna live in Boston when I graduate next year.
I'm gonna apply to college."

"That's good," Rose says, seeming bored, as if
Christina has just announced she's on the honor roll
again. "Patsy wants to know if you're gonna try out
for cheerleading. We're all gonna."

"That's good. Because I'm not. I consider that shit
fun for the feeble-minded."

Rose slips on her shoes and stands, smoothing her
dress. "I'm goin' downstairs," she says, and leaves,
closing the door.

Christina pulls out her notebook, but she can't concentrate. She gets up and lifts the arm of the record player and sets it down in the groove for the last song on the album. When "I Am a Rock" starts in, she sings along, taking a fierce pleasure in the words that seem to be written just for her.

Revitalized by singing her heart out—"*I have no need of friendship, friendship causes pain*"—Christina picks up her notebook and goes back to her play.

Joan, wearing a brown monk's cowl to symbolize her renunciation of all things worldly, sat on the bathroom floor and played her dulcimer. Through the bathroom door came the idiot sounds of a party of fools going on.

She hears the toilet flush in the bathroom across the hall. The door to her room opens just as Christina, from weary habit, yells "KNOCK," to no avail.

Her mother stands in the doorway. "You comin' downstairs? You godmother's askin' for you."

There is a loud burst of laughter from downstairs. Rose's infectious giggle soars above the others.

"I have a lotta homework."

"How come Rose don't have homework?"

"I don't know. I do."

Her mother's temper flares. "Good. Stay 'ere then all by youself. An' take those dirty pants offa my spread!" She leaves, slamming the door.

Christina picks up her pen, as if she really does have homework. But she can't summon that other place, the bathroom sanctuary, the calm aloofness of the girl in the monk's cowl. She looks at the door. A burst of stupid laughter seeps through the keyhole.

Joan begins to play a magical incantation on her dulcimer, a piercing tone that opens the pipelines of the entire apartment building and unleashes a tsunami of sewage, drowning out the party of fools and delivering unto her the sounds of silence. Joan smiles blissfully, in peace at last.

Christina's jeans begin to feel itchy and tight. She slips out of her clothes and sits on her bed, naked and free. She looks at her closet and wonders if she should put on a dress and go downstairs and join the party of fools.

RANSOMING THE CAPTIVE

B abe is looking like shit these days. The glamour that has clung to her even at St. Lucy's Home for the Aged Blind is floating away in feathery puffs like the moldering pink boa Babe still keeps in her closet, a relic of better days and hotter nights. It makes Christina depressed, and she worries that Babe will disappear any day now into one of her elaborate alternate realities and become a ghost herself.

Christina watches Babe, her eyes closed, a circle of light hitting her face like a cue to go onstage, a twitchy smile tugging at a corner of her defiantly red lips. Christina sees clearly the lipstick running in crazy tributaries along the descending wrinkles of her mouth, but Babe doesn't look clowny or grotesque or Baby Jane–ish, like the horror movie. She looks like an ancient icon, a sibyl who can impart secrets. Christina still wants Babe's approval with the same nine-year-old fervor she felt at their first meeting, when Christina believed she brought a fairy-tale creature to life with her magical summoning. Babe's white, almost see-through hand holds her cigarette in an elegant pose, fingers fanning out like a veil as she lifts it to her mouth. Babe will die, Christina thinks. Babe will die, and there is nothing she can do about it. As if reading Christina's mind, Babe convulses. She leans over and collapses in on herself, a rag doll someone has thrown carelessly on a chair. Her shoulders shake and Christina freezes. She half rises, poised to run for help. Then Babe snorts, and Christina sees that she is laughing silently.

She turns to Christina. "Oh God, I can't stop laughing every time I think of it."

"L-laughing?" Christina squeaks. She is still processing the fact that Babe isn't dying in front of her.

Babe cocks her head. "Eudes."

Christina remembers the scene at the entrance to St. Lucy's and the unfamiliar, withered apple–faced nun who greeted her instead of Sister Eudes, the usual ferocious gatekeeper. This nun had been, like Eudes, unsmiling and unwilling to let Christina past the reception desk. Christina had briefly forgotten Babe's real name and stood there, marveling at the crisscrossed lines on the nun's face activating and spreading, like a windshield hit by a rock. Finally, Babe's real name came to her.

"Miss Fogarty. I'm here to see Miss Fogarty," she had said, her voice shaky.

"Miss Fogarty is in her room," the withered apple–faced nun replied, dismissing Christina.

"What happened to Sister Eudes?" she asks Babe.

Babe snorts. "You're not gonna believe this." The years are dropping away. She becomes flirtatious, a girl again. "She took off." She howls, not even waiting for Christina's reaction. "Yeah, after fifty years she decided she just couldn't hack it. If she's lookin' for a boyfriend now, she's gonna have to explain the dent in her forehead."

"The dent?"

"Oh yeah, honey," Babe says, now earnest. "You think fifty years of that wimple diggin' into her face won't leave a dent? We all have scars, honey, we live long enough. Life leaves scars."

Babe doesn't like Joan Baez. Christina sings "Butcher Boy" for her, a beautiful sad song about a girl who kills herself because she is pregnant. Babe says if she wants to sing the blues, there are much better songs than ones about drippy girls who let themselves get knocked up. Then she starts singing "Gimme a Pigfoot," which grosses Christina out, even though she can see glimmers of the girl Babe once was, the one so confident of her own power she didn't give a shit what anyone thought. Christina can't help admiring that long-ago girl. She starts to feel virtuous about lifting Babe's spirits. Christina's performing good works, visiting the sick. If she still believed in the redemption promised in the catechism (which she doesn't, not anymore). Good works merit serious time off in purgatory. She ticks off the good works in her head: to feed the hungry, give drink to the thirsty, clothe the naked, harbor the harborless, ransom the captive, and bury the dead. She figures giving cigarettes to the smoker should fit in somewhere between drink for the thirsty and food for the hungry. She loves *harbor the harborless*. It reminds her of a big, untidy summer cottage in Green Harbor, redolent of late nights, fried clam dinners, and endless sunshiny days at the beach.

Babe doesn't want Christina to read to her, either, she informs her, not if it's gonna be more grim poems by Baudelaire or Rimbaud. She reminds Christina that she has been asking for *Peyton Place* since last summer. Something with a little zing, a little sex, something besides stories about people who are dead or wish they were.

Babe hates *The Group*, which depresses Christina, who had pictured the woman elaborating on the sex parts of the book that were vague or unclear. "If that's what college does to you, I'm glad I never went," she proclaims. "Buncha complainers. Rich-girl complainers!"

Babe tells Christina that it's exactly the kind of book she pictures Christina writing, if she ever writes a book someday, something so draggy and depressing it would make you want to take gas.

They are on a terrace at the Biltmore Hotel in Coral Gables. Babe went to Florida once on a wild weekend before the war and she remembers everything about the view: palm trees, pink sunsets, flamingos, endless flowing champagne, the mad music, the dangerous and handsome men. Christina blows smoke out the window and gazes at the scuffed linoleum in Babe's room. She is flattered that Babe thinks she could write a book. Christina shivers as a gust from the window cloaks her, insisting that instead of Florida, it is a sad late-November day in Massachusetts, and the actual view outside is of the denuded trees crouching against the unforgiving wind. She wishes she could be on a balcony basking in warmth and watching pink sunsets through a haze of strong drink.

"I'm gonna go to college," Christina says.

Babe shrugs. "Maybe that'll cheer you up."

Christina has not realized she really is going to college until she announces it to Babe. How will she ever make that happen? Her parents do not have high hopes for her future. They want her to be like her aunt Connie, only choose a better husband. Maybe work in an office until she meets her improvement-on–Big Dommie life partner. That would mean going to St. Catherine's after graduation next year, the secretarial school around the corner from Precious Blood High. If her parents have their way, it is entirely possible she could finish the two-year business course at St. Catherine's, work at Desimone Insurance across the street from Falcone's Café, get her wedding dress at La Sposa, marry the not-Dommie, and eventually be waked at Carmello's across the street from La Sposa without ever having left the neighborhood. St. Catherine, Christina remembers, has an instrument of torture named after her, the Catherine wheel, a spiked device a martyr was hung on after her limbs were broken and threaded through the spokes, left there to die slowly as vultures picked at her still-living remains and crowds of self-righteous onlookers cheered. When, if ever, will she stop associating first names with torture? She can't wait to go out into the wider world, to meet non-Catholics, Protestants, Buddhists, Jews. Her Old Testament knowledge is practically nil. Isaac brings nothing to mind, nor Jonah, except something about a whale. David is the statue her mother has a gilt-framed picture of in her bedroom. Bring on the Jews.

"That book is a dud. Tell me a movie," Babe demands.

Christina thinks of the last movie she saw at the Brattle. She skipped school on Wednesday to see Ingmar Bergman's *The Seventh Seal*. She doesn't think Babe would like the story of Antonius Block, a disillusioned medieval knight who plays chess with Death. And loses. Christina loved it from the first stark black-and-white shot of a lonely beach to the dance of death at the end. She was transfixed during the heart-stopping moment when Antonius goes to confession and pours his heart out to Death masquerading as a monk. Antonius, who is Max von Sydow in real life, has a skull face and an underbite and is blindingly blond, even in black-and-white. Antonius tells Death, "Life is a preposterous horror," a sentiment Christina currently shares. In addition to this essential truth of the cosmos summed up in a sentence, the film has an epidemic of the Black Plague sweeping the village and a young girl burned at the stake for being a witch and consorting with the devil. In other words, it has everything, a kaleidoscope of Roger Corman horror combined with bleak Scandinavian *weltschmerz*. Christina plans to investigate more of the Swedish worldview. She hopes the Brattle will do an Ingmar Bergman festival.

The four o'clock buzzer sounds, announcing the rosary, chanted daily for the elderly residents of St. Lucy's. Babe and Christina both jump reflexively.

"Well? Ya got any movies to tell? If not, today's the Joyful Mysteries, an' I could use a lift."

Babe flicks her cigarette butt in the general direction of the window and it sails outside, just grazing the sill. Christina watches the airborne cigarette and wonders for the thousandth time just how much Babe can really see. Even now, Babe's mermaid-green eyes are scanning Christina's face with unsettling focus.

Christina clears her throat. "Um . . ."

"Ya got one?" Babe prompts. "What's this one about?"

"Sometimes . . ." Christina says. "Sometimes, Babe, it's like you can really see. Like right now. You're looking right at me."

Babe cackles. "I'm an old bat. I can see in the dark."

If Babe can see even a little, what is she doing buried at St. Lucy's instead of living on the outside, raising hell with her friend and fellow ex-stripper, Twirly Shirley? Babe has more secrets than the CIA. Christina decides to visit Shirley in her Brighton store and ask her all about Babe, all the things she longs to ask but doesn't dare. Babe doesn't belong here, a prisoner in a place where no one laughs. *Ransom the captive.*

"I wish I would come here someday and you'd be gone," Christina says.

"I'll be dead soon enough. What, are you tired of waiting? Tired of doin' your good deeds?"

"I mean, I wish you didn't have to pretend to do all these things. I wish you really could live in a fancy hotel in Florida." The words come in a rush. When she sees Babe's reaction Christina wishes she had swallowed them. She has broken the unwritten rule of their friendship and talked about Babe's actual circumstances. Babe hates even a whiff of pity.

"I think we should take a little break, kiddo," the old woman says after a long pause, her voice neutral, as if asking Christina to close the window.

"What do you mean?" Christina says. But she knows. Babe is kicking her out.

Babe sighs. "Come back when you've got a story for me." The kindness in her voice is a dismissal.

"Okay."

Babe is looking right at her again. Christina gathers her things, burning with humiliation, as self-conscious as if Babe were checking her head for lice.

Out on the street, Christina's sturdy Frye boots beat the drum to her angry thoughts. *Hey, Babe, you wanna hear a story? I'm never coming to see you again because you only want stories from me but you won't tell me your own story, so you can just stay hiding in your room that you pretend is a palace and fuck off. And I'm going to college anyway, some college far away from here, and then I'll have some stories for you, if you're still alive and can get someone else to read them to you, if you're even really blind. Because I'm not coming back.*

She is breathing heavily, and her nose is running. Christina rummages around in the pocket of her pea-coat for a tissue and finds a disgusting crumpled relic from a few days ago. She watches as the bus pulls up to the stop at the end of the street, a hopeless distance to run. Max von Sydow is right: life is a preposterous horror.

SWING TIME

The junior class of Precious Blood High files out to the schoolyard and onto the buses. It is tradition that the junior class goes into town for a Catholic-themed movie every year near the end of the school year. Even though Christina is not looking forward to the two-hour treacle-fest that *The Sound of Music* promises to be, the class excitement at having a half day and heading into Boston is contagious and she is thrilled at the thought of going to a big downtown movie theater, a palace, really. The bright spring day holds the tangy portent of an afternoon free from chemistry lab and trig problems. The bored drivers huff open the doors and the class boards, girls on one side, boys on the other. Christina sits with Rose, who casts longing glances at Danny, sitting across the aisle with Dennis Dempsey. The cheerful caravan pulls out of the schoolyard, en route to a day of entertainment.

"Raindrops on roses and whiskers on kittens . . ." Cecilia's confident soprano soars over the subdued bus chatter, serenading them with the ickiest song in the entire *Sound of Music* repertoire.

Every girl on the bus knows the song because they have all been dragooned into singing it in preparation for the upcoming Precious Blood May Chorale, an annual fundraising event for the school. The boys are required to audition, but not every boy is selected. Only the girls, regardless of talent, are drafted to be in the choir. For two months prior to the concert, every high school girl has to be at school a half hour early to rehearse and then stay again after school for an hour every day. They stand on tiered risers in the dusty auditorium singing "Climb Every Mountain" over and over in a trance of boredom, the tedium relieved only by the occasional fainter or Dennis Dempsey's Hitler impersonation which consists of him whipping out a pocket comb and sticking it under his nose while raising his hand in a *Heil Hitler* salute, all performed when Sister Theodorine, the ancient choir conductor, looks down to check her sheet music. No one protests the blatant unfairness of the girls-only draft. Monks in Vietnam are setting themselves on fire and protests against the escalation to war are growing in the nightly news. The Civil Rights Movement is in full bloom, but none of this social consciousness has any effect on the girls of Precious Blood High, although Christina seethes with resentment every morning upon rising a half hour earlier, and is even surlier than usual to her mother over coffee. This year, like every year, the concert will be recorded and PB students will be required to press the Orwellian-titled *Glad Voices Sing* album on friends and relations for three or four dollars (the amount goes up every year, like

PB tuition). Her mother shelled out the bucks, peeling them from her stash, complaining bitterly: "Fockin'-a nuns! Always lookin' for money."

All the drippy girls in Cecilia's clique sing along with her, obedient drones swarming the queen bee. Sister Coronada stands at the front of the bus and glowers at the rest of the class, stifling the rolling groans that have arisen with Cecilia's first notes. The nun raises her arms for everyone else to join in, looking every inch the banana republic dictator, minus the medals and shoulder fringe.

"Jesus Christ," hisses Patsy, who is sitting with Mary Agnes in front of Christina and Rose at the back of the bus. "Isn't it enough we have to sing this shit every day before school? Can't we just relax for a change?" At least they all have seats in the last rows of the bus, far away from the epicenter of song and nun; they had pushed ahead of their better-behaved classmates to score places far from Coronada's evil eye.

"Fake it. She can still see us," Mary Agnes side-whispers.

The girls all mouth the words to the song while across the way, Dennis Dempsey makes fart noises. "Ugh! Awww, whew! MOSHER CUT ONE," he whisper-yells, pretending to be overcome, waving his hands, gagging, but staying expertly just under Coronada's radar.

Patsy and Mary Agnes try to stifle their explosive giggles. Timothy Mosher, sitting in front of Dennis, blushes a deep maroon, but keeps right on singing, his girlish tenor swooping just under Cecilia's bell-like soprano.

Christina stares at Dennis, thinking how little he's changed in three years. He has altered his hairstyle, attempting a Beatles 'do, but the end result is Moe from the Three Stooges, instead of dreamy John. Like a fortune teller peering into a crystal ball, Christina can foresee the trajectory of Dennis's whole future, the early marriage after he gets some girl pregnant, the series of shitty jobs, the drinking problem, the beer gut, the plot unfolding with the dull inevitability of her mother's soap operas. And yet, when Dennis looks at her, it's always with something like pity, ever since that summer he had clumsily kissed her, then dumped her the next day as if she had contracted leprosy like that girl in *Miracle at Carville*. He calls Christina "Edna" now, for Edna St. Vincent Millay, after the Ferlinghetti incident in English class that he triggered. She dreads standing in front of him during lunch, waiting in line for the fried baloney and rock-hard mashed potatoes, the usual food-atrocity menu, or walking past him on her way out of the schoolyard. "Ednaaaah," he singsongs in a doo-wop falsetto, followed by an idiotic zombie laugh. But beneath the horrific singing, Christina senses that Dennis feels somehow as if she is the one who has dumped *him*.

Christina averts her gaze before Dennis sees her looking at him, narrowly escaping the name-calling and false laughter. She pulls *A Season in Hell* from her macramé bag. "*My heart has been stabbed by grace,*" she reads. Rimbaud, ur-genius teenager, would drive a stake through Julie Andrews's saccharine heart. Rimbaud is her hero, a rebel poet from the last century who smoked opium and flaunted every one of society's rules. He was in love with a man, too, like Oscar Wilde. She had never even heard of being in love with a man if you were also a man before reading James Baldwin and can't remember the nuns mentioning it either. It has to come under sins of impurity, though, she is sure of that. She opens the book to a random place and begins reading. *"And springtime brought me the frightful laugh of an idiot."* She slides her eyes over to where Dennis is sitting. *See?* Christina thinks. Poetry does what God is supposed to do: read your mind and produce an answer, a sign that you are with Him as One. And not in a creepy voyeuristic way, either, like the God the nuns are always threatening you with, the deity watching you randomly, like while you're in the bathroom, just to catch you breaking one of His rules. Poetry just hangs around waiting for you to notice, too cool to step forward from where it slouches in the corner. Once you discover poetry, it manifests itself to you as God, like the burning bush or Jesus appearing to Magdalene, the Fallen Woman, after his death on the cross.

She risks another glimpse of Dennis. At the front of the bus, Cecilia has moved on to "Do Re Mi" and Dennis is mindlessly singing, *"Fa, a long, long way to run,"* and looking out the window, like a bored child at a birthday party that isn't his own.

Christina checks out the ladies' room first thing when

they arrive at the theater and is delighted to see that there's a comfy armchair in a fancy anteroom adorned with sconces and flocked wallpaper. The movie theater has a venerable past as a vaudeville house and its huge stage is adorned with wedding-cake scrollwork and dusty plum-colored velvet draperies.

"It's beautiful!" sighs Rose, her hands clasped as if in prayer. "Lookit the size of that screen!"

The class is herded to the mezzanine level where they scatter and find seats together. Patsy and Mary Agnes grab seats in the first row, and Rose contrives to sit next to Danny in the second row. Christina notices none of the fancy trappings or the movie screen twice the size of the one in her neighborhood theater. Her sole mission is to get a seat at the end of the aisle in whatever row is free, so she can flee when she is finally overcome by lederhosen. It's only a matter of time, she thinks. She nails a seat at the end of the third row beside Lillian Farrell.

To Christina's surprise, she gasps along with everyone else when the camera soars like a bird over the Austrian Alps. She is even stirred by the opening song, swept into a current of swelling emotion right up to the moment when the nuns begin singing and acting cute. Then she crashes to earth with a thud. How do nuns always get such great exposure in movies? Why are they always kindly or wise or beautiful or sweetness incarnate? Christina has yet to meet one of these cinematic nuns in real life. They probably have some deal going with the movie bigwigs, like Catholics won't give them the Legion of Decency seal of approval unless the nuns get to be saints or gaspingly beautiful every time you see them. They have an unbelievably good deal going for them, with movies proclaiming every single nun on-screen to be just great. Christina wishes she had some way to get everyone who meets her to automatically assume she's great from seeing repeated adorable Christina prototypes in movies.

The nun musical number brings her out of her trance. A gaggle of them are singing and performing the necessarily restrictive kind of choreography cute sisters can execute, whipping their hands in and out of their habits and walking in lockstep. The number is meant to be a charming interlude, but Christina is ready for the ladies' room again and the overstuffed chair. Before she can gather her things and bolt, she notices snickering coming from somewhere to her right. A civilian, someone not part of her school group, is sitting alone in the middle of the first row on the right-hand side, divided by the aisle. From the back, it looks like a young man with longish black hair. His shoulders are shaking and he is shrinking into his seat, giggling. She looks at the screen. There is nothing funny going on up there. The nun musical number is mercifully over, and now it's Julie Andrews telling the abbess, "But Mother Superior, I can't seem to *stop* singing." The giggling gets louder. Christina catches it like a virus. It is ridiculous. It's true, how could you not laugh at this girl who is too perky to be real?

Who is this guy? She is curious to see the giggler

from the front and plans to get a good look at him on the way out to the lobby and the plush ladies' room armchair that awaits her. Christina slips out of her seat and walks down the aisle. She stops and pretends to tug on her socks when she gets to the first row on the right, sure she is rendered invisible by the half wall in front of the rows of seats. She peeks up in the general direction of the laugher. He is leaning forward, resting his arms on the ledge that separates them and looking right at her.

"Good morning, little schoolgirl," he says, leering. His slightly tilted brown eyes look huge behind his wire-rimmed glasses. Christina has no idea he is quoting a song. She flees, cursing the stupid uniform that brands her as a schoolgirl, but somehow exhilarated at the way this strange googly-eyed boy looks at her.

Forty-five minutes later, Christina is sitting opposite the mysterious young man at a greasy table in a little Chinese restaurant across the street from the movie theater. She watches him expertly use chopsticks to eat something unrecognizable. She keeps an anxious eye on the entrance to the theater so she won't miss the crowd of Precious Blood students exiting after *The Sound of Music*. He waited for her outside the ladies' room and introduced himself as R.T., but his real name is Robin Truesdale White. Christina burst out laughing when he said his name; it sounded like a foofy English character from one of her Oscar Wilde plays.

"I'm a Mayflower descendant, my dear," he replied, mock-offended.

"Well, my descendants came on a much later boat."

He walks with a limp and carries a silver-topped cane like a dandy from another, better time. He has hemophilia, he tells her, thus the limp. *Like a Hapsburg prince*, she thinks. He is so exotic she feels like she has slipped into an alternate universe she has created with her own irregular brain waves, the ones her mother is always mislabeling as *pazza*. Best of all, he goes to Harvard. Okay, it's just part-time, or as he tells her, "taking a few classes," but still. A college boy has sought her out. He is interested in her. He wants to get to know her. She pictures telling Patsy and Mary Agnes and Rose she's dating a guy who goes to Harvard (she will leave out the part about only taking a few classes). She needs to impress him. *Say something*, she commands herself.

"Why were you laughing in there?" she dares to ask him as he wolfs down rice dotted with some kind of black sauce. It looks horrible but smells delicious. She wishes she were brave enough to ask for a bite.

"I ate a magic brownie for breakfast," he tells her. "It lasts way longer than a joint," he explains, when she looks confused.

His answer does nothing to lift the veil. Christina is still parsing the connection between a magic pastry and a "joint." R.T. laughs.

"You really are a little schoolgirl. How old are you?"

Christina's face shutters. The tilted eyes are kind, though, so she answers, keeping the edge out of her voice, "I'm graduating next year. So I'm probably not much younger than you are."

Two yellow school buses lumber around the tight corner onto Eliot Street and park in front of the theater. Christina stiffens. R.T. smiles.

"What happens if you miss the bus?" he asks, challenging.

Christina stands up nervously, bobbing her head for a better look. "I can't. I can't get in trouble again. Ferlinghetti almost got me expelled."

"Tell me."

"I got caught reading blasphemous poetry in school. I got sent to the monsignor."

R.T.'s eyebrows lift adorably. She has impressed him! "And what did the monsignor say?"

Christina smiles. "He told me to read John Donne."

"Did you?"

Christina pulls out *A Season in Hell* and hands it to R.T. "Yeah. And I found another Catholic poet—Rimbaud." R.T. pulls a face, about to say something. "I mean, he was French and I'm sure he was baptized, so he's technically Catholic, but I know he's the opposite of Catholic, I know that, I hope you know I know that," she babbles. She takes a deep breath. "The monsignor also told me to go to dances and have a swingin' time because boys don't like girls who read too much poetry." She pauses. "But I haven't been able to have a swingin' time yet." The buses rev their engines. Christina looks anxiously toward the theater entrance.

R.T. reaches into his green army-navy bag to retrieve a pen. He writes something in her book and gives it back to her. "I can help you with the swingin' time."

Christina's Precious Blood classmates spill out the door of the theater.

"I have to go."

Christina bumbles her way out the door, stealing a few backward glances before running to her bus, the pumpkin that will transport her back to Derby Street, away from her Hapsburg prince. She scrambles onto the bus and finds a seat at the back, grateful no one else has boarded yet. Breathlessly, she opens the Rimbaud. He has written, *For a swingin' time, call Robin Truesdale White.* His phone number is scrawled below. She clutches her pounding heart, stabbed by grace.

All her fever dreams of a swingin' time with R.T. have been put to rest at the beginning of the summer. It takes a month for Christina to get up the nerve to actually call the number R.T. scrawled on the title page of *A Season in Hell,* and when she does finally call on the upstairs phone, clearing her throat and looking around to make sure her mother is nowhere within hearing, R.T.'s snotty little sister answers.

"Who's calling?" the girl asks, an adult presence eerily belying her kid voice.

"A friend of his, Christina," she replies, attempting an airy delivery but sounding more like a child younger than the little sister on the other end of the line.

"He's backpacking in Europe this summer. I thought all his *friends* knew that," the sister informs her.

Christina replaces the heavy black receiver without another word.

Every weekend Christina takes the trolley to Harvard Square. She isn't looking for R.T., she tells herself. (And she definitely isn't looking for John Patrick, who she's nearly forgotten about.) She is rehearsing for her life after high school. But why does she never ever see R.T., not even once? The little sister knew, with the dead-on perception of evil children everywhere, that Christina didn't belong. Why is she such a coward, afraid of a little sister? Why is she so stupid? Why hadn't she given him *her* number? But he would never have called her. He has probably forgotten all about that day in Boston. Maybe she will see R.T. next weekend, buying a scarf at the Coop, or rifling through the secondhand books at that open stall on Mass Ave.

Or, now that summer's basically over, she could call him again.

Her mother is watching *The Edge of Night* when she gets home. A pile of naked dolls lies beside her in a heap on the sofa, like victims of a genocide in Toyland. Rita is crocheting toilet roll covers, her new side business. Offending bare toilet rolls are covered by pastel crocheted yarn that become the full skirts of dolls plunked down in the middle of the rolls. The finished toilet roll dolls wear a hat that matches their skirts. They are hideous and people are buying them like crazy.

"Where's Vinny?" Christina asks, without a greeting. Her mother doesn't answer. The ominous music filling the room means someone is revealing something life-or-death about someone. This information is crucial to Rita for some reason Christina can't fathom. The soap opera has been running on the same infinity loop of scandals and infidelities since she was in elementary school, and every morning Rita discusses the previous day's episode with Aunt Connie over coffee like the events have happened to her. It is, in a way, Christina thinks, more tragic than the melodramatic events on television.

Her mother holds up her hand, her eyes still on the screen, and gurgles her irritation, a nonverbal warning to back off. Christina stomps up the stairs to her room. Vinny is nowhere around—good, she'll have an iota of privacy for once. She grabs her diary and takes it into the bathroom, which has the only door in the house with an actual lock. She pulls the heavy black hall phone into the bathroom with her, checks the number in her diary, and sits on the pink toilet seat cover. She stares at the matching pink crocheted toilet roll cover with the doll in the middle on the shelf opposite the toilet. The doll has black hair and a superior blank gaze, as if Christina can't possibly understand that the doll is a work of household art. Christina begins to dial, the whirring sound of each circular finger sprocket calming her a little. He answers on the second ring. She was expecting the snotty little sister and has to clear her throat.

"Is this R.T.?" she asks. She sounds like some breathless Beatles fan, she thinks, her voice high-pitched and girly. "I met you last May at *Sound of Music*, remember?" She inhales sharply.

After a moment of suspense, R.T. responds: "The little schoolgirl! How could I forget! You are forever etched in my memory—the quaintness of your native costume, your knee socks . . ."

Christina listens to his low, somewhat nasal voice with gushing relief. She giggles and remembers to exhale. "You wrote something in my Rimbaud book, do you remember?"

"Uhhh—"

"You wrote, *For a swingin—*"

The phone clicks and a rough voice intrudes: "Oo's that?" her mother grunts. Christina has been a fool to think that a mere locked bathroom door could prevent Rita from crashing into her world like a random asteroid obliterating all forms of sentient life.

"I'M ON THE PHONE," she screams. "Mother, please hang up," she then says in a lower voice, impersonating people from families she has read about, polite families who don't barge in rudely on other people's conversations like cops busting a dope dealer.

The phone clicks again.

R.T. laughs. Christina stares with venom at the doll. She grabs it and turns on the faucet, holding the doll's head under the flow. Then she sets it back on her toilet roll perch, its blank eyes now obscured by the soggy hat drooping over its face.

"I'm having a party tomorrow night," R.T. is saying. "You could be my hostess. We'll be the lord and lady of the manor."

Christina nearly forgets to breathe again but remembers to write down the address. She is going to a party in Cambridge with people who go to Harvard. She will hold this secret inside her all day tomorrow, ignorning her friends' endless bragfests about boyfriends and cars and the Harvest CYO dance, and she will be the Secret Lady of the Manor, sharing none of this with Rose or Patsy or Mary Agnes.

A boy is hurling on the lawn when Christina gets to the address she has been nervously checking and rechecking since she got off the trolley at Mt. Auburn Street. The house, a white clapboard colonial, is ablaze with lights. Christina sees a side door and scurries toward it, avoiding the person on all fours vomiting into the patchy grass like a barking circus seal. She has chosen the only outfit she ever wears outside of her Precious Blood jumper, a uniform of another sort: boots, blue jeans, black turtleneck, and, in cooler weather, a peacoat. She stands before the side door, wishing she had a mirror to check her appearance. What if R.T. doesn't recognize her in civilian clothes? The music of some rock band she doesn't know blares suddenly as a disheveled guy opens the door and reels past her. A small, slender girl about Christina's age is at the door shouting after the person who stumbles away.

"You're leaving before the cake!" the blond girl cries. She is very pretty, with bulgy hazel eyes and a fetching mole at the corner of her mouth. She turns her attention to Christina. "We're making cake," she says, by way of invitation inside.

Christina follows her into the kitchen where the distracted blond girl, who introduces herself as Penny, starts sifting an oregano-like herb into some cake batter. The kitchen is empty, except for what must be R.T.'s little sister and a husky bearded young man sitting at the table and poring over an encyclopedia-sized book. R.T.'s little sister is placing the little pans of batter into her Easy-Bake Oven and adjusting some dials with the air of gravity of a physicist calibrating a nuclear device.

"This is Althea, and that's Alfred over there, studying runes," Penny says.

Althea, who looks around eleven years old, avoids Christina. She appears resentful at having to share Penny with anyone. Alfred flashes Christina an off-kilter smile from the table, white teeth glinting through a forest of reddish facial hair. He seems older, like a professor.

"I'm Christina," she announces. "Is R.T. around?"

Loud whoops of laughter echo from the living room, punctuating the strange music Christina later finds out is the Doors.

"Can't you hear him laughing? He laughs like a cat in heat," Althea says, her eyes on the toy oven.

Penny laughs. The oven dings.

Althea pulls out a miniature cake and hands it to Alfred. "Try it," she orders.

Alfred rakes his fingers through his beard, then takes the tiny cake and breaks it in half in a strangely familiar, priestlike gesture. He hands it to Christina. She notices tiny flecks of food in his beard and her stomach lurches.

"So, he's . . ." she points toward where the noise and music is coming from, addressing Penny.

Penny licks some batter from her finger and nods, smiling. Althea mimics Christina's timid pointing and repeats, "*So, he's* . . ." her bad-seed child's voice capturing exactly Christina's uncertainty.

Christina hurries through the cluttered hallway, forging ahead before she loses her nerve. She leaves the cake in a wicker basket crammed with circulars and mail at the foot of the stairs. To her left is the living room, a large open space with bare wood floors and a few rya rugs scattered about. Huge trailing plants hang in hairy rope holders in front of floor-to-ceiling windows at the front-facing part of the room. Christina counts at least three sofas and a few overstuffed chairs. Every sofa and chair is occupied and there are more kids lounging on the floor. Some are gyrating to the music, their heads thrown back in what looks to Christina like pictures she has seen in her father's *National Geographic* magazines of tribal shamans in distant lands enacting strange rites. No one moves like that at the Precious Blood CYO dances. But then, no one at a Precious Blood event ever came dressed like these kids, like characters who have stepped out of a Renaissance painting. The girls wear flowy long skirts and peasant blouses.

Of course, Christina thinks with an inner snort, their ties to peasant forebears are safely hundreds of years away, and no Romani caravan ever transported these sharp-featured girls with their Puritan-forefather genes etched into such merciless bone structures.

Christina finally spots R.T., resplendent in a maroon-velvet jacket, a *costume*, really, she thinks with delight. His hair has grown over the summer and now he looks Byronic, with his long black hair edging the high collar of his jacket. He sits reclined into a plush sofa, his arms around a faux-blond girl on either side. Christina moves so that she is standing opposite him, on the other side of a coffee table littered with rolling papers and cigarettes and a baggie holding what she realizes with horror and excitement is *dope*. R.T. blinks at her, his tilted brown eyes puzzled behind the affected round wire glasses. He doesn't remember her, she thinks, and all the pleasure drains out of the moment. He smiles, though, and looks happy to see her. That emboldens her.

"*The hills are alive,*" she sings in a comic falsetto, "*and it's truly frightening.*"

R.T. laughs, a startled gasping sound that is both charming and slightly upsetting and nothing like a cat in heat. "Little schoolgirl," he says. "I didn't know you in civvies. Come and sit with me." He pats the divan.

One of the blond girls moves sulkily out of the way. R.T.'s stick-thin legs shift to make room for Christina. He looks vulnerable and powerful at the same time and she wants nothing more than to kiss him right then, that very moment. Instead, she leans in close, all she dares. He smells of an alien spice, sharp and swoon-inducing. He's nodding to the thrumming music when he turns all at once to Christina. She feels herself blushing. Had she inhaled him out loud?

"Come with me," he whispers, his smile insinuating. To the party at large, he makes an announcement: "Revelers! Feel free to party on, but the lord and lady of the manor are retiring!" He smiles at Christina, struggles to his feet, and holds out his hand to her.

Christina tries not to gloat as she leaves the room with R.T. She should get a long skirt, she thinks dreamily as she follows R.T. up the stairs. But she won't buy a peasant blouse. She would probably look like an actual peasant in a peasant blouse.

Forty minutes later, Christina and R.T. are wrestling joyously among the stale bedclothes. They giggle and grope and kiss until Christina looks up and sees Althea staring at them from the doorway. Christina shrieks.

"Mother's home," Althea says.

"Get out, spawn of Satan," R.T. answers, without raising his voice.

Christina notices for the first time that the sound level outside the bedroom has lowered. She slides off the bed and picks up her peacoat. "I better go."

"*I better go,*" Althea echoes, still staring at Christina. She does look like the spawn of Satan, standing there with a blank expression that reminds Christina of the blond cyborgs in *Village of the Damned*. R.T. raises his cane at Child Zombie Althea in a mock-threatening gesture, but she doesn't budge. Nor does her facial expression change.

"I'll call you," R.T. whispers in Christina's ear.

Christina looks at the spawn standing there in the doorway, then kisses R.T., turning her back on the girl. "Bye," Christina says to R.T., shrugging on her peacoat.

"*Bye,*" Althea says, blocking the doorway.

The doll inside the toilet paper roll, Christina thinks: same artificial-looking black hair, same blank eyes. She pushes past the doll-child and tiptoes down the stairs.

BEWRAYMENT

Christina barricades the door to her room with Lamby, Teddy, Minou, and John Lennon, just a subset of the millions of fucking stuffed animals her mother keeps buying for her. She lights the sandalwood candle she got in Harvard Square. It's time. She sits on her twin bed and flings back the quilted pink bedspread. She puts the album of Indian chants on her record player, the one that drives her mother mental. She lays out her tarot cards in a hurry, eager for the outcome.

It is a sticky late-summer evening that feels more like August than September, the night before the first day of school for her final year ever at Precious Blood High. The last card, the outcome of the reading, is the Fool. She will graduate with the Class of '68 and step off into the world, like the Fool in the picture on her tarot deck, a young man looking forward, his head tilted in the air, carrying a stick with a bundle over his shoulder with all his worldly goods in one hand and a single rose in the other. The sun shines behind him, so luminous that the ghostly outline of the moon is present, too. The beautiful young man never notices he's standing on the edge of a cliff. But there's a little white dog on its hind legs by his feet. And the dog will warn the Fool, Christina feels sure, before he falls to his death. No, the Fool will hear the dog and step back to gaze at the whole world spread before him. He will not fall. Neither will she. And at the end of the school year, she, too, will have a knapsack over her shoulder and a flower in her hand and she will step off into the world. Because the meaning in the book that came with the deck is for people who aren't spiritual and will succumb to the "folly, mania, extravagance, intoxication, delirium, frenzy, and bewrayment" (*bewrayment*?) it describes. For Christina, and Christina alone, the meaning is different; the outcome means she should take a chance on things because she is too spiritual to be extravagant or delirious. But maybe it means she will meet someone who will be intoxicated with her. Or *bewrayed*, whatever that means.

The doorknob to her bedroom turns. Her mother tries to push the door open and only manages to get it opened halfway. "*Che cazze*," she says, irritated. "You playin' with teddy bears now?"

Christina jumps up to remove the bedraggled family of oversized stuffed animals retrieved from her closet.

"'Ang this up." Rita thrusts Christina's freshly pressed uniform at her. She looks around the room, taking in the tarot cards on the bed. There is an awkward silence.

Christina wills her mother to leave, tamping down

her annoyance. If that spark shows, it will detonate into a fight within seconds.

"*Smother Brother* comin' on," Rita says, her voice falsely gay. She sounds grotesque, Christina thinks.

"Yeah, I'm coming down," Christina replies, turning her back to her mother and hanging the uniform on the closet door.

Rita stands in the doorway like a warden. She is always urging Christina to watch more television. She thinks it's the one normal thing Christina does. Rita doesn't even get half the jokes on *The Smothers Brothers Comedy Hour*. Her mother lingers at the door.

"What?" says Christina, working hard to keep her voice even.

Rita jerks her chin at the tarot cards. "What's that?"

"It's for telling fortunes."

"Oh yeah?" Her mother brightens, edging closer to the cards. Rita loves her version of the supernatural as much as she disdains the priests and nuns and their rites of the Church. She consults regularly with Mingucc', the local *strega*, believes in dream messages from her dead parents, and practices the anti-*malocchio* and other arcane rituals, like suspending a needle over a pregnant woman's belly to determine the gender of the baby, or scattering salt over the doorstep at the entrance to the house. She imparts the secret chant for warding off the evil eye to Aunt Connie at midnight on Christmas Eve, the only night deemed safe for the transfer of her power to another person. Christina has been declared too flighty and too young to receive this power, which stung when Rita announced this at dinner in front of the whole family, but Christina has no interest in her mother's old-world guinea superstitions.

Rita reaches for a card.

"Don't touch them. Only I can touch them."

Her mother withdraws her hand and folds her arms across her chest. She assesses Christina. "You gotta get up early tomorrow." Rita looks pointedly at the uniform hanging on the closet door.

Christina doesn't answer. She sits on her bed and starts collecting the cards.

"You gonna walka with Rose tomorra?"

Christina stays silent.

Her mother shakes her head sadly. "You got no friends no more."

"Yes I do," Christina says. She won't look at Rita, give her the satisfaction of knowing she speaks the truth. But her resolve lasts only a few seconds. She peers sidelong at her mother. Rita is staring at the Fool, the last card, the answer to Christina's question. Christina can read her mother's thoughts: *I never should've let you out of my womb. You don't know nothing. You never look where you going. You gonna fall down, like the blond* stupidone *on that card*.

Rita shakes her head and mutters something unintelligible. "Put those away," she tells Christina. *YOU GONNA FALL DOWN* is left unsaid but Christina can read it in every feature on her mother's face. "*Smother Brother* comin' on an' you gotta get up early tomorrow." She turns and leaves the room, her arms still crossed, like someone warding off a vampire. Christina is surprised she hasn't forked the anti-*malocchio* fingers at her cards, casting her dark spell, skewing Christina's future plans.

Christina closes the door on her mother's retreating back. She thinks of pulling another card, a random one, just to back up her interpretation of the Fool's message. She decides against it in case she draws the Nine of Swords, a really gruesome one that shows a person lying prone, stabbed in the back with nine huge swords. Christina feels sure her mother's lingering presence in her room would draw the Nine of Swords. She is sticking with the Fool and his personal message for her. *Bewrayment*, she keeps thinking, the word pricking like a nettle. What does it mean? She hopes it means *bedazzle*. She would like to bedazzle people next year when she starts her post–Precious Blood life.

She runs downstairs to the dictionary in the bookcase. She looks up *bewrayment*, then immediately wishes she hadn't. It means *betrayal*. Maybe she should wait until the end of the week when she can lay the cards again. Her mother has skewed the reading by coming into her room and mixing her dark aura with Christina's. She will do another reading, she decides. She doesn't like that word.

"What the hell happened to her? She's like someone from *Invasion of the Body Snatchers*," Patsy says.

They are walking home from school, and Sister

Bernadette's sad, reduced state is all they can talk about, has been the topic whispered over school lunches and screeched on after-school walks and pondered during evening phone calls. It's only the second week of school, but the Precious Blood seniors all have appointments with Sister Bernadette, the newly appointed guidance counselor. Patsy, Rose, and Mary Agnes have already seen her in the little cubbyhole office designated as *Guidance*, though it is really just a stockroom with a desk and a chair and a crucifix on the wall. Christina's appointment is the next day, but she knows what to expect.

Mary Agnes calls the depressed nun "Bernie the Zombie Queen" and does a perfect imitation of her dead-sounding, staccato speech. "*What do you plan to do next year, Mary Agnes?*" she drones.

"She always looks like she's gonna cry any minute now," Rose says. "Remember how pretty she was?"

"Big deal. She's a nun. She might as well be hideous," Patsy replies, matter-of-fact.

"I think she had a nervous breakdown or something and she can't teach anymore," Mary Agnes says. "That's why they made her guidance counselor. She just tells everyone the same thing, anyway."

"*Christina, do you plan to attend beauty school?*" Christina says in a dead voice. "At least that's what she says to the Italian girls, probably," she says in her own voice.

"That's what she said to me!" Rose shrieks.

Christina shrugs. "I rest my case."

"Good luck tomorrow," Patsy calls, as she and

Mary Agnes turn off toward their respective streets.

"Yeah, tell her you're gonna be a brain surgeon!" Mary Agnes shouts.

Sitting opposite Sister Bernadette, Christina tries not to stare, but her eyes are drawn to the young nun's face like it's the site of a three-car pileup. Which it is, if you count getting the youth and beauty and joy sucked out of you in, what was it, four years since eighth grade, when Sister Bernadette had been Audrey Hepburn incarnate? The Sister Bernadette who giggled and preached to them about love like a giddy newlywed? The Sister Bernadette who couldn't stop talking about her bridegroom Jesus and love, love, love?

The black pouches under her eyes are shocking; she looks like she was in a death match with a demon from hell and lost. Sister Bernadette stares at the piece of paper in front of her. She has been staring for so long Christina is in the place of no-time limbo she goes to during school pep rallies or the recitation of the rosary in church. But she can't stay there, lost in her own thoughts, not sitting so close to this scary replica of Sister Bernadette. She feels panic rising, as if she were three years old and her parents had just left her alone at the hospital to get her tonsils out, with a scary nurse leading her away to a white-tiled room.

Finally, Sister Bernadette speaks, not in a zombie voice (then, Christina feels sure, she would know she's trapped in a terrible dream) but in such a muted one, Christina barely can hear her.

"Excuse me, Sister?" she says in an equally hushed voice.

Sister Bernadette finally looks up. She sighs. "We're here to talk about your plans after high school. Have you decided on anything?"

"I'm not going to beauty school," Christina says, then laughs a little to show she's joking. Maybe humor will wake up Sister Bernadette, make her shed her thousand-year-old mummy guise, and just snap out of it.

Sister Bernadette looks at something over Christina's shoulder and sighs again. They each sit there in silence. Christina feels trapped in someone's deranged amateur art movie, Sister Bernadette staring, sighing, dead-voiced, the same frame playing over and over until the film or your brain gets shattered to bits. Sister Bernadette isn't going to wake up.

Christina tries to move it along, desperation mounting: "Uh, I dunno. I think I'm applying to UMass. In Boston."

"It's my responsibility to tell you that we don't give recommendations for non-Catholic colleges," Sister Bernadette replies, the words all jumbled together, like a penance prayer you get out of the way after confession.

They won't help her get into college. Christina almost laughs. What did she expect? Well, she doesn't need them, either. "I'm going to go, because I think . . . I think I can really do . . . a lot of things I've been thinking about doing for a long time and I think I'm going to go," she says in a burst.

She stops. Sister Bernadette's eyes are closed and silent tears are seeping from under her reddened lids. Panic flutters in Christina's chest and her heart beats like a trapped bird. What is she supposed to do now? She wants her mother. She wants Rita to come in and tell Sister Bernadette to leave her alone, she's only a kid for Chrissake, to slap her frozen face and tell the nun to wake up and stop acting like a *stoonad* and scaring the shit out of kids.

"I, uh, my grades are good, and I think I'll probably qualify for a scholarship, like from the Sons of Italy or something, and, uh, so, uh, I think that's okay," she babbles, feeling hot, then cold, then faint. It is stuffy in this supply closet. Christina can almost see the air. She can't breathe. She has to get out. If Sister Bernadette keeps crying she will just leave. She pictures the sister tottering after her, the mummy awakened.

Sister Bernadette takes a deep breath. "Do your parents approve of this plan?" she asks with great effort.

"Yes, yes, they do. They're so happy. Really, really happy. So I, uh, thank you, Sister, uh, for all your help. Good afternoon, S'tah." Christina uncurls her hands from their death grip on the arms of her chair and clunks out of the room, her schoolbag grazing a stack of yellow lined pads on a shelf and knocking them to the floor. She starts to bend down and pick them up but notices Sister Bernadette staring at a spot on the wall just below the crucifix. Christina leaves the notepads scattered on the wooden floor and hurries out, her right foot skiing on one of them. She regains her balance just before she goes into a perfect cheerleader split. Patsy would be proud.

No one cares about Christina's dramatic meeting with Bernie the Zombie Queen on the way to school the next morning. When she tries to describe the episode in the supply closet, giving the reveal of Sister Bernie's madness the slow build of a horror movie, Patsy interrupts her right in the middle of the story: "Toldja, she's a basket case." Sister Bernie is old news, even though her descent into madness is way more interesting than the never-ending topics of cheerleading and boys. Mary Agnes says she dreads the pep rally scheduled for that afternoon because she's already exhausted right now at this ungodly hour before school has even started. Patsy is worried that she won't be able to lead the Indian cheer because her voice is hoarse. Mary Agnes snipes about Carol, the little cheerleader who tops the pyramid, always being late climbing up and leaving them all looking like assholes or dogs on their hands and knees for what feels like hours. Patsy, Mary Agnes, and Rose all wear their new letter sweaters, slouchy white cardigans, striped with the colors of Precious Blood, purple and gold, royal-purple for Jesus's blood, Christina supposes. The letter sweaters are a blanket thrown over her friends, like the tent forts they used to make when they were little, the private spaces created for huddling together and telling secrets to each other. Now, though, Christina is outside the tent; there are no confidences, no giggles in the dark. Her friends' voices are tamped down, made indistinct by the heavy letter sweaters. They plan their cheers and gossip about the other girls on their squad and complain about the football team losing every game so far this season, indifferent to Christina's presence, uninterested in her stories about poetry and redemption and the *demimonde*, a word she overuses, she knows.

"You gonna be reading a book during our rally today?" Rose challenges.

"I always watch you," Christina says defensively.

"Riiiiight," drawls Mary Agnes. "Like I care anyway, as long as Bobby's lookin' at me." She addresses Rose and Patsy as if Christina isn't standing there. "She should try lookin' at a boy for a change, instead of a book." Mary Agnes uses her sincere voice, the one she brandishes when she feels the need to draw blood. Christina braces herself. "A boy might even look back and she could finally get a boyfriend and everyone might stop calling her Edna St. Vincent Millay."

They arrive at the iron gates marking the beginning of Precious Blood property. The girls all adjust imperceptibly, readying themselves for the daily gauntlet that is high school. Everyone except Christina unrolls her skirt to regulation length. Christina never bothers to roll hers up. She doesn't see how rolling up the skirt of her uniform a few inches on the way to and from school makes it any less hideous. They join the swarm, and Christina tells herself that her patron saint, Christina the Astonishing, levitating above the crowd and looking down at them, could not tell Christina apart from anyone else. But she is different. She is going to live in an apartment and go to UMass Boston next year. Even though she doesn't believe anymore, in anything, she will honor her mad name saint.

Christina pushes open the battered screen door that leads to the cramped kitchen of Falcone's Café. She slings her book bag onto the worktable and peeks through the half door into the bar. She remembers her little-girl shyness at the threshold of that room, the rowdy voices and barks of laughter luring her inside because the loudest laugh belonged to her father. There were no mothers or aunts to keep order in that dimly lit space, only men in a smoky world all their own. She sees again her father's delight when she appeared at the door one afternoon, as if she were a princess in a ball gown instead of a little girl with scabby knees in a navy-blue uniform. He roared her name, the special one just for her: Dolly, because she was his little doll, his pixie girl. She was his pride, because she belonged to him. He lifted her onto the bar and she sang "Que Sera, Sera" for the men, who laughed and gave her quarters and called her sweetheart. Her father whooshed some ginger ale out of a spout like a magician and gave her a glass of the golden drink with tinkling ice and a maraschino cherry. Conjurer. Source of all light and warmth. When had she stopped orbiting his sun, exactly? Was it when she became a "young lady" that the eclipse had occurred and the world got a little colder? She got her *friend*, as her mother and her own friends called their periods, always with a wry downward turn of the mouth indicating that this friend was not welcome and that the name was a sham. Christina remembers how angry and ashamed she was when her mother told Joe that she was a "young lady" now. Her father looked uncomfortable, that's what she remembers, how everything shifted at that very moment. And now she is no longer a pixie but a messy girl who can get pregnant and bring shame to the family with the same power that once brought smiles and approval and silver quarters from the laughing men at the bar. She is a woman now, or a potential woman, and suspect.

Now, non-pixie present-day Christina steps into the bar. Her father is talking with a wholesale liquor salesman she remembers dimly from her glory days as a tiny lounge singer. The rest of the bar is quiet, with only a few men hefting bottles and making conversation in the booths at the back. Joe smiles at his daughter and points her out to the salesman with pride.

"My oldest, Christina. Remember her? Graduatin' this year. Then, in a few years, I'll be walkin' her down the aisle."

Christina tries to hide her scowl, but it isn't necessary because the salesman only gives her a perfunctory once-over, gazing up from the papers spread out on the bar to flash a distracted thin-lipped smile. She guesses there'll be no quarters coming from this guy.

"Get yourself a tonic, honey, and I'll see you in a minute," Joe directs her.

"I just dropped by, anyway, you know, to say hi. I'll see you at the house," she says.

"Okay, honey," Joe replies, already back to his business with the salesman.

Christina walks to the corner and pounds the button on the traffic pole harder than necessary. She approaches the branch library at the top of her street, sneering at its puny one-story size. She has read every book in the place, practically, she thinks to herself. *Get yourself a tonic, honey.* Her father didn't even look at her, but he takes Vinny fishing and to Fenway Park, just because he's a son. *In a few years, I'll be walkin' her down the aisle,* as if he can't wait to get rid of her, hand her over to some neighborhood *whyo* and unload her for good. *Graduatin' this year.* She knows there'll be a car for a graduation present; he has been hinting about it for months, teasing her at family dinners like she's a puppy with a just-out-of-reach chew toy. A used car he'll get a deal on from Rose's father at the Chevy place. She doesn't want a car. Anyway, he's supposed to be taking her driving on Saturdays so she can learn to parallel park and he never does. So what. She doesn't need to be a good driver. She will take her bike into town and get an apartment and ride to UMass through the Boston Gardens every day like a free spirit.

So. Her father has no time for her. Her friends aren't even her friends anymore, they're just cheerleaders now and that's all they ever talk about unless it's Rose's wedding plans or Mary Agnes going to nursing school or Patsy's new red convertible. Mary Agnes will enjoy being a school nurse, Christina thinks, sticking needles into terrified little kids.

She looks back. That pathetic library. The reception desk takes up most of the space in there, and they don't even have microfilm. A perfect library for her neighborhood of proud know-nothings. She feels like throwing a rock through the window.

"No daughter of mine leaves this house unless it's with her husband," Joe decrees with the force of Zeus hurling a thunderbolt.

"You wanna give him a heart attack?" Rita yells. "Why? Why you wanna kill you own father?"

"You're gonna live in Boston? Murderers, rapists, perverts on every corner!"

"I useta work there. A man, he wave his thing at me! *Sozz'*!" Rita makes an obscene gesture in the vicinity of her crotch. Christina shudders.

"I gotta be up nights worryin'?"

"He ken' sleep now!"

"An' you don't even know what you wanna study!"

"Oo studies just to study? *Tu sei pazz'*!"

"Whatta you gonna waste time and money studying for you don't even know what! You'll be married in a couple of years!"

"I pity you poor 'usband!"

"You can go to St. Catherine's, live at home, do bookkeeping right across from the bar—"

"Why you gonna go there for, in town? Whatta you gonna do there you can't do 'ere, uh?"

"A young innocent girl—you gonna live on your own?"

"*Disgraziata*!"

"You're goin' to secretarial school, you hear me?"

"Nice. You wear nice clothes, no work 'ard."

"St. Catherine's. That's it. I don't wanna hear no more about it."

Christina withstands the barrage in silence, her mouth set in a grim line to restrain her traitorous tongue. She follows the rules of a prisoner of war, like in all those late-night black-and-white movies: she will not cooperate. Rita discovered Christina's great escape plan by opening a letter addressed to her from the University of Massachusetts. That this act was a heinous invasion of Christina's privacy and an actual federal offense is totally lost on Rita, who can't comprehend where her persona ends and Christina's begins. Christina has irrefutable evidence of this strange quirk. Rita called her "Mammà" in tender moments until she was ten, as if Christina and her mother were interchangeable. Then, as the tender moments waned in direct proportion to the ascendancy of Christina's sulky adolescence, Rita switched over to Vinny and began calling him "Mammà."

The letter from UMass confirmed her acceptance and informed Christina that she would begin classes in September and asked for a deposit on her first semester's tuition. Rita went straight to Joe and together they stoked each other's outrage until they could present a united volcanic front to their daughter who isn't their daughter, but a cuckoo in the nest, a stranger, a betrayer who went behind their backs and plotted to stab each of them in the heart and bring utter disgrace and ruin upon the family.

Christina watches them as if from a distance, even though they are standing on either side of her, screaming in stereo as she sits at the kitchen table. Ashy gray flakes swirl against the windows, the March snowstorm adding a background sucker punch for the family feud. Vinny decamps at the first sign of shouting and Nonno is emitting faint, ineffective "s'all rights" from his chair in the living room. She sees her parents as a stranger would: their foolish Abbott and Costello routine, their silly hectoring voices, spittle flying, faces exaggerated into grotesque commedia dell'arte masks, Rita grabbing her crotch like a crazed streetwalker. They are ridiculous. They can't stop her. She will get a job on weekends and a full-time job in the summer, and she will pay her own tuition. And she will get an apartment and study in an actual place of higher learning instead of an indoctrination camp, and then—her imagination begins to sputter and fail. *Who studies just to study?* No. She will have an apartment and live like a bohemian. *You'll see perverts on every corner! Rapists!* She will go to coffeehouses and bars and walk back to her apartment late at night, a cosmopolitan girl who belongs in the city. She will wear a miniskirt. No one will bother her. *Whatta you gonna do there you can't do 'ere?* Break every single rule. Be a fool and try anything. Walk off the edge of a cliff just because she can. She will succumb to folly. The card predicted it. She is the bewrayment, she realizes. That's what it means. She is the bewrayment.

UNDERCOVER AGENT

Christina refuses to go to the prom, even after a surprise invitation from shy, goofy Richie Donnelly. Everyone says she will regret missing the prom for the rest of her life. She tells all her friends, sneering, that she wouldn't dream of imitating some forty-year-old and dancing to Lawrence Welk music, but the truth is that she doesn't want to go to the prom with Richie Donnelly. R.T. is her boyfriend, sort of, for people uncool enough to use that word (and she certainly isn't one of them). Christina isn't sure anyway if R.T. would agree to go to prom and she's afraid if she asks him he'll think she's a high school twerp who wants to go to prom. She knows he will go with her to the after-party at Winifred Mahoney's family cottage on White Horse Beach.

At the after-party, R.T. brings beer and they lie on a blanket apart from the others, kissing, sensing her classmates' disapproval, their faraway grimaces a strange aphrodisiac for Christina, whose giddiness increases in direct proportion to the distant scowls on the faces of her classmates.

A gritty wind begins blowing sand around, and kids straggle toward the Mahoneys' beach house and the protection of the screened-in porch. R.T. and Christina trail behind, two longnecked bottles of beer dangling from R.T.'s aristocratic hand. They trudge along, their heads down to avoid being blinded by the pinging sand. When they look up, a disapproving adult colossus is blocking their path, his arms folded in the universal bouncer's "no-go" symbol. He stands at the wooden gate to the Mahoneys' cottage, wearing giant-sized madras shorts, which flap like sails in the now–gale force winds. He is young for an authority figure, with a sunburned bulbous nose and meaty cheeks. He looks vaguely familiar.

"Who are you?" he says. He is speaking directly to R.T., ignoring Christina.

"Who are *you?*" R.T. asks cheerfully.

Christina loves that R.T. isn't intimidated by adults.

"I'm Father McMullin," the man pronounces, as if that's Christina and R.T.'s cue to drop to their knees and kiss the hem of his madras shorts. *Now* she recognizes him. Out of his man-dress and under a baseball cap with sunglasses on, he looks like just another generic harassing parent, but he is, in reality, the official clerical chaperone of the after-prom party.

"What are you, an undercover agent for God?" R.T. asks.

Christina's heart swells. Oscar Wilde beams at

them from the afterlife. R.T. is the love of her life, even if she isn't sure about going all the way with him.

Being banned from the after-prom party doesn't dim Christina's ardor even though she has been fantasizing about showing off her new boyfriend to her classmates and intoning the magic name "Harvard." They return to the sandstorm and, on a blanket rolled out in a frenzy behind a dune, she awards R.T. with bare skin for the speed and wit of his comeback to Father McMullin. She is unable to distinguish her excitement from her fear as R.T.'s hands roam over her breasts now liberated from her new quilted-top two-piece.

Father McMullin calls a "special assembly" for girls only on the morning before the last day of school to deliver a lecture on the evils of young women who behave indecently in public, young women who think nothing of breaking the law of the sixth commandment and putting their mortal souls in jeopardy. He fixes his watery Prince Charles spaniel eyes directly on Christina, who stares back, unmoved.

On and on Father McMullin drones his tired incantation. They are leaving the sanctuary of Precious Blood, going out into the world. Christina feels a surge of happiness when she hears this. The priest continues, his voice rising as if to counter the tide of joy that ripples through the audience of about-to-be-liberated girls. They are to conduct themselves as "little Marys" as they go on to fulfill the purpose God has in store for them. They are to be credits to the holy Catholic

Church. But some of them don't seem to understand that. Some of them don't know how to conduct themselves as little Marys. Some of them are shaming the two-thousand-year history of the Catholic faith. He is speaking to Christina now, and Christina alone. All the girls know this. Some of them half turn to watch her reaction, and Mary Agnes swivels all the way around in her seat.

Christina sees and hears all this, and she doesn't care. She doesn't care. It is the morning before the last day of school. And she isn't going to St. Catherine's Secretarial School in September. She is going to UMass and she is going to live in Boston. And Mary Agnes can rotate in her seat like a demon-possessed whirligig for all she cares. The day after tomorrow, she will pose beside Mary Agnes and Patsy and Rose for pictures snapped by overexcited parents. She will smile and feel silly in her white graduation robe and then she will probably lose touch with all of them except Rose. She will never see this auditorium again. This is her farewell to Father McMullin and his obsequious harem of Precious Blood nuns. She wishes them all well.

She smiles at Father McMullin.

She is an undercover agent for love.

THE SEND-OFF

Babe sits on her wheelchair throne surveying her empty realm. Her white hair is no longer in a stylish gamine cut; now it is long and witchy and pulled into a messy bun at the nape of her scrawny neck. She still looks elegant somehow, even sitting in her shabby room, the sacred heart of the martyred Christ hanging in His designated spot on the wall, trying in vain to get Babe's attention, pointing to His barbed-wire heart.

"Babe," Christina calls.

Babe raises her supernatural-green eyes and stares in her direction. "Well, well. The return of the native," she cackles. "What took ya so long?"

At the sound of that familiar tough-girl voice, something wells in Christina. "I'm glad you called me. I have so much to tell you."

"Well, do it while you're pushin' me outside. I've been stuck in here all day, lookin' at Tyrone Power on the wall over there. I know, I know, it's Jesus H. Christ. But to me he's Tyrone Power." Babe's signature cigarette cough/laugh fills Christina with joy.

"Shirley's comin' with gin and tonics to celebrate you graduating."

They sit in the dwindling afternoon light of the dormant garden, savoring the faint scent of the burgeoning earth and listening to the otherworldly sounds of the peepers from the weed-choked pond. Shirley rounds the corner, toting a cocktail shaker and wearing a shimmery blue dress that shows off the goods, a little fuller now, but still on display. She plops down on the stone bench beside Christina. From a voluminous carpet bag, Shirley retrieves three tall glasses which she sets down between her and Christina. She pours and hands the first glass to Babe, then to Christina, then takes one herself.

"Party time, girls! Bottoms up!" Shirley declares, then drains her glass. She repours and holds her glass aloft. "To our future coed, Christina Falcone! May she earn her MRS if that's what she wants, or, if not, may she have a blast and get some ass in the hallowed halls of the University of Massachusetts!"

They all toast again.

Shirley turns to Christina with her usual greeting: "What's the tale, nightingale? Let's hear it."

It is a week after the forced retreat Precious Blood High School makes seniors go on if they want to graduate. Christina tells Babe and Shirley about the criminally belated sex-education film and the face-to-face confession.

Shirley leans in. "I woulda made him squirm."

"Didja make him squirm?" asks Babe.

Christina realizes, with a sinking heart, that the thought had never even occurred to her.

"Wrong team," Babe croaks, and Shirley screams with her, their seagull calls rising like hosannas in the garden of St. Lucy's Home for the Aged Blind.

Christina eyes Shirley as she drinks her third gin and tonic; she fervently hopes she won't be tapped to drive her boat-sized Buick home. Christina has only recently gotten her license and is still petrified with nerves behind the wheel. Driving Shirley back to Brighton is unthinkable; she can barely navigate beyond the parking lot where her father has, after much whining and sulking, taught her the basics.

Babe slides a chunky white envelope across the bench. "It's for you. From me and Shirley. Don't spend it all in one place."

"Thank you," Christina says, too shy to pick it up.

"Open it!" Shirley barks, nudging Christina, who takes a big gulp of her gin and tonic. Shirley lights cigarettes for herself and Babe. Both look at Christina, waiting, gleeful.

Embarrassed, Christina tears open the envelope. Inside is an oversized, glossy card with a picture of a graduation cap on the front. She opens the card and five hundred-dollar bills fall out. She looks at Babe and Shirley, agog.

"First and last month's rent, plus security," Shirley says.

"For your apartment when you go to school," Babe adds.

A metal key ring slides out of the envelope. Shirley holds it up, demonstrating. "And this is where you keep your keys. Lookit this, I love this." The metal clockwork attached to the key ring features a man inserting his coppery penis in and out of a woman on her hands and knees. "This beats your sex-education film!" She laughs, and Babe adds her signature croak in agreement.

"Thank you," Christina mumbles, overwhelmed, both by the generosity of the five hundred dollars and the vulgarity of the key ring. Shirley and Babe glow, the joy in their eyes scalding her. "This is a lot of money, you guys," she manages to say.

"Aaaah, shaddup and go to school!" Shirley yells, then rises unsteadily. "I gotta pee like a racehorse."

Christina watches her waver off. She'll definitely have to drive the Buick.

Babe is watching her with that uncanny mermaid stare. She smiles at Christina. "Don't worry, you can do it."

Christina hopes she is talking about driving the Buick. Starting school and finding an apartment now seem like a breeze in comparison. "I'm gonna still come and visit you, Babe."

"Nah, you probably won't. But that's okay, kiddo. Drop me a line once in a while and tell me your story. Make it juicy."

Christina nods, unable to speak.

BREAKING THE SEAL

Dear Father Generic Irish Name:
(I can't remember your name or face, just your collar and ankle-length man-dress.)

I'm not good at keeping secrets, Father. Right now, as a side note, I want to assure any friends that somehow happen to read this—for other people's secrets I have extreme, Sicilian-level *omerta*. But for my own? Not so much. I'm a blabbermouth by nature and an actress by trade so I don't have many good secrets left at this point because they've all been blabbed.

But I feel like it is time to break the seal of the confessional.

When they told us at the retreat that due to the new rules of the church, confession is now going to be a face-to-face deal—I'll admit it threw me, the face-to-face thing. I was seventeen years old and about to graduate from the parochial school I had gone to since kindergarten. All the girls in my class had spent a weekend at the Holy Family Retreat House where we were supposed to be praying and getting ready for our roles as Catholic wives and mothers in the outside world after high school. It was the late sixties. There were no other options at the time, except nurse or teacher or secretary. The night before the face-to-face, you and some of the other priests had—inexplicably and creepily—screened Fellini's *La Strada* for us, a film with Giulietta Masina and Anthony Quinn. Anthony Quinn is a strong man in a circus who buys Giulietta Masina from her impoverished mother. He is brutal to Giulietta Masina, and he abandons her in the end but this drives him crazy. Nobody got why we were seeing this film, but I got that I wanted to do what Giulietta Masina was doing, shine like I was lit from within and make people laugh and cry. I made her my patron saint of acting, so thank you for that. Now I knew what I wanted to do after high school.

The face-to-face confession was supposed to be the last holy ritual we did before we were able to go home. It was a required thing, like when you go before a parole board.

At the time, I finally had a boyfriend who wasn't monosyllabic and who read books and could quote Oscar Wilde and Edward Gorey at will, which made me love him. We were romantically dry-humping in rooms heaped with coats at teenage parties and I was writing profane poetry for him about chalices of flesh, inspired by Rimbaud and Baudelaire and Sylvia Plath. For this required confession I had kind of been counting on the usual setup that even non-Catholics have seen in films or read about—the little booth, the blackout curtain, the darkness, and the further anonymity of the face-level grate that distorts your features so that you're unrecognizable afterward in a crowd of other girls. Instead, you opened the door to a prissy living room with two pale satin-upholstered chairs facing each other. I was awkward and confused and the lace mantilla I was wearing got caught in my mouth and made me choke. You looked eager and smiley. Was I supposed to kneel before you while you sat? No, you informed me, I could sit in my chair facing you while I said the ritual words: "Bless me father, for I have sinned."

I realize that when I told you about the boy touching me, it was partly because of my impulse-control issue and partly due to my being an incorrigible show-off. I kind of wanted to brag about my new boyfriend who wasn't even Catholic and had a grandfather who was Chinese and wore his glossy black hair long and had an upper lip that mesmerized me because it curved into a natural sneer. You weren't impressed, as I recall. You got right down to business and asked if I let the boy touch me and I said that I did (I was absurdly proud of this; most boys just told me "You're weird" and walked away at Catholic Youth Organization dances). You got very serious and killjoy and told me that you couldn't grant me absolution unless I promised to never do it again. And the way you said that! That you, as the agent and direct representative and mouthpiece of God, would deny me forgiveness, and the idea that I would remain forever tainted by sin, unforgiven, with a compromised, blackened soul—that terrified me. For about a minute.

And then, for the first time in a long time, I listened to my mother, even though my mother and I were mortal enemies at the time. Do you know what a *mangiapreti* is, Father? The literal translation is "priest eater" in Italian. It also means anticleric. My mother was from Italy and she was a *mangiapreti* even though she sent me to Catholic school. She thought it had to be better because you paid for it. It wasn't. It really wasn't. I remembered when I was a little kid and cried because she never went to confession and I was afraid she would burn in hell and not go to heaven where I planned to reside for all eternity. She was rolling out the Sunday macaroni at the time and she cut off two strands and twisted them together. She showed them to me and said they were called *strozzapreti*—priest stranglers. Because when she was in Italy and they didn't have much to eat, the priest would invite himself over for dinner and he would eat a big plate of *strozzapreti* that was supposed to be for the whole family and they would end up going hungry and he should choke on it and that's why they're called priest stranglers. I told her that you were the human representative of God on earth and strangling a priest was murder, but then she said that the priest making them *morta di fame* was also murder, just slower. She said to be careful around priests and never to let them touch me. I thought she was crazy and prayed for her and hoped her craziness would spare her from the eternal fire.

Turns out, she's smart, my mother.

So, you may be wondering why I talked about breaking the seal of the confessional at the beginning of this letter, when you're the one bound to secrecy. Well, Father, I want to thank you: that confession was the beginning of a transfer of power. I took the power from you to stand in for God as Her representative. And that's why it's me breaking the bonds of the confessional and not you, so no worries on your part.

On that day, I told you that I would never do it again. Only I didn't specify that I would never let the boy touch me again. I just agreed that I would never do it again.

And I didn't even really know at the time that when I said I would never do it again that it would mean that I would never again, in the dark or face-to-face in full daylight, confess my sins to a man who claimed to be standing in for God.

Sincerely,
Christina the Astonishing Falcone

PART 4

PART 4

TRANSFIGURATION

Rita comes on the subway, all the way into town, to see Christina's apartment for herself. Christina knows that the visit is also to gauge how much her changeling daughter has changed in the month since she packed her bags and left Derby Street and the home where she was born. Rita has dressed carefully for the trip into the city in a tailored gray suit and frilly white blouse. Christina smirks when she meets her mother at the Park Street entrance to the Boston Common. Rita senses the disrespect immediately and, without any greeting, shakes her head at her daughter's outfit. Rita is presenting her best self to the world, something her daughter doesn't understand, she has informed Christina, the need for a *bella figura* to protect one from scorn. She tells Christina that she invites scorn with her rags and her feathers, like a village *pazza*.

Christina and Rita have lunch at the place that serves the ninety-nine-cent clam dinners across from Filene's Basement. Mother and daughter sit facing each other like strangers forced to share a booth during the lunchtime rush and, like strangers, say little besides *Pass the salt* or *Hand me a napkin*. It is the first time they have ever eaten in a restaurant alone together. They are calmed by the bustle of the lunchtime crowd, the clink of china, the indifferent voices of secretaries and shoppers that swaddle them in silence. Rita orders a whiskey sour and after it arrives she gulps it down, and seems instantly high. She looks blearily at her daughter.

"You father's not doin' good. He's worried. About you. Not sleepin' good. He sayin' it's my fault you move away before gettin' married."

"It's not your fault," Christina says. "I wanted to go to college and live in town."

Her mother shrugs. "Eh, the girl belong to the mother an' the boy to the papa."

Now Christina shrugs with irritation, unconsciously imitating Rita. "That's fucked up," she says. "I don't belong to you or him. I belong to myself."

"You aunt Connie no like either," Rita says. "She say you doin' a lotta things here she no like."

This enrages Christina. "What does she know? She got married when she was my age! And now she *belongs* to the biggest *stupidone* in the neighborhood!"

Rita shakes her head and orders another whiskey sour.

Rita lags behind Christina on the stairs to her fourth-floor apartment, giggling and repeating "I'm drunk" louder and louder with every flight and calling for Christina to 'elp. Christina finds her mother's drunk routine fake and not funny in the least, though her mother keeps acting like she should think it's a riot. Her mother has had two drinks as far as Christina can recall and is now jeopardizing her daughter's relationship with everyone else in the building on Anderson Street, a tenement on the wrong side of Beacon Hill. Christina is skittish about how her mother, whose tastes run to the baroque, will react to her bare-bones apartment. Her roommate, Penny, who works at the Bread and Bowlery, has brought home some random pottery and candlesticks for the living room (where she also sleeps), but Christina's room is no-frills: a mattress on the floor covered by a yellow Indian-print bedspread, a candle beside the mattress, and two grimy uncurtained windows that look out onto the backs of other tenements. Rita runs to the bathroom and is even now, Christina guesses, staring in queasy wonder at the eye collage Penny and Christina slapped on the walls after smoking a joint and collapsing in hysterics at their own cleverness in creating a bathroom that is an Argus.

Christina's mother emerges unsteadily from the bathroom and takes her first look around. "Nice," she pronounces insincerely. "You get the light." This is a blatant falsehood, since the apartment is at the back of the building and it is often hard to tell day from night, or a gray day from one bright with sun. Rita smiles and gestures toward the tiny room beside the "living room" which holds Christina's bed. "You sleep-a 'ere?"

Christina opens the door. Rita's smile wavers and

she begins to blink rapidly once she takes in the mattress on the floor and the dungeon-like essence of the room, amplified by Christina's mad-looking slogans scrawled on the wall, quotes from Rimbaud writ large in black marker.

"Yeah, but I'm never here. I'm always at school. Or at work." Christina has two jobs, the cool one at the coffeehouse on Charles Street and the prosaic one at the Mug 'n' Muffin, also on Charles Street. Christina feels the need to babble, to forestall the tears threatening to spill from her mother's tormented-saint eyes. She asks about Connie, Rose.

Rita shrugs, unable to speak.

"Want a cup of tea?"

Rita nods.

Christina disappears into the tiny kitchenette to boil water. Rita sits at the rickety table, trying and failing to compose herself.

Christina returns with a thick blue mug and sets it before Rita. She places one for herself on the other side of the table. "It's herbal," she informs her mother. "Chamomile."

Rita grasps the bobbing life raft of a familiar word in this unfamiliar place. "*Camomilla*!" she says, with pleasure. "My nonna used to give me!"

"Oh yeah? You never told me about her. Maybe that's someone in the family I'm like. You're always saying I'm not from this family."

Rita takes a fortifying sip of her tea, then looks up and smiles. "You better make sure you not like her."

"Why?"

"Because," Rita says, beginning to giggle, "she was *pazza*." She laughs this time for real.

Christina laughs, too, relief making her laughter giddy. "What was her name?" she manages to gasp.

"I forget," her mother says. "Nonna?"

This makes them laugh harder. They give themselves over to their laughter and it echoes and rises higher and higher, bouncing off the bare apartment walls.

When at last it ebbs, Rita gets ready to go, blotting her lips with a tissue fished from her giant purse, primping her hair. She turns to Christina. "I'm makin' homemades for Sunday. You comin'?"

"I'll let you know. I might have to work at the coffeehouse."

"Yeah, okay," her mother says, shrugging.

Christina understands then that when she next returns home for Sunday dinner, nothing will be the same. And that makes her both happy and a little afraid.

EATEN BY PIGS: A CHRISTMAS STORY

"**E**ATEN! EATEN BY PIGS," wails Christina. She twists her face into a mask of horror and stares at her friend Kyle's oversized rubber head, now dented and covered with stage blood. She leans against the doorframe of her Spanish-peasant hut, fake-rending her garments. She hopes she looks insane with grief and lost financial opportunities. Kyle is playing her nephew, a hydrocephalic little person, in Christina's first-ever performance on the shallow auditorium stage that her cash-strapped state university uses as a theater.

The play is *Divine Words*, a Spanish translation of a grotesque rumination on greed, lust, and death that goes over the heads of most of the eighteen-year-old players, including Christina. Her drama professor likes to think of himself as edgy and that is the reason for this production of *Divine Words*, or *Divinas palabras* as he likes to proclaim, rolling the title salaciously on his tongue, and the reason she is screaming onstage about her nephew being eaten by pigs just three days before Christmas.

Christina loves acting with her friend Kyle, the first gay person she has ever known, if you don't count the snickering and whispers about Father Mc-Mullin. Kyle is flamboyant and doesn't give a shit, his high-pitched giggles a happy release from the droning of the Hare Krishnas and the SDS chanting against the Vietnam War outside the campus library. Christina thinks her entire life would have been different if she had met Kyle in high school. No one at Precious Blood High understands people with artistic temperaments. Christina and Kyle have posed backstage, vamping with haughty expressions and holding cigarettes aloft as if they're about to perform Noël Coward's *Private Lives* instead of an obscure play from the 1920s by Ramón María del Valle-Inclán.

In Act I, Kyle masturbates onstage while the girl playing his mother dies of syphilis, collapsing awkwardly to the obscene rhythm of her son's rocking cart. The climax of the play displays Katharine Feeney, the lead actress, standing center stage in a nude scene as some kind of symbol, the meaning of which is lost on Christina. The effect of the nude scene is blunted by the fact that their drama professor chickened out at the dress rehearsal and made Katharine wear a nude-colored bodysuit instead of actually going naked. The professor's qualms about the nudity and, more likely, the fate of his tenure track, only adds to the absurdity of this surreal play about nineteenth-century peasants who make a living exhibiting their deformed nephew at local fairs.

Christina, the grieving aunt, is basically an extra

in the climactic fake-nude scene. She thinks meanly that the bodysuit makes Katharine look like a giant knockwurst. Christina is also guiltily aware that she would be afraid to stand nude before an audience, especially one with her mother, Aunt Connie, and Connie's loutish husband sitting in it. Dommie is their reluctant chauffeur tonight, because Connie is afraid to drive in the city and her mother can't drive at all. Joe has to work late at the bar; Christina is glad. The nude scene would make him start harping on her all over again to quit college and live at home and go to secretarial school and marry some *divya* from the neighborhood and start pushing out babies.

Christina rushes out to meet her mother and aunt as soon as the curtain falls, still wearing her costume and greasepaint. Her goal is to hustle her family out of the auditorium before any of her friends emerge from backstage, possibly wanting introductions. There is to be a party afterward at the professor's apartment in Back Bay. Christina pictures herself drinking wine and tossing off airy put-downs of her philistine relations to the appreciative titters of the crowd around her.

"HEEEYYYY! HERE SHE IS!" Dommie's voice carries over the murmur of the people in the hall waiting for the actors to emerge. It looks like most of the audience is either related to or friends of the cast. Christina shepherds her group away from the crowd. She kisses her mother and Aunt Connie.

Connie shrinks away and pulls a tissue from her voluminous purse. She begins scrubbing at her face.

"Jesus Christ, watch it! What color is that makeup comin' off you, purple?"

Dommie nudges Christina. "You didn't tell me I'd be lookin' at nude chicks! I'm comin' back tomorrow!" Connie tells him to shut up and Dommie snickers. He pulls a comb from somewhere and adjusts his Elvis-style pompadour.

"Hey, Dommie, thanks for coming in," Christina says.

"We hadda go the North End anyways. To get the eels for La Vigilia," Connie interrupts before Dommie can answer.

"Where . . . where are the eels now?" Christina fears that they are in a bucket close by, swimming creepily in circles, awaiting their doom on Christmas Eve a few days from now.

"Hey, eels woulda fit right in with that friggin' play," Dommie says. "I shoulda brought some up onstage during the nude scene."

"They're in the car, for Chrissake. Whadda we look like, *gavones*?" Connie's jaw is jutting dangerously. "You're comin' home for Christmas, right?" she asks, more a challenge than a question. "You can help your mother with the squid."

Christina notices that Rita is crying. This does not disturb her. Her mother cries often, especially at public events, where she feels it is expected of her.

"Did you like it, Ma?"

Christina is actually curious. She thinks some of the bizarre happenings in the play might have resonated with the few freakish stories she has heard about her mother's early life on a garlic farm in Abruzzo.

"It remind me of the pig I have in Sulmona," Rita replies, her tragic Anna Magnani eyes glistening with tears. "They make a salami outta him." The tears give way to sobs.

Connie throws Christina a look that means *Hug your mother, you little shit*. Christina pretends not to see her. Connie puts consoling arms around Rita, sending death-ray glances at Christina over Rita's shoulder.

Kyle bursts through the stage door, his head now a normal size. He is wearing an antique morning coat and a long white silk scarf flung around his neck. "Darling!" he calls to Christina. "I was looking for you!"

"*Il fidanzato?*" her mother says to Connie out the side of her mouth, tears suddenly forgotten.

Christina freezes. Does her mother think she's invisible, rudely speaking in another language about Kyle in front of Kyle? She notes with relief that Kyle, who is appraising Dommie like he's some mythical creature, appears not to notice her mother's comment.

"Is it time to leave for the party?" Christina asks, beaming an SOS to Kyle in their private eyebrow code. She turns back to her family. "Our teacher is throwing a cast party, so I have to get ready to go."

"Make sure you wash that shit off your face," Connie says. "You look like the Wicked Witch of the West."

"But her face was green."

"Who?"

"The Wicked Witch of the West."

Connie stares at Christina for a long minute, then shakes her head. "That mouth."

Christina stares back at her aunt. She grabs Kyle, not breaking eye contact. "This is my friend, Kyle, everyone. He's helping me get ready for the party. And we're late and I don't want to show disrespect to the teacher."

Kyle finally gets the message. He throws his arm around Christina and starts walking her back toward the stage door. "Hi, everyone! And byeee! Gotta run or we'll be late for the party!"

Christina turns back to her mother. "I'm sorry about the pigs."

Her mother shrugs. "You were good. Good screamin'. Like Philomen' when she jump in the coffin. Go 'head. Go see the teacher."

"Okay. I'll see you on Christmas Eve."

Her mother has a smudge of Christina's purple greasepaint under one glistening eye.

They don't hug or kiss any goodbyes.

Christina refuses a hit off the joint Kyle offers on the way to the professor's apartment. She is paranoid enough around her teacher after what he said to her in acting class: "You will never be an actress, because you can't take direction."

A pronouncement from on high, ex cathedra. His sonorous voice like the oracle at Delphi. She changes her mind and takes a covert hit, just to relax before the party. Christina hates her professor, the phony. She can spot a phony from the moon, that is one good thing about growing up blue collar. She takes another hit of the joint. Just because she isn't a fucking puppet. She desperately wants the professor's approval. She hates herself. Fuck him. Her mother liked her performance and she could relate, because of the pig. Christina giggles, thinking of the pig. Shit, now she's really stoned.

The party is in full swing when Kyle and Christina finally arrive at the Marlborough Street brownstone, almost all the way to Mass Ave., the unfashionable end of Back Bay. They're some of the last to arrive, having stopped for hamburgers, ravenous after Kyle's weed. The professor's cramped apartment has floor-to-ceiling books and art prints on the wall. There is a bay window, wood paneling, and highly polished oak floors. Christina thinks of the religious pictures with dried palm fronds in the shape of a cross and posed baby pictures that dominate the décor where she grew up, book-deprived, except for the encyclopedia her mother got at the supermarket and her father's collection of *National Geographic* magazines dating back to the fifties. She and Kyle head over to the drinks table that by now contains only the dregs of some mouthwashy-looking off-brand rosé and a near-empty sangria bowl with tiny flotsam rafts that were once recognizable pieces of fruit.

Christina goes to the kitchen for some water. Kyle follows her. The professor is holding forth on Brecht and Ramón María del Valle-Inclán to some rapt student suck-ups, his arm draped casually over his star, Katharine Feeney.

"Ah, the venal aunt and her doomed nephew finally appear," he intones. All heads swivel obediently their way.

"My mother really loved the play," Christina says. "She's . . . European, so she could, uh, relate."

"Especially to the pigs," Kyle pipes up, devilishly.

Christina glares at him and totters to the sink. She turns on the tap and drinks almost a full glass of metallic-tasting water.

The professor leans in. "What part of Europe is your mother from?"

"Uh, Italy," Christina answers.

The professor walks her out of the kitchen, away from the others. "I want to give you a note on your performance tonight," he says. "Don't worry, you did well. But I think for tomorrow's performance you should add something to your big scene. You should tear at your hair, but not really, of course." He smiles at her. "It's all for show, you see, with these peasants. I'm sure your mother has told you about the *bella figura*, basically putting on an act for people. So the audience can understand that it's theatrical, for effect." He touches Christina's long, wild hair. "You wouldn't want to really pull out your beautiful hair." His hand travels down the back of her head and lands on her ass, where it lingers.

Christina moves away, shocked. "Uh, okay, I'll tear out my hair tomorrow night." She chances a look back at the professor. He is still smirking, ogling her behind, his expression dreamy and satisfied.

Christina and Kyle run down Arlington Street toward the subway, fugitives from academia. "I can't believe he grabbed my ass!" Christina screams. "What a male chauvinist pig!"

The weary Santa by the Arlington Street station pauses his bell-ringing and glares at Christina, as if she has just named and shamed him.

"Eaten! Eaten by pigs!" Kyle yells back. They scream as they run down the subway stairs, their laughter echoing off the dirty, ancient tiles.

FOOD FIGHT

At the age of twenty-three, Christina knows how to *kasher* a dishwasher, information that wasn't in the rubrics learned at Precious Blood High School. She also knows what you call the divider between men and women at an orthodox shul (a *mechitza*) and how to write the Jewish date and year on a letter. Today is 4 Sivan, 5734, or May 25, 1974.

Christina is working as a long-term temp at the Rabbinic Fellowship of New York, situated incongruously in a brownstone on the Upper East Side of Manhattan. She is "long-term" because she hasn't yet scored the paid acting job that would free her from the mind-numbing secretarial duties that consume her days at the fellowship. The rabbis agree that Christina can go to her infrequent auditions and not be docked for pay if she will stay on as the chief rabbi's secretary. They also allow her to wear jeans at work, which is tsked over by her elderly office mates, but somehow allowed, possibly because Christina doesn't know any better.

Christina's duties at the fellowship include operating the many antique business artifacts, like the mimeograph, a first-edition Xerox machine, and a gigantic beige Dictaphone. She also answers the community help line phone. There are daily calls from sobbing grandmas whose grandsons are marrying *shikses*, making Christina feel vaguely guilty even though she is an ex-Catholic and her current boyfriend is a WASP. She is required to climb atop a file cabinet to adjust the air conditioner at least twice a day, since she is the only staff member under sixty-five, except for Risa, the manic-depressive receptionist. Risa is thirty, four eleven, and morbidly obese. When the manic part of her disorder kicks in, she disappears on her lunch break and returns hours later with five or six shopping bags, raging at the world, and on one spectacular occasion throwing tampons at the rabbis, who hid in their offices.

"So, Sarah Heartburn, when am I gonna see your name up in lights?" This is Goldie's standard greeting after any of Christina's auditions.

Christina's response to the "joke" is always a weak chuckle, barely disguising the homicidal rage Goldie's question arouses, especially since Christina is usually humiliated at these auditions in ways that would make her elementary school nuns titter nostalgically. Back at her desk, Christina distracts herself by staring at Goldie's feet, much the same way you would rubberneck at a particularly gruesome car wreck. Goldie's toes, shamelessly flaunted in the plastic sandals she invariably wears, resemble nothing so much as the talons of a large, flightless bird. The toenails are a murky, jaundiced color, curved, and, apparently, indestructible. Christina has never actually seen Goldie's legs, since she wears polyester pantsuits every single day, but she can vividly picture them: thin, bright orange, and scaly.

Goldie has other birdlike qualities: she daily consumes what appears to be twice her weight in food. She has also been known in the past to roam freely throughout the office snatching other people's lunches and snacks. Just in the past week, Christina returned from the local coffee shop with a coffee for Goldie ("light, dolling, make sure") and a tuna on rye for herself. Before she had completely unwrapped the sandwich, Goldie came to claim her coffee and advanced on Christina's sandwich, swallowing much of it whole, before grunting out, "You don't mind, dolling, if I have a bite," as a rhetorical question. It was an impressive feat, considering the fact that Goldie has at least forty years on Christina, who towers over her at five foot three, and at 110 pounds is evenly matched in weight. The first time Christina was body-blocked by Goldie for food, she was so stunned at her boldness that she was rendered mute, not even able to muster her weak chuckle.

Christina can't tear herself away from Goldie's daily feeding ritual. Every day at five minutes to noon, she hears a dry, rasping sound from Goldie's desk, conveniently across from hers. Somehow this sound penetrates through clacking IBM Selectric typewriters, ringing phones, and the constant screech of voices discussing the details of unsavory physical ailments, mostly involving bowels. The rasping sound is Goldie rubbing her hands together in anticipation of her lunch. The first time Christina sees this, she feels like she is watching an old-timey play, as if next Goldie will twirl her mustache (she can, easily) and laugh diabolically. She makes a note to tell her acting teacher. Once riveted by the hand-rubbing, Christina is doomed to witness the entire rite. After the hand-rubbing comes a deep, cleansing breath. Then, in one swooping dive, Goldie grabs her brown-bag lunch from under her desk and positions it in the exact center of the desktop. More gastronomic foreplay as she hesitates for another long minute, gazing tremulously at the bag. By now, Christina is gripping the sides of her Selectric with tension. Without warning, Goldie rips aside brown bag and waxed paper in one violent but neat move. She then sinks her teeth into whatever it is she has brought for lunch (Christina is never able to determine the exact food source). Shortly afterward, Goldie will emit, along with her energetic chewing, orgasmic Brooklynite moans of delight. This is the point where, every day—every fucking day—Christina will be driven to wonder about the medical possibilities of clitoral transplant. Goldie has lived her entire life with her gorgonian mother in a tiny apartment in Sheepshead Bay. Has Goldie, realizing her dismal prospects in the world of mating and dating, somehow managed to perform a switch? Is there now located in the middle of Goldie's palate a tiny button that becomes erect every day at 11:55 a.m.?

* * *

The Blueberry Muffin Incident forces Christina to move beyond the weak chuckle as a coping mechanism. Christina always avoids joining in the byzantine confrontations waged with relish by the fellowship staff. Set off by some secret signal Christina cannot detect, cries of "Oy!" and "Feh!" bounce off the green office walls like radio signals from a distant planet, growing in power and intensity until culminating in the traditional coup de grâce: "*Gai kaken oifen yam*!" (*Go shit in the ocean!*). While the drama student in her appreciates the gladiatorial combat from afar, the Little Sisters of Sadism have imbued Christina with a hard-core prisoner-of-war mentality that has taught her the way to live under the radar in this kind of group situation. She understands that she is no match for these tight-permed ladies who can go from smiling-granny types to raging Godzillas on a dime. She gives one-word answers to daily inquiries as to what she is cooking for dinner (*Uh, nothing?*), acts deaf to urgent demands that she "cover her neck" before venturing outside in sixty-degree weather, and looks glazed when they demand details about her boyfriend. She never picks sides in the simmering feuds. Instead, she usually runs into the rabbi's office and takes the occasion to tidy up. Safe from the fray, Christina and Rabbi Warmflash smile at each other, chuckling weakly.

On the morning of the incident, Christina is searching the rabbi's appointment book for something in his office, when out of the corner of her eye she sees someone sneak over to her desk, then quickly scurry away. When she returns to her desk, the blueberry muffin she's brought to work that morning is now reduced to a few crumbs. She is finally outraged. "What happened to my blueberry muffin?" she asks the office at large. She sounds querulous and whiny even to herself. The question hangs in the air, unanswered. Goldie exhibits all the classic signs of guilt in keeping with the melodramatic hand-rubbing and mustache-twirling. In a lightning-like move, her head shoots downward to her desk, and she appears entranced by a pile of paperwork.

Goldie doesn't look at Christina for the rest of the day and her lunchtime ritual lacks the usual flourishes. Her palpable guilt is even starting to make Christina feel guilty. She is glad to be tied up with Rabbi Warmflash for the whole afternoon as he dictates and redictates overdue thank-you notes to Solly or Rivka for invitations to long-since-consummated marriages or bar mitzvahs that by now are but a faint, dyspeptic memory.

Christina is curled up on her ratty sofa, staring at Ida Lupino in black-and-white instead of finding a new monologue to work on for auditions. She can't resist *They Drive By Night* whenever she happens upon it. The phone rings, just as Ida has her shameful meltdown after killing her husband. It's Goldie. The fact that Goldie has Christina's number is as disturbing as hearing her on the phone.

"Dolling," the women croaks in her basso profundo, "I feel so guilty, I had to call."

On the blinky-black-and-white screen, Ida Lupino screams, "The doors made me do it! The doors made me do it!" Ida has lowered the garage doors on her passed-out-drunk husband, leaving him to die of carbon monoxide poisoning.

On the phone, Goldie's voice drops to a low rumble: "Dolling . . . *I* ate your blueberry muffin. I insist on replacing it. I insist."

Christina stares at Ida on her television screen as she hears Goldie make her confession and wonders if the synchronicity is a sign from somewhere about something she can't yet fathom. Maybe this absurd coincidence means she will get an acting job soon and be freed from the fellowship? Maybe Goldie will never call her Sarah Heartburn again.

A piece of stale pound cake appears on Christina's desk the next morning. Neither Christina nor Goldie acknowledges it.

THE INEVITABLE NUN

Maria Callous adjusts Christina's white habit, her hands fluttery and graceful. She spells her name C-a-l-l-o-u-s, but Christina has never heard of the opera singer, so the joke is lost on her. Maria Callous is working part-time as wardrobe mistress in the fifty-seat off-off-Broadway gay theater where Christina has scored her first acting job since coming to the city. Miss C is always kind to Christina, no matter how clueless she acts. They are both crammed into the tiny bathroom that also serves as a dressing room. Miss C's partner, Roxy, does makeup. Christina, who never wears makeup, is fascinated by the perfection of Miss C's plump red lips and her astonishing, spidery eyelashes, Roxy's *specialité*, as she likes to proclaim. Roxy pokes her head in. Tonight she has a retro hairstyle—a full pompadour with bumper bangs. Her entrance is preceded by an aureole of smoke from one of her ever-present Virginia Slims menthols. Christina is thinking of taking up smoking from sheer admiration. She dreams of perfecting the art of speaking while bobbing a cigarette from the corner of her mouth like Roxy, who looks like a gun moll from a forties movie. She is waving today's edition of the *New York Times* that has a picture of Patty Hearst on the cover, dressed in her battle fatigues and sporting a huge machine gun.

"The FBI nabbed her. Looks like it's the slammer for Miss PattyPoo," Roxy says. "Poor little rich girl."

Maria Callous leans over to take in the headline. "Love the beret, though."

Roxy finally puts the paper down and looks at Christina. "You need just a dab of Love That Red lipstick, sweetie, and some fabu lashes, and you'll be dazzling, Audrey Hepburn in *The Nun's Story*."

"I don't think nuns are allowed to wear makeup, Roxy," Christina ventures.

"Oh, fuck that noise, sweetheart, you'll just vanish onstage without lipstick and lashes."

"Okay," Christina concedes at once. She is in awe of Maria Callous and Roxy, at how they turn into beautiful women with makeup. If only makeup could transform her into someone else, someone stunning. Maria Callous and Roxy are magic; good witches who scattershot wisecracks like sacraments. Christina stares at herself in the mirror. Her white wimple and habit do not make her look like Audrey Hepburn. She practices a shy smile, raising her eyes heavenward, going for a generic madonna look, like the Virgin Marys on the half shell in every backyard where she grew up, a constellation away from Tribeca in New York City. Her own nun teachers at Precious Blood wore witchy black and not one of them had ever seemed to embody the sacred, like Maria Callous and Roxy. Christina looks at herself again, hoping for a last-minute Audrey Hepburn glow, summoned by the power of drag queens. In her periphery she sees the photos of erect penises that decorate every inch of the bathroom walls. They are even on the ceiling.

Roxy follows her glance. "You touch one for luck before you go onstage, honey. It's a theater tradition."

"In *this* theater, darling," Maria Callous says. "Our theater." She smiles at Christina in the mirror above the grimy sink.

"Next victim!" Roxy yells, opening the door. To Christina, she makes a sign of the cross in the air and says, "Break a leg, Sister Slutface."

Christina bows her head, accepts Roxy's blessing, and touches the nearest penis. She is about to go onstage in her first New York City off-off—face it, below Canal Street, really off—Broadway show.

The night before, Christina almost runs away from the production, stalked by the inevitable nun. There is to be an attended dress rehearsal, and she still doesn't know what she's doing. She will be terrible. She will disgrace herself. She will fail in front of fifty people. Who is she?

Christina has no lines at all in the play. She is to spend her entire time onstage sitting at a table in the pub which is also a bordello. In the first act, a spotlight will highlight her as she sings "The Foggy Dew" a cappella. The play is *The Hostage* by Brendan Behan. The theater's founder, Brick, claims Brendan Behan for the team, since he is said to have been bisexual. Brick is large and imposing and dressed always in black leather. He moves with conviction through this world he has created, trailed by smoke from his ever-present Parliament cigarette, the chains on his motorcycle jacket a herald of danger possibly coming your way. During rehearsals he sits in the front row of the empty theater, knitting furiously and somehow managing to smoke at the same time, like a many-handed Indian god.

During the run-through before the attended dress, Christina wants to ask Brick about her character's background—like what was a nun doing hanging out in a pub and a brothel and why doesn't she have any lines?—but she is—face it—just too intimidated. Brick can be volatile. Anyway, she tells herself, isn't that her job as an actor, to create her own backstory?

Christina paces the balding linoleum in her Yorkville tenement, a redbrick stand-alone building that hasn't yet been replaced by a high-rise. After the attended dress, she had slogged home in time to run into the frenzied occupant of 1B on the ground floor. Christina has never learned the name of the attractive, middle-aged woman, who is always on edge, like someone fleeing cartoon men in white coats with a butterfly net. She wonders if the nameless catwoman had once been an aspiring actress. She asked Christina in her scarily vacant voice if she had seen a kitten anywhere, then turned away before Christina could answer. There is a huge clan of semi-feral cats living in 1B, the cause of the overwhelming smell that hits you like a blast of congealed evil the minute you cross the threshold. Christina had trudged on to the second floor, to her own tiny apartment with the bathtub in the kitchen and the only slightly more welcome fried-chicken smell from the restaurant window that abuts her bedroom and invades her dreams.

There isn't a nun in the original production of *The Hostage*. Brick looked at Christina and decided she would be a nun after her audition. Why had her audition for one of the prostitutes made Brick think of her as a nun? In her junior year at college, she hitchhiked all over Ireland and took a theater class in Dublin, where she was assigned a role in Austin Clarke's play *Sister Eucharia*. She was given the title role, a nun who had visions and spoke with the souls in purgatory. Why is she being typecast as a nun? In Ireland she had laughed about the role she had been assigned, and she had vamped in her habit, posing suggestively, raising the skirt of her habit for the theater's lust-struck Irish photographer, who followed her everywhere, snapping picture after picture.

She is no longer laughing. She clomps around her kitchen, her nerves fraying, as she pictures an acting career where the only characters she ever gets to play are people who have sworn off sex forever and dress in body-obscuring robes. Is she sexless? Does she come across as Miss Prim, her mother's most stinging (and accurate) nickname for her? She worked as hard to erase her parochial schoolgirl past in the first year at her state university as she did to get on the dean's list, her hip bones jutted landmarks always pointing south, picking up boys at bus stops and going home with them, spending wild weekends in bed with total strangers, taking her life in her hands to kill Miss Prim and stop her from ruining Christina's post–high school future. Miraculously, no one had threatened or assaulted her, and the worst she had taken away from her casual sexual encounters was a case of crabs she discovered while meditating cross-legged and naked on a visit home. She had even escaped the herpes outbreak the entire cast of *Our Town* had suffered. And now here she was—despite the double-digit lovers, the random meetups at concerts and love-ins—Miss Prim, stalked all these years later by the inevitable nun.

There is a soft but insistent rapping at the door. Christina opens it to her across-the-hall neighbor, her doughy face a familiar rictus of Teutonic pain. Her German neighbor has left Christina hectoring notes a few times about the noise she makes walking across the floor of her apartment or rattling pots and pans while throwing dinner together (a rare occurrence, since Christina lives on takeout). It is amazing, when you think about it: despite the ever-present roar of the city, her neighbor can only hear the footsteps of 103-pound Christina as she crosses her tiny apartment floor.

"Pliss. Die boom boom boom." The neighbor extends a pair of ratty slippers toward Christina. "You vill vear, pliss. My head. Die boom boom boom. You must vear."

Christina draws the rage around her like a cloak. "You want—you want *silence*? In New York? Join a CLOISTER," she screams.

She slams the door and stares at it. She hears the door across the hall unlatch furtively, then silence. Sudden tears blind her. She can't even yell at someone without invoking nuns! She is possessed!

She isn't really a nun, Christina thinks, tossing in her single bed. Maybe her nameless character is a revolutionary impersonating a nun so she can run guns to her IRA comrades. Yes. Good note. Christina's character is possessed by the ghost of fierce Maud Gonne, muse and out-of-body mad sex lover of W.B. Yeats, and she is a spy.

"What is wrong with you?" Roxy says. She peers at Christina over her cat's-eye glasses. "You're in a bordello. In Ireland. You're the kinky-nun fantasy for twisted Catholic boys." She takes a dramatic pause, staring at Christina and bugging her eyes, making a *Duh* face at her. "Don't be an airhead, darling. You're an Irish hooker dressed like a nun."

They are sitting in the first row of the theater, smoking Roxy's horrible menthol Virginia Slims. Christina has arrived early so she can get Roxy's input on the elusive, inevitable nun that has kept her up all night.

"You look stoned. Are you stoned? You have to go on in two hours. It's opening night!" Roxy pretends to smack Christina across the face. "Snap out of it!" She takes a long drag on her cigarette and exhales lustily. "I'll take a large black decaf with two sugars. My fee. And go to the good place on Broadway. The one with the delicious counterboy."

Idiot. Idiot. Idiot. Idiot. Every clacking step of Christina's Dr. Martens rings out a mortification tattoo. She is too stupid to live in New York, much less make it here as an actor. She plods past the Canal Street subway entrance. She pauses, thinks briefly about going down the grimy stairs, getting on a train to Port Authority, and taking a bus home to Boston, leaving it all: her apartment, her shitty temp job, her fantasies of being on the stage. Aunt Connie's grimly satisfied face becomes a full moon over Manhattan. No. No way would she have that face looming over her as she moved back into the family scrum. She runs the lines of the song over in her head as she races across Canal against the light.

Twas down the glen one Easter morn
To a city fair rode I . . .

After Patrick plays the opening chords and the spotlight hits, she is in it, right there where the hooker nun lives, in that seedy bar where all her misspent passions can go. The song is her story and the struggle is not the unholy blasphemies of the boys she seduces at night but the ones lost forever to the revolution, and she is so intoxicated by the lift of her own voice she can't even hear the metallic rustlings of the Fist Fuckers of America who have sold out the house on opening night. The inevitable nun has been exorcised.

* * *

The Fist Fuckers of America give them a standing ovation.

Michael's Thing is a gay periodical and Christina hears from Roxy that they had sent someone to cover the play. She rushes over to Sheridan Square on the day the review is supposed to come out and picks up a copy. The cover of *Michael's Thing* has two men dressed in leather, happily entwined. She quickly pages the little periodical until she comes to the review, ominously titled "Gay but Not Good." She gasps, not because of the title. She doesn't care about the title because there, opposite the review, is a full-page picture of a nun sitting at a bar table dressed in a white habit. Her character, Sister Ignatius, in a magazine. The picture is of such poor quality that she looks pretty. She will tear it out and send it home, first checking the other side to make sure there are no entwined men in leather (Aunt Connie's disapproving face looms again, momentarily).

She floats out of the newsstand, past Marie's Crisis, and down the steps to the subway, where she almost trips over a nest of rags in front of the turnstile that is actually a drunken woman who looks up at Christina, her face a commedia dell'arte mask of disgust.

"YOU AIN'T QUALIFIED," the woman prophesies. Her sibylline voice roars, enhanced by the cave-like depths of the Broadway line.

TAKING UP SERPENTS

C hristina is hoping for snakes. She is visiting her boyfriend who is working at a regional theater in a small Southern city. She is delighted by the otherness of everything including the pasta, which comes in a box with a brand name that implies rescue, a big red cross on a brilliant yellow background. It is amazing to her that pasta even exists below the Mason-Dixon Line in 1979. Her boyfriend is staying in a deliciously seedy rooming house, with sailors and shouting from other rooms. Christina and her boyfriend are in their twenties and not yet terrified that seedy could become a lifestyle.

One night when the boyfriend is performing, Christina wanders the streets surrounding the rooming house. It's obviously a poor part of town, with cafeterias and pawnshops and broken sidewalks. The entire area has a toxic smell; something unseen is belching noxious fumes nearby, perhaps a tannery. She stops for coffee at one of the garishly lit cafeterias and a man with two heads rings up her order. On second look, she sees that one of the heads is a huge goiter. Christina smiles perkily at him, hoping for an authentic conversation full of homespun wisdom and alien idioms. To her disappointment, he seems totally uninterested in her, pointing to the coffee urn without a word. Two old women sit at a table cawing at each other good-naturedly in regional birdspeak, exotic and unintelligible. Christina takes a seat nearby, hoping the old ladies notice her and invite her to tell her story to them, but no one in the cafeteria even looks at her. She starts to get self-conscious and leaves.

It is late autumn and it is disconcerting to have the trees bare and no bite in the wind. Christina sees a group of people milling around a small storefront with dirty windows. There is a blinking electric sign that advertises: *Penial Revival Center*. She wonders if the storefront is named after the penal code and is a misspelled sanctuary for ex-cons. Or after the pineal gland and a misspelled haven for spiritualists.

A big bald man with the face of a prizefighter invites her inside. "C'mon in," he says, gargling the words at the back of his throat. He seems more proprietary than friendly. Christina ignores a tinkle of alarm and follows him inside.

Christina and the gargle-voiced giant sit at the back of the room. A skinny-throated preacher leads a service. People are testifying, waving their hands. One young girl weeps and talks about Jesus. She has her back to Christina and her slip is hanging at an odd angle under her skirt. Christina is the only woman in there wearing pants. She is also the only woman in the place wearing lipstick and eyeliner. People turn their heads and openly stare. The bald man never leaves her side, gazing down at her like she's a prize heifer at the county fair. She wonders if they think she's Jewish (she is dark-haired and her eyes are almost black).

There is someone playing piano and pounding out stern Protestant hymns. Christina is used to grandiose cathedrals with walls of carved white marble, lurid statues of mutilated saints, and censers wafting incense. After a few minutes of testifying she begins to get bored. Everyone seems to be grateful to Jesus, but for what she can't tell. They are all emotional wrecks. But the revelations produce no juicy details. She has heard more exciting confessions in her mother's kitchen over coffee with Aunt Connie, tales of a failing marriage, casual details about sex. She glances around for the exit, but she's stuck in the middle of a packed row with Baldy. She pictures his arm shooting out and locking her firmly in his prizefighter's grip if she tries to leave. The testifying is getting repetitive. She wonders if there will be a central event, like communion, finally ending this service that is longer than a High Mass.

Christina is really hoping for snakes. She has seen a documentary on people handling poisonous snakes in a backwoods church somewhere in the Deep South. It was fascinating and scary, the way the vipers and the handlers had identical pitiless stares. Christina is terrified of snakes. Once, when she was twelve years old, she had run screaming from a big black racer snake incongruously coiled on her aunt's front doorstep, waiting like it was a guest at one of her aunt's weekly stitch-and-bitch parties. The unnerving thing about racer snakes is how quickly they can move, even though they are supposedly harmless. The old Yankees who lived next door to her aunt said they could book ten miles an hour. Christina knows she can probably race five miles an hour, and then only if death were looming. But she doesn't think they do snake-handling in the city anyway.

At last, the testifying and singing come to an end, and there is a commotion at the front of the hall. People are surging forward, though Christina can't see what's going on. The prizefighter turns to her and barks out something that sounds like "Broo svd?" His manner seems vaguely threatening. Christina thinks she should placate him. She smiles politely, nodding vaguely. He repeats himself, this time more intensely: "BROO SVD?" Christina stretches on tiptoes for a better look up front. People are collapsed onto their knees and the preacher is standing over them, tenderly raising them up.

In a moment of Zen clarity, Christina has her own revelation. Big boy is asking, "Are you saved?" He wants her to go up there and get reborn. He wants to bring a Jew to Jesus. Or someone who could possibly be a Jew. Or at least a pope-worshipping Catholic. Like a bounty hunter about to slap on the cuffs, he begins to guide Christina by the elbow. The people beside her in the row shrink back, lest they impede her path to glory.

Christina briefly considers doing it as an acting

exercise. After all, she is a perpetually out-of-work actor and her boyfriend is the one getting roles. Her main experience is in acting class and this would be a noncritical audience. She is always accused of being over the top when she does monologues in class. Her hand-waving during one particular scene was deemed "amateur night" by her teacher, which had resulted in Christina quietly sobbing at the back of the class for the rest of the evening. This group would expect nothing less than a balls-out barn burner of a performance, and hand-waving would be welcomed. She would have to do without applause, though. After testifying, teary-eyed people are just led back to their seats where they lie in a heap, sobbing quietly. That is disappointing. It is, actually, a deal-breaker. Christina decides it isn't worth it. Once her keeper gets her to the end of the row, she will find a way to escape.

Instead of heading for the altar, Christina squirms out of Baldy's grasp just as they get past an ecstatic old lady waving her arms like she's bringing in a Boeing 747.

She slithers like a racer snake out the door, booking it.

CHRISTINA THE ASTONISHING

On a large television screen, a silent film is in progress. We see a stone chapel in a wooded copse, a fairy-tale setting come to life. A little girl opens the wooden door. Inside, it's dreamlike and spooky, candlelit and murkily beautiful. The walls are lined with female statues of the saints. The camera moves to St. Lucy, holding a golden salver with her eyes on it. The camera slides over to St. Agatha in her own niche, holding a plate with her severed breasts on it. Next in line is St. Apollonia, patroness of toothache sufferers, holding up a pincer containing a tooth, symbolic of her torture when the pagans pulled out all her teeth. St. Rita lies under a glass case like Snow White, looking like she is sleeping, with a thorn embedded in her forehead. All the saints have plaques with their names on them.

The little girl stands before the statue of St. Lucy. She approaches warily, afraid of the eyes on the plate. She looks back longingly at the door to the chapel, but she stands her ground. She knocks on the base of the pedestal and smiles at St. Lucy. Nothing. Suddenly, the little girl executes a tap step, a simple flap ball change. No response from St. Lucy. The little girl steps up the routine, executing a full turn.

St. Lucy's foot begins tapping and the little girl claps her hands with excitement. St. Lucy pops her eyes back in, jumps down from the pedestal, and imitates the little girl's dance step. The girl laughs with delight and goes on to the next statue, St. Agatha. She knocks on the pedestal then performs her routine—

Rita shatters the silence, her voice a Mediterranean crow circling above roadkill: "Nobody talk in this?"

Christina shushes her mother.

On the screen, St. Agatha flings the plate and whips the two breasts in a full circle, then stuffs them in her gown. She jumps down from the pedestal and follows St. Lucy and the little girl.

Now Christina's father is getting in on the act: "I got some background music for you. VINNIE, switch on the stereo."

Christina's hulking brother casts a black shadow across the television screen. A few seconds later we can hear the musical stylings of Bent Fabric, and the tinkly sound of "Alley Cat" fills the living room.

"DADDY! Turn that off, would you PLEASE!" Christina yells.

Onscreen, St. Appollonia discreetly turns her head, pops in her teeth, then smiles, jumps down, and follows the chorus line of saints led by the little girl.

"Okay, honey, sure. VINNIE, SHUT IT OFF!"

Vinnie's large dark shadow crosses in front of the television again. The music cuts off abruptly.

On the screen, St. Rita struggles to overturn her glass case. St. Apollonia, St. Agatha, St. Lucy, and the little girl finally push the case open and St. Rita joins them.

At last, the little girl comes to the statue of Christina the Astonishing, dressed in rags bound with saplings. The character of Christina the Astonishing is played by Christina.

There is a loud gasp from her family, watching in the living room and at the same time shoveling in Easter ricotta pie, replenished by Rita at the pace of someone in the throes of a manic episode. Her mother is especially careful to overfeed the boyfriend Christina has brought with her from New York for the Easter visit. The boyfriend, raised on tuna noodle casserole and other WASP atrocities, is bedazzled by the food and entertainment provided by her family. She has warned the boyfriend, but she can see that he can't take his eyes off Rita and is probably wishing that Christina would have a go at some red lipstick and wondering why she didn't inherit her mother's shape.

"That's YOU!" Aunt Connie notes unnecessarily.

On-screen, Christina the Astonishing jumps down from her pedestal and picks up the little girl, kissing her. They twirl round and round together.

A priest comes out onto the altar, enraged. He storms toward the dancing saints, pointing to the pedestals, demanding that they return to their immobile positions. The saints, led by Christina and the little girl, dance around and past the priest, knocking him to the ground, laughing at his sputtering fury.

"It's really good, honey. Deep," her father says, using his bullshit voice, the lower register reserved for people he thinks are phonies. He's been using it all day with the boyfriend.

"Yeah," her mother chimes in. "You gonna leave-a like this?"

On-screen, the saintly entourage reaches the door of the chapel. There's a moment of panic when the little girl can't get the heavy door open. The priest is back on his feet and gaining on them. At the last moment, and with all the saints helping, the little girl finally gets the door open. The saints all run out, laughing, led by the little girl. The screen goes to white, and then "Dedicated to the memory of my friend Babe" scrolls across the screen.

Aunt Connie hauls herself out of the comfiest chair. "Joe, some Anisette?" she asks her brother, then smiles warmly at Christina. "You savin' up for a nose job? You should, if you're gonna do this for a living."

"Connie, I have two words for you, and they're not Merry Christmas," Christina replies.

Rita immediately unleashes, as if she's been waiting for this all day: "You tell you aunt fock you?"

"Barbra Streisand," Christina replies, to the bewilderment of all present, except the boyfriend.

"She directed some movies and she won an Oscar," he says. "Also, she, uh, has a good-sized nose."

Her family says, "Ooooohhh," collectively, as if they understand.

Acknowledgments

This book has had many incarnations and I am most grateful that it has been reborn finally at Akashic Books. I am so happy that Johnny Temple and Johanna Ingalls have given my novel a home in the best place it could ever be. And I am thankful to Ann Hood for introducing me to this great publishing house through her imprint, Gracie Belle.

Many, many thanks to my agent, Colleen Mohyde, who has backed this story from its inception (and sent me a picture of herself in her parochial school uniform!). Thanks also to John Sayles for his very helpful suggestions, and to Tom Perrotta, who gave me encouragement and an early quote about the book. Thanks always to early reader Andre Dubus III, for his ever-generous and constant support.

Lastly, I guess I should thank the Sisters of St. Joseph for giving me way too much material, enough for a sequel.